DOMICILE 41

A JACK DYLE THRILLER

DAN PHALEN

Creston Hall Press

It's Lies All The Way Down

To understand what actually happened, you had to be everywhere at once. A lot of what follows is guesswork, since the dead don't talk and every man, woman, and digital entity left standing will lie to avoid prosecution. To be honest, I bend the truth a bit myself. For the same reason.

1

A Late Disruption

Central-Alameda is not the shiniest part of Los Angeles, but few can match it for surprise endings. Saturday night was turning quickly to Sunday. I was in the shop late, gas welding a parabolic seam in a fender from a junked '40 Ford, and looking forward to a quiet, uneventful finale. Not the one I was going to get.

My weekend playpen, four walls of mismatched corrugated steel hugging the butt end of a bricked-up furniture factory, was unpainted and unbranded, a study in rust boasting touches of greasy chic—in many respects, a lot like me. A roofing supply building across the alley blocked the street light, casting the shop in deep shadow. I'd strung a cordless drop light from a rafter to save electricity and avoid the heartbreak of lacerated flesh.

A daytime high in the nineties hadn't backed off much, so I'd stripped to the waist and left the door rolled up. On the floor, a vintage boombox graced the air with ninety-mile-an-hour Bluegrass from Sweet June Dowd and the Pine River Mountaineers. Darby Kettle's washtub bass had my head bobbing like a chicken pecking corn. All was right in my world, rolling smooth as a bulk oil hauler, when the side door banged open.

I looked up and saw a chesty redhead in street duds. She had a steady grip on a 9mm automatic aimed at me, center mass. On my night off. In my shop. Without a hall pass.

"Please point that thing elsewhere," I said. "You've brought offense to the sanctuary."

"This is Central-Alameda, dude. High crime rate, safety grade D any day or night."

"Granted, an enclave for treachery, but I hope you didn't barge in here with mugging in mind. As the door sign clearly states, we do not carry cash."

The gun did not move, the eye behind it stayed on target. "There's no sign on that door. It's covered with rust."

"That's the grunge motif, very in right now. You just didn't look closely enough. Sign's clearly printed in six-point Helvetica. How about you go back outside and check it while I make myself presentable?"

"You *are* Jack Dyle, right?"

"I'm not sure any answer I provide will alter the circumstances."

"Yeah, you're Dyle. I was told you have a lip." She released the trigger and lowered the weapon. "What's that you're doing with the torch?"

"Well, I was *trying* to weld a parabolic seam on this fender before you broke my concentration. Now look what you made me do, Ollie."

She ignored my allusion to vintage film comedies—I like old-timey movies, even the silents. Old cars too, not so silent. Some say I was born a hundred years too late.

The gun went into a plain leather shoulder bag. She was tall with a largish nose and close-set eyes a little on the hard side—the kind that size you up right the first time. Might be taken for a lady lawyer if you didn't know she was carrying. Despite a severe set to her jaw, I held out hope for my usual five-star approval rating.

"What's with the hillbilly kerosene lamp?" she said.

Rodney Dangerfield got more respect.

As I am particularly sensitive to the term *hillbilly*, I adopted a belligerent attitude.

"Who's asking?"

"Minnie Glover."

Just as belligerent, if not more so. She flipped out a business card and snapped it down on the bench top. "Do you always work in the dark?"

"Just on Saturdays when I'm not expecting intruders."

Minnie Glover walked over to my forge table, picked up a piece of twisted bar stock, examined it, put it down. Looked around the shop at antique smithy tools hung from rail spikes. I let her take her time. My night was shot anyway.

"What can you tell me about that?" she said, pointing at the '40 pickup shoved against the back wall and half hidden by a tarp.

"Project car," I said.

"Looks creepy old."

"It's a relic, owner found it in a chicken coop in Ontario, brought it here two years ago and left it."

"And you haven't moved it."

"Need a front-loader for that."

"Or a small crane. You know Deacon Hood."

Clever, that quick switch.

"Never heard of him," I said, which was untrue because in a past I was trying to forget, Deke Hood had roped me into extracting fugitives from bad people in bad places, representing himself variously as FBI, CIA, Treasury, or Homeland. The difference mattered little, as the relationship between us was uniformly strained and the support irregular.

Glover apparently knew all of that. "Deke speaks highly of you. We're working together. Partners, you might say."

"Only if I cared."

She switched gears again. "You rent this hole from Gabriel

Cooley, right?"

I gave her a level look. "Maybe."

"Right, and maybe you know he was found in Hollenbeck Park early Friday morning."

"No, I hadn't heard that."

"Beaten and murdered the night before." Glover lifted her chin. "Don't you watch the news?"

"As seldom as possible."

Gabe Cooley was what's affectionately called a slumlord. He rented out a string of aging crackerbox houses in South Central, plus my Central Alameda shop and a few adjoining commercial wrecks on the same block. For protection during his collection rounds, Gabe sometimes hired one or two gym rats from a sweat parlor in East Los Angeles. The man was not liked and didn't mind a bit.

Glover anticipated my next question. "The police don't have any suspects yet—or they won't say. Hey, it's lovely Boyle Heights, Gangbangers Incorporated. Gabe was found on a footpath near the lake. I mean, what was he thinking, going down there after dark?"

"Look, Miss Glover, what happened to Gabe is a shock, but all it means to me is a new name when I pay the rent."

"Deacon says you should know Cooley was cooperating in a sting op. Deke couldn't make it down here tonight himself, he's so tied up with Beltway bureaucrats, so he asked me to make sure you were still here."

"Where's the good Reverend now?"

"Somewhere within a ten-mile radius of this spot."

"Why is ten significant?"

"One of the conditions of parole. I'm wearing an implant."

That one stopped me cold.

"Also a safety measure," she added, "or so I am assured. Isn't that a laugh? Anyway, the funeral is Monday. We'd like you to attend."

"I have a day job."

"You mean the one where you play detective for insurance companies?"

According to the State of California I was a certified marine investigator, licensed to check out insurance claims for boat theft, boat damage, boat title transfer. Strictly boat stuff. Well, sometimes I did that, like sometimes I quarterbacked the Rams. My CMI tag was in serious jeopardy of being revoked for gross neglect.

"No, I mean the one where I get a weekly paycheck."

"That's Briggs Speedline, right? You build hotrod showcars?"

"Street rods. Early Fords mostly—"

"I drive a '48 Ford fastback, myself. Not around here, though. Runs a 383 Chevy stroker, Turbo 350 tranny, B & M shifter. Body's dropped and shaved, with a $12,000 pearl chameleon paint job. Side slash gradient goes Tangelo Sunset to Claret Red. Kinda like me on a hot date."

While I struggled to close my mouth, Glover reached into her bag and pulled out a wad of cash. "Here you go," she said, thumbing off a few Ben Franklins. "Three, four, five hundred. That cover your day?"

I kept both hands at my sides. "What happens if I don't show?"

"Then Deacon brings certain facts from your past to the attention of people who might use them against you."

"He doesn't have any such facts."

"We're talking Deacon Hood, don't forget."

"Now, look just a minute—"

She thumbed two more bills.

"No, wait," I said, "I wasn't fishing for—"

"Good, then we're square at five. We'll have people in the area but not on site. Oh, and a question of more immediate concern."

I was getting mildly steamed. "Significant of what?"

"His face was disfigured. No dental records, no priors, DNA

lab's weeks behind. We're looking for some other way to identify the body."

"I don't do autopsies either."

"There's an open casket viewing at eleven. Get yourself on that list, and don't show up in mechanic's overalls. That okay for you?"

"Which cemetery? There's about a hundred to start with."

"We don't know yet. Use your investigative powers and just be sure to show up."

"This is a drastic departure from my weekday routine."

"Gabe probably had the same thought Thursday night." Minnie Glover pointed at her business card on the bench. "Call me before you get any ideas otherwise."

I ditched my leather apron and walked her out to the street because we were in a designated combat zone. A hard case in a leather vest and biker tats stood unscathed beside a '71 Buick Riviera low-rider, also unscathed. Ten grand in the mag wheels, fifteen for the navy on pearl paint, ten for custom upholstery, another fifty in custom bodywork.

Nevada plates.

"Who's your friend?" I said.

Glover opened the passenger door and got in without a word.

The biker scowled, got back behind the wheel and turned the key. A blast of supercharged power rattled the neighborhood—five-liter Coyote mill at twenty-five grand. Rounded out to a six-figure ride.

In Central Alamurder.

I watched the frenched LED taillights until they turned the corner. Then I whipped out my phone and called my most trusted ally.

"Actually, you know," I said to the empty street, "a closed door as such means *you knock before entering*. Don't need a freaking sign, you myopic Mata Hari."

My zingers always arrive late like that.

Some things are worse than getting mugged in Central Alameda. One is getting beaten to death in Boyle Heights, but another is saying yes to a gun-toting dame telling a story with more holes than a pub dartboard. I'd agreed to her demands out of sheer overwhelming curiosity. However, unlike the proverbial cat, I seldom land on my feet.

2

Hired To Snoop

With Minnie Glover's shakedown blinking my lights, I was done working metal for the night. I locked up my *studio d'art* and drove home on autopilot—home being three cargo containers joined at the hip and parked at the back of Tobey Auto Salvage, a chain link and razor wire bastion of urban blight charming the hell out of residential Los Angeles.

Owner Doug Tobey's defensive line, a Rotweiller named Yankee, leaped from his canine abode, a Dodge van on blocks, to inform me that he hadn't had a regular meal in the last hour and might expire at any moment. The ring of crumbs in his water bowl belied that claim, so I gave him only half a bag of Doctor Dawg's special mix. It was gone before I reached my front door.

With too many what-ifs knocking around in my head, I turned on the TV and sat my frame in the recliner to let a movie rerun take care of it.

An hour later I was jarred awake by my phone. The number that flashed up was not one I recognized. Having cancelled my spam detection service, I answered.

"Tobey Salvage," I said. "You break it, we take it."

A quavery woman's voice said, "Is this Jack Dyle?"

"It is, but my insurance is paid through 2099 and I signed up in advance for AARP, so goodbye and never darken my door again."

"Wait! Please, oh please!"

Not your usual scammer stall, so I said, "Whut?"

"My name is Sheri Burke and I know it's awfully late, but I'm calling about Gabe Cooley."

I sat up straight. "Who is this again?"

"Sheridan Burke. Gabe is my uncle—or was. I don't know if you've heard, but he—"

"I've heard," I said. "Tell me quick what this is about or I'll hang up right now."

"No, please! I don't have much time and it's important that we talk."

"It's past one a.m. and I've got church first thing in the morning."

She didn't buy one subatomic particle of that fabrication. "Uncle Gabe gave me your name as someone I could count on to handle a delicate matter."

"Miss Burke, I'm an auto mechanic. Delicate I am not."

"You're also an insurance investigator, according to the card you gave Gabe."

I never knew a business card could metastasize so quickly.

"And you trust Gabe Cooley when he tells you to trust me."

"Dependable, was the word he used."

I made a mental note to add "Dependable" to my card slogan.

"This is about something personal," she went on. "A confidential matter I'd rather not discuss over the phone."

"Probably a good idea these days. What do you have in mind?"

"I'm at work in Westwood right now, but I can zip away for a bit."

"Who works Sunday morning in fun-filled L. A.?"

"I do. And not by choice, believe me."

"Why the rush, Miss Burke?"

"It's Sheri, please."

"Okay, but only if you call me Jack."

"Oh, thank God! I was so worried. How far are you from Santa Monica, Jack?"

"I can be there in thirty minutes without breaking the law."

"I've got ten past, so let's make it 1:45 at the Broadmore Motel."

"Don't think I've heard—"

"It's an out-of-the-way place I know about through work. I'm in motion pictures—production, actually—most of the time."

"And you want me to meet you in a motel room. What's wrong with a business breakfast at Denny's?"

"Too many eyes."

"Of course. What was I thinking? A Hollywood luminary can't be too careful."

"Um, I didn't mean—"

"Tell me which part of Santa Monica we're talking about."

"Near the beach, Pico and Lincoln. I know the proprietor there. They have a conference room where we can talk."

"A beach flop with a conference room. I'll bring donuts and coffee."

"Would you? I haven't eaten since lunch and I'm starved. Oh, and when you get there, check with the desk and ask for Madison."

"Who's Madison?"

"It's a password."

"Oh, right. Should I wear sunglasses and a trench coat?"

"Jack, please, no joke. Things are moving fast and scary serious." Her voice trailed off at the end.

"Sorry, I can do serious."

～

I took Alameda north to an all-night donut shop under the

freeway. With the requisite fortification in hand, I climbed onto the I-10 west and stayed on it all the way to the Lincoln exit. When Lincoln dumped into Pico I turned toward the beach.

The Broadmore was an unassuming establishment from the 1940s. Two rows of unattached cottages formed what they used to call a motor court. Each unit sported a red tile roof and white stucco siding, small but tidy. The venerable property, crammed between a tire store and a two-story apartment complex, definitely had missed the upgrade to "motel."

The desk lady had a smoker's cough and pinned-up orange hair under a red calico bandana. I said I was looking for Madison, and she said my party was waiting in the executive suite. I found the alleged suite lurking at the back and looking like all the other units from the outside. I gave the door two raps and waited.

An attractive honey blonde opened and immediately threw her arms around my neck with a breathy, "Oh, Jack!" A perfectly natural greeting I've learned to expect on first sight from female strangers across the land.

She backed into the room with a hand to her face, apparently late to realize the awkward impasse that bloomed and filled the tiny room. I was thrilled.

A maple dinette table with four mismatched wooden chairs occupied the center. Shoved against the back wall were a child-sized wet bar and a brown-corduroy futon designed for discomfort. A door on the left stood open to a bathroom sink and toilet. The clever renovator had simply yanked the double bed outa there and dropped a Goodwill conference ensemble in its place. Unaccustomed to displays of such class, I restrained my enthusiasm.

"You didn't have to go all out like this," I said. "I'm just as comfortable chatting on a park bench."

Sheri composed herself and waved a hand for me to take a seat at the table. She was young, maybe not yet twenty-five, blue-eyed runway model perfection, tall with a regal arch to her neck, an air of graceful self-possession as she smoothed her skirt before sitting. No resemblance to "Uncle" Gabe Cooley on any account.

The table was set with two picnic plates and plastic forks. A sheaf of papers and a fat neon-orange ballpoint pen lay to one side. I set the pastry box down, opened the lid, and got busy with a blueberry scone. Sheri selected a cinnamon raisin bagel and, after a dainty bite, got right to the business on her mind.

"You could be in movies."

I get that a lot in pickup bars. My usual response is, "Your place or mine?" What I said to Sheri was, "You too."

"What I mean is, you frame well from several angles. It's something we're trained to look for."

"In production?"

"In everything. Mostly learned in film school."

"Which one?"

"UCLA. I couldn't afford SC."

"That's still a pricey curriculum."

"Gabe picked up the tab. At least I think so. I learned early it was best not to ask where money came from."

"Good old Uncle Gabe."

"Good to me, anyway. At least in that regard."

I mentioned the obvious physical discrepancy with my usual sensitive touch. "Speaking of faces, Gabe was a freaking toad. You, on the other hand, have one of those faces every camera loves."

Sheri pressed a finger to her lips while she swallowed a bite. "Thanks for the flattery, but I know my limitations. Assuming I could act, which I can't, they'd have to shorten my nose and give my bustline a lift. Anyway, don't look for any resemblance. Gabe's more of a Dutch uncle. He and my dad were in the military together."

"Marine buddies?"

"Not that close, but the same outfit, years apart. Later they connected over something else and we had him over to the house for dinner a few times. Gabe didn't have family of his own. He always brought a gift for me, something small and thoughtful, never extravagant."

That didn't sound like the Gabe Cooley I knew, but I withheld comment and got intimate with an orange glazed while Sheri went on.

"We lost touch, my mom and dad split, she remarried. I got wrapped up in film school at UCLA. After graduation I couldn't find work anywhere in Hollywood. Finally got a job as a typist in a realtor's office. One day, out of the blue, Gabe shows up and takes me to dinner at a nice place, says he's going to be a better uncle. A couple weeks later I get an offer from Five Dragons Productions."

"Gabe behind it?"

"I asked him and he said he wasn't, but not long after I started I was out at the studio lot and I saw him across the way talking to an assistant producer."

"What did he say about that?"

"I didn't ask him. It was too awkward."

"And he never brought it up."

"Right."

"Fast forward to the present. Why are you and I talking about this?"

"Let me explain a few things first. Last Friday morning, before I left for work, I got a visit from Uncle Gabe's lawyer, Weldon Latimer. Never met him before, he just shows up at my door. First words out of his mouth: Gabe was killed last night. I mean, we're still at the door, I'm not sure I heard him right, and he rattles on, like, Sorry for your loss, the police don't think it was suicide, things are happening fast, can I come in. Just like that. He flashes his driver's ID, so I show him inside, and while I'm recovering from the shock, he opens his phone and points out the news squib and goes right on telling me the funeral's already set for Monday at

some obscure graveyard in Pomona. He hands me a list of names
with phone numbers and says I have to call all these people and—
"

"What kind of people?"

"Most I don't know, but quite a few are big Hollywood names
associated with Five Dragons. I'm supposed to invite them all to
the funeral. Anything else, talk to no one but him. And he'll get a
good criminal lawyer to handle the police. I go, Why should I
worry about the police? And he goes, Where there's murder
involved, you always worry about the cops."

"Sound advice. I'm liking this guy already."

"Next, he informs me that I'm executor of Gabriel Cooley's
estate. Well, Gabe never told me that, and I when I say so, Latimer
says it was a very recent decision, sort of a hasty afterthought.
While I'm digesting that one, he pulls out a paper list this long
detailing 'Properties To Which Decedent Owns Title' and points
out that one of them is a small warehouse about a mile from the
park where Gabe was found."

"No big surprise. Neighborhood fits the Cooley property
demographic."

"I suppose, but the next thing, I'm leafing through this
mountain of paperwork, stuff I've no idea what it means, and I
start to ask a question, and Latimer up and bails on me."

"What do you mean? He just left you hanging?"

"He gets a text message on his phone, says to me, 'Gotta see a
man about a horse,' and goes out my front door, jumps in his car,
and drives away. I'm left with this huge stack of legal documents
and no idea what to do with it. I mean, the papers look really
important but I can't dig into all that stuff." She reached across the
table and grabbed my hand. "For God's sake, Jack, I already have a
job! I can't handle two!"

"Easy, easy. What'd he say when he came back?"

"That's the scary part. I haven't seen or heard from him since.

Not one word, not even a phone text."

"Well, his client just got murdered, so he has a lot of legal work on his hands."

"But he just dumped all of Gabe's records on me."

"Okay, maybe it was something else. That was early Friday. Anything else go down at all?"

"With all these papers to go through, I called in sick to work and spent all day Friday going through property titles and lien notices and balance sheets and parties of the first part till I was cross-eyed. And still no Latimer. I go out for a pizza, just to get away from it all, and the minute I get home, my phone rings. I'm hoping it's him, but it's a woman. Says she's Weldon Latimer's secretary and do I know where he is. I tell her the S.O.B. was here for a quick minute and left me with all this paperwork. She says she's calling the police right now, and she hangs up. Well, I figure he's a lawyer, busy man, can't bother checking with his office every hour, and I let it go because I've got a ton of phone calls to make."

"Sounds like you need an accountant. So again, tell me what I'm doing here."

Sheri shoved the donut box aside and dropped a contract in its place. Then she leaned both elbows on the table and flashed a pretty smile.

"I want you to find out who killed Uncle Gabe."

3

View And Identify

The Broadmore Motel's executive suite suddenly felt even smaller than it looked. I bent forward in my chair to address the young woman suffering from acute information overload.

"Sheri, the L. A. cops are already on Gabe's case. What am I going to find that they can't?"

"Maybe nothing, maybe a lot. One thing I did learn from the file is Gabe was just awash with debt, something he ever let on to me."

My mind was awash with doubt. According to my neighbors around the shop, Cooley ran his collection rounds in a chauffeured Cadillac sedan, showed up at each rental shack in a tailored Italian suit and paisley tie, jotted notes on a monogrammed iPad with a flashy gold stylus. I tried not to make my disbelief too obvious to Sheri.

"You say he put you through film school. All four years?"

"Just the last three. I took General Ed my freshman year at Santa Monica College. Worked odd jobs to pay my own tuition. When I graduated from UCLA, I couldn't get any film work until he intervened."

I nodded that I understood the Hollywood employment culture. "I suppose the rental business is yours now?"

"Looks that way, but I don't know how much it covers or where the money goes. I don't even know how to find some of these banks. This one's in Geneva, that one's in Nicosia, another's on some Caribbean island—"

"Did you say Nicosia? As in Cyprus? Sheri, Cyprus is one of the places you shovel capital gains to avoid taxes."

"I guess I missed that in Econ One. I don't know who to ask about the balance or how to withdraw money or—or anything! I'm not some hedge fund manager with world-wide connections. I'm little old Sheri Burke from Monrovia. I vet novels and screenplays for an assistant to the assistant producer. All I see of the movies we actually make is what I get on Netflix, same as everyone else."

I browsed the top page of a boilerplate contract for investigative services Sheri had probably downloaded from a web site. The names for the parties of both parts were already typed in. I pushed it toward her a couple of inches.

"This is a police matter, Sheri," I said. "You'll bury the man in a couple of days. That's as done as done can be."

"I know, but there are so many details left, and I just need someone who knows how to check them out."

"As in, where's the money?"

"Maybe, but more like, what was he doing so far from his own place at that hour of night?"

"Could be certain amenities were lacking at his own place. Where is it?"

"A fricking hotel-sized Frank Lloyd Wright castle in Holmby Hills." She thumbed through a sheaf of documents. "Says it was assessed last year for taxes at five million-three and change."

I ran a quick check on my phone. "Market value would be closer to nine mil. Monthly P. I. T. would be pushing fifty grand."

Sheri gave her pretty head a shake. "I can't even deal with

numbers like that."

I knew Gabe Cooley had money. Otherwise, he wouldn't have owned an entire slum block in lovely Central-Alameda. But Sheri was talking a night-and-day gap my mind failed to leap.

"You want me to run down this Weldon Latimer, who is the subject of another LAPD investigation?"

"And also talk to George."

"George who?"

"I don't know, just George. He's a houseman or caretaker. Lives there full time, drives the Benz, keeps the bar stocked. Big guy, maybe six-four. I got the impression he was Gabe's bodyguard sometimes."

"You know this how?"

"Been there myself, once to pick up Gabe for a dinner date, and then I took him to the airport a few times. Gabe flew a lot for business, you know."

My thoughts drifted back to my dialogue earlier with Minnie Glover. "Does his will stipulate a cemetery for his interment?"

"Yes, Guiding Light Memorial in Pomona. Is there a problem?"

Not on the face of it, but I found it strange that a certain federal analyst already knew about it.

I had another consultation with my phone, this time asking for images of Guiding Light—something I should have done earlier. One look at the photo gallery spoke volumes. I turned the phone around so Sheri could see.

"This is a street view taken less than a year ago." I pointed out the palm fronds littering the entrance, scrawny shrubs, relic headstones, brown grass, dead trees here and there. "You might call it an Econo Lodge for eternal rest."

"You're suspicious."

"Gabe had his pick of a hundred better places in L. A. If he kept house in a nine-million-dollar mansion, Guiding Light doesn't fit."

"See, that's why I need you. It bothered me, too, but I'm running around in fifty directions. And speaking of the funeral, Friday I barely managed to email invitations to studio people who knew him. I'm expected to show up Monday morning in a limousine. You're a car guy, can you help with that?"

My first reaction was to cringe a little inside. No way do I drive limousines. You can't hide a stretch limo on stakeout, even at night. If you cut a sharp right on red you'll take out a mailbox or a pedestrian or a light pole, maybe even a homeless tent. To shop at the mall you need two opposing parking spaces, when it's hard enough to find one. And a freeway chase is hell for sudden lane changes. But I'd just had a chat with a guy who wasn't bothered by all that.

"Look, my friend might come up with a limo. I'll have to call him to make sure. If not, I'll just boost one from the nearest Costco parking lot."

"Okay, super."

Rolled over that one like Steph Curry jogging back from a three-point swisher.

Sheri pushed the contract back into my dining space. "So how about it?"

"What am I looking for specifically?"

Sheri made a face. "I dunno, it's all very fishy, but maybe you can find a logical reason for everything."

"For starters, how about an address for this Holmby Hills palace of his?"

"Sounds like you're on board." She scrawled a few lines on a note card and handed it across the table. "This eases my mind so much, Jack."

"Well, I'm all for that, but you realize there's a fee involved."

"How much?"

I told her, and she laid down cash for retainer and expenses. "There's more in the bank," she said.

"Gabe's money or yours?"

"Mine, but I'll get access to his checking account by Wednesday." She pointed a dainty finger at the contract. "Sign it."

I did that, and we stood up from the table and brushed cheeks like all the movie people do. I was out of Santa Monica before the surf was up.

And that was how I became Chief Investigator for the estate of Gabriel Madison Cooley, deceased. Yeah, the "Madison" coincidence explained—maybe. First time I'd been chief of anything. I wasn't kidding myself, though. When things go wrong, the chief of anything gets fingered for the fix.

Every. Single. Time.

4

Being Available

Coffee and donuts at two a.m. are essential to surviving a nightlong stakeout, but the sugar high fails to serve normal nocturnal activity, such as sleep. On my way back from the Broadmore, I stopped at a Denny's to have that businessman's breakfast—with Gabe Cooley's dossier for company. After a thirty-minute read, I could only conclude that Cooley was a bag man for several other parties.

Such documents as he did keep showed rental income received for twenty-seven apartments, houses, lofts, and garage conversions. Another nine were small businesses of the mini-mall type one finds tucked between the dry cleaners and a vacant H&R Block. Remitments were invariably recorded as cash. Final disposition of funds was never mentioned, but the considerable air travel Sheri had mentioned earlier indicated Cooley transported the cash himself out of state, implying access to private or leased air services not requiring baggage inspection.

Also, I saw no evidence of funds disbursed for taxes, utilities, or repairs, nor any documentary evidence that Gabriel Cooley owned a single dwelling himself. Whether the properties were encumbered by mortgage debt I couldn't tell, as any purchase contracts or deeds were likely kept in corporate files neither available nor of interest to the bag man. A corporate accountant would pay taxes and negotiate repairs with contractors, as no expense of either kind appeared on Cooley's books. The clogged sink in my shop washroom was a testament to the familiar urban predator policy: buy distressed, house the oppressed, spend zilch. So, what to do next?

A friend of mine needed bothering, so I phoned and caught him in an idle moment. I asked him where he was and told him I was not far away and was buying. Fifteen minutes later he stepped through the Denny's glass door, terrorizing the two counter patrons and the entire night staff.

Lacleef Jones cut his eye teeth driving thugmobiles for a Crips gang lord. Then one day a kindly law figure convinced him the straight life's yawning boredom offered better prospects than the place he was headed. These days he drove for Uber, went six-three, two-twenty, gave new meaning to the word "intimidating." His eagle stare drew furtive glances when he entered a room. Got the nickname "Scarf" from the way he made food disappear without adding a millimeter to his waistline.

Despite his background, Scarf had style. When he showed up for a fare in a black Caddy CTS, tailored conservative suit, Italian shoes, white shirt and tie, jaws dropped. I once asked how the natty attire and a backseat chrome-and-walnut beverage bar paid the rent. He said, "On balance, things take care of themselves."

I took that to mean that, despite four years of college and six in black ops, he hadn't severed all ties with his darker past.

The waitress, a round-and-brown soul with "Louella" on her badge, came over with coffee and a menu. Scarf called her "sister" to leaven the atmosphere and ordered a steak-and-eggs Signature breakfast with a "side" of Texas toast.

"I'm not one for maple syrup so late in the day," he said to the gal. "You got anything stronger?"

"Blackstrap molasses."

"Deal."

He turned back to me when she was gone. "Mind telling me what keeps you up at this late hour?"

"Just got in from Santa Monica," I said. "Lady in distress. l told her I'd attend a funeral for her. But a couple of hours before that, I had a woman poking around my shop."

"After dark?" he asked. "In that neighborhood? What'd she want?"

"Well, she *said* she was referred to me as an investigative expert. Might be other reasons. Also told me about Gabe Cooley. You remember my landlord?"

"Hard to forget. What about him?"

"Got himself killed Thursday night," I said. "Boyle Heights."

"Ooh, nasty turf." Scarf straightened his table setting. "Other than being your landlord, what's it mean to you?"

"The last call on his phone was to my number."

"What'd he say?"

"I missed the call, didn't notice until the dame mentioned it. But that's not what I called you about. This other woman I met in Santa Monica, Sheri Burke, has a tight connection to Cooley. She's handling his estate, and there appears to be a lot of money and property involved. She's burying him Monday at eleven and needs a limo and driver. You want the gig?"

"Shee-it, man. At that hour my body is still locked in cathartic torpor."

"Doggone, Scarf, you are such a master of verbal nuance. Cuth-ar-per—I can't even say it."

"That's because you're a tongue-tied wrench ape. Edified gentry such as I hire servile drudges such as thee."

"Well, Massa Edified, can you make it Monday, or do I have to bale that cotton all by myself?"

"I'm good for it, son. Whereabouts?"

I gave him Sheri's address in West Hollywood. Scarf's primary interest being maps and routes, he came up with an immediate correlation.

"That's directly odd," he said. "Picked up a fare last night at Kingsley Plaza, Wilshire Center. Tall specimen in a tailored suit, silk shirt. Parked him just a hoot and a holler from that lady's place."

"What's your point?"

"Guy asked if I knew Jack Dyle."

I'd got a hot neck from Minnie Glover's surprise. This one prickled my scalp.

"Where'd you drop him off?"

"Beverly Hills Hotel. I get me some stylin' clientele time to time, but hardly any do the Beverly. Place taps you for a hundred dollars every time you turn around."

"Uh-huh."

"How do you suppose he got your name?"

"No idea. What'd you tell him?"

"Whattaya think, Jackson? I told him no, with a straight face. Guy tipped me a C spot anyway. Gave me a number to call if I hear anything."

Two probes in a matter of hours, one involving murder, both throwing money around. Not likely connected, but the combination was troubling.

"Don't suppose you got a name to go with that number."

"Nope. You must've made somebody's A-list. Anything going down?"

"Not that I know of, which is scarier than knowing."

Scarf poured an obscene amount of molasses thick enough to hold an I-beam in place. "Back to this funeral business," he said. "Where am I taking the lady?"

"Guiding Light Memorial." I gave him that address. "I appreciate you doing this because I've got to put in ten hours at the shop tomorrow."

"You're still working for that prick Sheldon Briggs, aren't you?"

"Yeah, still there."

Scarf put down his fork and gave me a long look. "I can't believe what I'm hearing. You got a brain, Jack, and a damn fine education. But you aren't using either one. You live in somebody else's ghetto to prove you're one of the downtrodden masses. Your head's stuck in the past with things you did in far-off places, so you live the low life to avoid standing out. And now this funeral for Coolio, a certified Class A prick."

"Thank you, Dr. Freud."

"Does this Sheri Burke know you?"

"Now she does—hey, I bought her coffee and donuts."

"So wedding bells are just around the corner. Where'd your first visitor come from?"

"Glover? Someone I worked with before."

Louella arrived with an armload she proceeded to offload. Once everything was in place, the array of dishes took up half the table.

Scarf rubbed both hands. "Hot damn and sweet pickles."

I gathered my papers and stood up. "Long day tomorrow. I need some shut-eye."

The first waffle did a quick disappearing act. "*Ciao, mon frere*," the virtuoso magician said around a wad of molasses-drenched toast.

"Scarf, *ciao* is Italian, *frere* is French."

"Actually, see, I knew that."

When I paid at the register, I got a baleful glare from Louella.

"He's harmless," I told her. "You couldn't be in safer hands."

She handed me the receipt. "Says a guy who cracks cement with a fist."

5

Chevy Nomad Recall

Yankee barked me through Tobey's gate until he realized the intruder was his occasional bringer of food. Doug Tobey was sleeping like normal people, so I took care of his needs. Yankee gave me a grateful snuffle and sent me off to a quick shower and bed.

Ordinary folk can sleep in Sundays without drawing a penalty. For me, Sunday started a new work week, six nines, so I clocked in at Briggs Speedline every Sunday morning. The promise of a share in the shop was added inducement, but financial independence was not just a walk around the corner. More like the other side of the world.

I arrived late with no excuse slip from my mommy. My foggy brain was working up a story when Sheldon Briggs came busting out of the office to announce in his quaint and colorful manner I was effing in charge while he journeyed to Montebello for an effing nine holes with some effing duffers. Briggs was a scratch golfer and a savvy hustler at the tee. And I think I just ran out of positives for the guy.

We had to get a '56 Chevy Nomad ready for the SEMA show in Las Vegas. Fabian Cerna had taken the shop van to church already—a time-saving gesture since afterward he would hop over to his cousin Siggy's to scrounge parts. He might watch a little ball over beers afterward. Grappo Gronowski lived to-hell-and-gone in West Covina, so he put in five tens with Saturday *and* Sunday off. For the nonce, I had the shop to myself.

The car was up on jacks because Aggie Agajanian's '57 Nova commanded the hoist. I was still working the steering setup from underneath. I grabbed the crawler and scooted in on my back to twerk the steering linkage around the 454 mill. You drop a heavy Chevy where a small block 256 used to live, and something has to give.

Due to the new geometry, I got to work miking the thing and before I knew it, I heard the clatter of shoes on the cement floor. Way early for Sheldon to be back from the course, so I wheeled out on my back.

It wasn't Sheldon. Two slick types in designer jeans with dark buttoned shirts and ties were standing beside the car, looking it over with a hard-eyed sweep that sucked in every detail and left nothing to chance. I figured they were trying to guess what the finished project was going to be, like most civilians faced with the wholesale reconstruction of a car made before their daddy was born.

The smaller of the two guys surprised me. "Nice stance on that baby. Who did the drop?"

I walked over to the bench and grabbed a hand towel. "Matter of fact, I did. How can I help you gents?"

"You're Dyle, right?"

"You can call me Jack."

"We're from Vic Straga," said the spokesman. He went about five-eight, maybe one-fifty in a downpour with galoshes and umbrella. I doubted he was the type to use either galoshes or umbrella. The clipped delivery, the stony look, the attitude all said Italian import—Fiat, not Ferrari.

"Who am I talking to here?" I said.

"We're outa New York."

"Good for you, I'm outa Afghanistan and damn glad of it. Names?"

"Sure. I'm Frank Sinatra, he's Louie Prima."

"Well, Frank, the boss has this whole place wired with cams like Chase Bank. Come back in a week and I'll have your real names, arrest records and identifying tattoos, and we can start over on a proper basis."

"Think you're funny, huh?"

"Not even trying."

Sinatra waved a hand at Prima. "He's Frank Diamond, I'm Anthony Lupato."

"Thanks, Mr. Lupato, but I've got nothing for you. You're here about a car?"

Lupato pointed at the Nomad. "That one."

"I see," I said.

Victor Straga, a.k.a. Vikko Sharra, ran a sweat parlor in East Hollywood known as Vic's Gym. I worked out there from time to time. Vic had done hard time back in the day, or so I'd been told. He had brought the car to me with paperwork to certify he was the car's bona fide owner, all well and good. But he'd fronted the rework with cash. Nothing wrong on the face of it, but not your usual deal. Sheldon Briggs likes cash, so none of us questioned the source. I hadn't known until now that Straga employed out-of-state wise guys as messengers.

As it sat, the Nomad had no window glass, no seats, nothing up front but a 454 short block. Appropriate décor for a salvage yard.

"As you can see, the build is coming along nicely," I said, and no, I didn't used to sell used cars.

"Vic wants it back," said Lupato. "Tomorrow."

He pronounced it *tamarra*. Maybe not New York, maybe

Jersey. Didn't matter, the wants-it-back part was the shot to the groin.

"What's that mean? The whole banana?"

"This car right here, whatever you wanna call it, all back."

"Not the stuff we've added, I hope?"

He pointed at the project. "This ain't the original stock."

"No, it's totally refabricated to handle the bigger mill and new drive train. We already discussed this with—"

"Notice you got a trailer out in the yard. Put the car on the flatbed and take it back where you got it. That's the deal."

Before I could explain that that particular trailer wasn't street legal, he pulled out a wad of cash and stuffed it in my overalls pocket. "To cover your labor plus transport cost. Vic wants it back in the Vernon warehouse, says you know where."

"Yeah, same place he sent me to pick it up. But what's going on? Is he pulling the plug on the project?"

"You got it, señor. Too bad, but that's how the cookie falls."

I ignored his mixed metaphor. "Is Vic pissed about something?"

"Nothing you need to worry about. Just deliver as requested."

"I don't know, we're going to have to work late just pulling—"

"Don't tell me your problems, 'kay, pal?"

"Sure—pal."

I reached into the top tool drawer and pulled out a pipe wrench, flipped it end-over-end once and caught the handle like I juggled those things for fun. Then I pulled my phone and thumbed the number I had for Straga's gym. I maintained eye contact with the Italian mini-stallion. He didn't like that. His second took a step closer.

"Hey, whatcha doin'?"

"Like you said, nothing to worry about," I told him, "but I'd feel better if I heard direct from Vic himself. Just a word, you know. He brought the deal to me in person. Always spoke direct before."

I got no answer from Straga, but I got one from his Italian wise guy.

"Vic's a busy guy. The car is just a loose end he wants tied up."

Lupato then jabbed my chest where he'd stuffed the cash wad. "You got your money, so don't try no mechanic's lien shit. Man wants his car, that's all. Warehouse on Boyle, tamarra. Got it?"

Most people who jab me anywhere get an automatic left hook nose-breaker. But if I did that to Straga's boy, I'd have to explain the mess on the floor to fastidious Sheldon Briggs. And Vic Straga would just send someone bigger next time. So I eased the wrench upward a couple inches and looked down at Anthony Lupato's finger still pushed against my chest.

"You might want to put that back in your nose before I do it for you."

We locked eyes until he removed it.

6

Sheldon Says Nix

Sheldon Briggs inherited a first-rate custom car shop from an uncle who was a hotrod legend. My rag-tag shop did not compare, and I entertained no thought that it should. Briggs' investment in tools alone was beyond my means and my interest.

To move the car, I would need the street legal shop trailer, a branded, fully-enclosed twenty-six--foot box on tandem wheels we used for hauling large parts and whole cars to and from the shop. It so happened the trailer was out on loan to a friend of Sheldon's. I couldn't begin the transfer without it, and I needed extra hands to lift and shove. That meant waiting and doing nothing to Straga's car until the boss got back from golf.

The shop was an all-male operation. A salty dog of seventy named Nobby Nash was a one-man office manager, outsourcer, and mentor to the crew. Until five years ago, Nobby had smoked three packs a day since he was eleven. His skin made ten-day-old road kill look good. These days he sucked bottled oxygen instead of unfiltered Camels.

Nobby had arrived while I played host to the visitors. I got along pretty well with him because we were both metal benders. I poured two cups of coffee and went into the office and sat down on the "sofa," a tuck-and-roll backseat out of a '55 Olds hardtop. Nobby raised his mug in salute and looked at me through the tops of his granny glasses.

"You didn't have to do that, you know," he said.

"Do what?"

"The clinic thing. They called last week, said I was set up for a year prepaid in advance. Trials on some new-fangled meds. When I asked, they said your name."

I shrugged.

"It means a lot, Jack. One helluva lot. Thanks."

"Make it count, Nobby, that's all I ask. We want you to get better."

"Ain't no 'we' in this place. Like for instance, those two skinny punks that just left." He pointed through the window to the shop. "I won't ask about your past, but I've seen you wipe the floor with bigger 'n them. Didn't look right."

"Nothing to do with my past," I told him.. "They belong to the guy who brought us the Nomad, or so they claim."

"What'd they want?"

"He's taking the car back, Nobby."

I pulled the cash wad out of my pocket and tossed it on the desk.

Nobby gave the money a dubious squint before he picked it up and counted it twice, as was his habit. He then tossed the wad in a drawer and slammed it shut. "An even four grand," he reported.

"Car's bought back and paid for, they said."

"Sheldon'll be the judge of that, with a good dose of my input. What the hell happened?"

"Something changed on his end. I don't know any more than that, and didn't care to ask. Straga could be bad news. Thing is, he wants the car back at his warehouse tomorrow."

Nobby's eyebrows shot up. "Tomorrow? That's crazy! Shel's got work jobbed out to a whole buncha places—rear end, tranny, upholstery, and that screwball instrument cluster for the dash. It'll take us days to put the brakes on all those jobs."

"Just passing along what I was told."

"Jack, you know what that'll do to SEMA. We're signed up to put three cars on the floor by November. That's like twelve weeks."

"Eleven."

"Okay, makes it worse. Shel's got the promotionals out for printing, Topo's doing the placards, Chewy's doing the lights, Artima's already ordered the paint for the car. Then there's all the swag—the tees, the mugs, the sponsor decals, everything."

"I know, I know, that's what I came in here to talk about."

"Don't look at me. I'm just a retired body-and-fender man. Never did any of this fancy custom rod stuff you do—channeling and frenching and chopped tops and all."

"So you say, but I'm more interested in what's inside your head. Briggs is going to remind me how I brought the car in with an all-cash deal and a prize money split. Now I'll have to tell him it's gone. I need ideas."

Nobby peered at me over his granny glasses again. "What you need, son, is another Nomad."

"Yeah, I'll just pick one off a tree."

"Can't you stall this guy? Or at least negotiate something reasonable until we shut down the outsource work? Call him back and tell him how this business works."

"Already tried, but he's off-line or something. Sent his boys to make sure I got the message. You don't say no to this guy, Nobby, not after he tells you what he wants."

"How'd you get mixed up with someone like that?"

"I work out at his gym sometimes."

"But somehow you found out how he operates."

"Only because I checked him out after I got started on the car."

Nobby sipped his coffee and stared through the window into the shop. One of the crew was back and moving around out there.

I hoped it wasn't Sheldon because my brain gears were not meshing right.

Nobby leaned forward in his chair. "So, Jackson, fill me in on this client before Shel gets back."

"What for?"

"For your own foolish good."

The word "foolish" is not a direct quote. I think Nobby inserted an expletive of his own.

~

The movement Nobby saw in the shop was Sheldon, back from the golf course. He came through the office door in as good a mood as I could have hoped for, having just made himself richer at the expense of a doctor and two of his neighbors.

"Twelve hundred cash, baby. Dogleg tee-shot I almost couldn't believe myself, then four chip shots for tap-ins. Kleinhauser ought to know better by now, but hey, sucker's got a medical degree, right?"

Into this ocean of prosperity and goodwill I plunged my trident.

"Vic Straga wants to stop the project," I said.

"Who the effing hell is Vic Straga?"

"The guy who owns the Nomad."

Good mood took wing and fled.

Sheldon made like he was just barely restraining the urge to paint the next project with my body fluids.

"I got news for you, Dyle. *I* own the effing Nomad because it's sitting in *my* shop. With *my* labor and *my* TRADEMARKED design work. State of California and every labor law in the country says that car belongs to me. Not effing what's-his-name. That Nomad isn't going nowhere!"

"He sent his people. Covered extenuating expenses with cash."

"Extenuating my ass! What's he going to do, barge in here with an eighteen-wheeler and a pickup crew?"

Sheldon embellished his tirade with a few four-letter curlicues. He stood not much taller than the guys who had just left, but he was doing his best to make up for it with hot air and foul words. His approach did have an effect.

I gave him the facts. "Vic Straga isn't somebody you run over with numbers and legal bullshit. He's a very powerful guy with a reputation for roughing up people who don't do as he asks."

"Don't threaten me, Dyle. I will not be intimidated by some two-bit…"

He interrupted himself and turned to Nobby

"How much do we know about this asshole?"

"According to a guy I know who knows such things," Nobby said, avoiding my gaze while he repeated the bio I'd just given him, "Vic Straga is a bigger asshole than you. Did some time for tax evasion back in the day. Alleged mob affiliations, alleged murder for hire, alleged casino stuff."

"In other words, a one-time loser with a rap sheet and all the wrong connections. Why didn't we find out about this guy before we made the deal? Where'd you find him, Dyle?"

"He found me. Through an acquaintance."

"Some acquaintance. What circles do you run in, anyway? Are you an ex-con?"

"No." I was practiced at delivering that answer with a straight face.

"Okay, here's the deal. You keep calling him until he answers. Meantime, the car stays here and you keep working on it like you're supposed to. I got too much invested in SEMA to throw it away on some asshole's say-so."

"What about the asshole's money?"

"I'll put it where it's safe until this gets resolved."

"And Straga's twenty grand deposit?"

"Stays in the bank. If those bastards show up here again, you show them the door and don't be polite about it."

I said nothing. I was nobody's bouncer, but my paycheck came from Sheldon Briggs, not Straga's Italian bag man. Let the boss find out for himself how the matter might play out if he pissed off Straga.

Sheldon grabbed the door handle and yanked. "Dyle, this is a dog turd on my doorstep I do not need right now. Take care of it or get used to working lube pits again."

His phone buzzed just then, and as he listened, his mouth widened in a humorless sneer. "Yeah, those're exackly the mags we want. How much?" He glowered at me, stuck out his chin. "Perfect for the Nomad. Bring 'em home."

Sheldon clicked off. "That was Grappo. We got one-off custom-billeted mags with the Speedline logo. Nobby, give me that money for the safe. Dyle, tell Mister Loser thanks for covering the cost of those wheels. They'll turn heads in Las Vegas."

I'd never worked a lube pit in my life, but I had a feeling one was reserved for my immediate future.

If I had one.

7

Lisa Pushes Hard

After a full day at work on the Nomad, I drove off the lot in zombie mode. Due to my work ethic—or Sheldon Briggs'—my personal time was limited to an eat-and-sleep regimen. Being in severe need of both, I decided to try my luck with dinner at a retrograde hole-in-the-wall diner.

Eight o'clock found me at my usual booth in the back of Mother's Mud, an off-off-Wilshire eatery of dubious worth and reputation. As usual, I was Mother's only patron. My head was down while I peered at something advertised as chili but closer to MRE in a rainstorm. I heard a noise at the entrance and looked up.

LAPD Detective Lisa Montero entered and crossed the floor at a relaxed pace. I was easy to find, so she slid onto the bench across from me, close enough to touch. Her expression clearly said touching was a bad idea.

I pointed at her. "Have a seat," I said, "why don't you."

Montero shrugged out of a soft-leather tote. "Thought I might find you here."

Sam "Mother" McCree came over with a clean mug and a stained coffee pot, poured, and left.

"He knows I take it black," she said. "Funny how people out of stir can pick up on a cop just like that." She snapped her fingers.

A while back, Lisa Montero and I had had a good thing going, a kind of us-against-the-world mutual appreciation with all the earmarks of a keeper. The end came from a misunderstanding over fenced diamonds. I escaped the cuffs, but the feds barred me from explaining my innocence to anyone, even the LAPD cop on the case. Lisa believed then and thereafter that she had evidence of my guilt, so I got the icicle treatment.

"What's this about, Madam Detective?" I said.

She was wearing tight denim pants and a tan summer jacket over a taupe scoop-neck top. I missed the easy smile she hauled out to endear herself to curmudgeons like me before dropping the hammer.

She swept a lapel aside to reveal the badge clipped to her belt. The heel of a Glock peeked at me from the other side. *We're here on business.*

"Where were you Thursday night between eight and twelve?"

"At home with Yankee, the Wonder Dog," I said. "We watched the Dodgers beat the Mariners three to one. My question still stands."

"What this is *about*, Dyle, is the guy you rent from. Gabriel Cooley was found dead in Hollenbeck Park Friday morning."

"So I've been told," I said.

"But wait." She swallowed coffee. "There's more."

"I hesitate to ask."

"The last call he made on his phone was to your number, close to time of death."

"Must've been late. I shut the damn thing off at bedtime."

"Ball game was still on. Eighth inning."

"How do you know it wasn't the ninth? Or the seventh?"

"Time track on the sports channel playback. Wonders of modern forensics."

I opened my phone and checked. No text message flag, but an

unanswered call indicator. I thumbed my recent calls—and there it was, just below Sheri Burke's call:

> Gabe Cooley   ⊙ ▤
> ✓ Mobile • Thu 9:21pm   ♪

Four nights ago, Gabe Cooley had called me after more than a year of radio silence. He usually just showed up at his convenience, not mine, but Thursday he'd found reason to make an exception. Due to my compulsive compliance with other people's priorities, I'd missed it.

I noticed I'd also missed a voice mail from him right after.

I pocketed the phone and said nothing.

Detective Montero watched my reaction with a seasoned investigator's intensity. I let the silence drag on until she broke the impasse.

"Nothing to say?" she said. "Not a word?"

"I hadn't noticed 'til now," I said.

"Don't you check your phone for missed calls?"

"Not for a while. I'm doing a frame-off rebuild for a demanding boss. Short deadline, long hours, custom parts to line up. Gives me a lot to think about."

"And what are you thinking about right now?"

"I'm wondering what took you so long to bring this up."

"Could you show a little concern for the victim? Maybe casual interest? After all, he was more than a passing acquaintance."

"Not by much. Hollenbeck Park is high crime territory, particularly at night. How'd he buy it?"

"M. E. says massive blunt force trauma to the head and torso, but cause of death was manual strangulation."

"Gangsta boys doing a take-down usually just shoot and run. Any suspects?"

"You know I can't tell you that. I spent half the day looking for you until I remembered this greasy spoon. I'm surprised to find you still hanging around these parts." She narrowed her eyes as if seeing me for the first time. "You don't fit the local profile."

"The rent's cheap. Look, Detective, this may be a helluva shock to you, but I worked all day and I'm very tired, so let's pick it up. What's your angle?"

Her squint sharpened. "Your card turned up in the victim's clothing. Any idea why?"

"No."

I was unhappy with that discovery, but more concerned that Lisa Montero, a Hollywood Division cop from day one, was asking questions about Hollenbeck's case. True, Hollenbeck's load was always heavy—occasionally so much so that another division might lend a hand. But would they send a Tec Two to investigate a park murder on the other side of town?

Montero found my terse reply unsatisfactory. "So it's merely a coincidence? How do you suppose the vic got your card?"

"It's all over town. When I'm on an insurance case I hand them out like Halloween candy."

She pushed her coffee aside and leaned her elbows on the scratched Formica table. "You're saying somebody set you up."

"I'm saying I don't like it, but nothing I care to say further."

Her lips tightened, then relaxed. I'd seen them pucker countless times when we got close like this, but always before we'd ended in a clinch. I felt the old magnetism surge forth and come alive. Lisa must have sensed the change, for she stiffened and backed off.

"You're so well-connected with the local indigents, any idea who might have it in for the guy?"

"Just twenty or forty pissed-off tenants," I said. "Maybe an angry Chicano got tired of his honky face showing up on their doorstep every month. Or a berserk meth freak from one of his crackhouses."

That got an eye roll and a smirk. "Gabriel Cooley, a crackhouse landlord?”

"Got one just a grenade lob from here, in South Park. Ask your colleagues at Newton Station. The man was no saint."

Montero sobered in the next breath. "So, you can't think of any reason he would call you prior to or during the assault?"

"Didn't know him that well. Every few months or so we'd stumble across each other on the street around here. Didn't talk much, and when we did, it was short and to the point."

"What sort of point?"

She was like a dog on a scent. I didn't think it would help her investigation if I mentioned that my landlord hated my guts. The man had wanted another undocumented beanbag he could toss around, but got me instead.

"As I may have told you in our forbidden past, the forge was my main reason for renting that hole. When I found out the gas hadn't worked since Pat Paulsen ran for President, I filed a complaint with the city."

"Cooley didn't like that?"

"Inspector came down to check it out, found toxic waste. Slapped him with a fine, started proceedings for violations discovered on the adjoining properties. Hell, Gabe Cooley has the deed to every bodega on that block and the next."

"You and he had a disagreement."

"A discussion. Landlord-tenant. Nothing ferocious."

"Any threats?"

"Nothing either of us meant."

"Would the neighbors understand it that way?"

"I can't speak for the neighbors."

"Let's talk about next steps. Cooley had a Nevada driver's license, but his last known address is a sixty-foot yacht."

"According to whom?"

"Not for sale. There's another question of more immediate concern."

I was getting mildly steamed. "Significant of what?"

Montero stuck both hands on her hips and glowered. "Why do you think I came down here on my Sunday off, Dyle? Because I find the neighborhood such a charming attraction? Did I have nothing better to do? Or am I simply drawn to the scintillating personality of a tough guy with an inscrutable past full of intrigue and string-pulling shenanigans? A guy who works the speed bag three days a week. A guy who hammers fender dents for a living, shoves engine blocks around like shoe boxes. A guy who gets a phone call from Gabe Cooley on or about the hour he's beaten and choked to death. Person of interest? You betcha, fella."

"You're about as subtle as a U-turn with a semi."

"One more thing, Mr. Certified Marine Investigator." She poked a sharp fingernail on the table to emphasize her point. "Cooley's boat is moored in Newport Beach, not Marina Del Rey."

"But that's way down in Orange County—oh, I get it. You think because we have a history, that makes me a pliant minion for the LAPD. Problem is, I do not feel the obligation. I don't care what was done to Gabe Cooley by whom for what reason."

She pointed at Sheri Burke's stack of papers beside my elbow. "I made another call on Honey Buns earlier today. She told me you're working for her. That's messing with evidence."

"Not really."

"Yes, really, since you stand to inherit a piece of the vic's estate."

"First I've heard of it. Care to tell me which piece?"

"She didn't say, but no difference, that's conflict of interest, a breach of your investigator's license. And the other thing—I don't know how you arranged it, but you're driving her to the vic's funeral."

"Not unless another party doesn't come through..."

"And Lacleef Jones is so reliable."

"Actually, he is. Anyway, my conscience is clear, so I'm not worried."

"Too bad, because you're in water up to your thick neck and the river's rising."

She slid out of the booth and slung her tote over one shoulder.

"Better hope I don't catch you playing that little bimbo for a sucker, Dyle, or it'll be the last scam you pull."

Sam McCree came out from the kitchen just then. We watched as Detective Montero left the building in high dudgeon.

"She didn't pay for the mud," he said.

"Add it to my tab."

"Big spender. You're in that booth so much, I'm thinking of charging rent."

"Will it include coffee?"

"You realize the price of Farmer Brothers roast these days?"

"You don't buy Farmer Brothers."

"I know, but the other stuff is catching up."

"Rising like the proverbial river."

I paid my bill and left. As I got into the truck, I remembered I hadn't listened to the voice message from Gabe Cooley. I brought it up and put it on speaker.

"Safety reminder, Dyle. You need a fifty-amp breaker to run that arc welder, or you could burn up the whole block. Get it done pronto."

I stared at the speaker icon for a few seconds. I'd just heard a man's last words, uttered minutes before getting beaten to death. The parting demand from a guy who wouldn't spend a dime to fix my clogged shop sink. Still too cheap to hire an electrician.

In a few hours I would help bury Gabriel Madison Cooley, a slum baron far beyond caring about any of us.

"Miserly Scrooge," I said as I fired up the C10. "Now you know for real that you can't take it with you."

8

Rite of Passing

Monday morning at Harmonious Rest Funeral Home, arguably the least homey place in Pomona, I was the only viewer present at Gabriel Madison Cooley's open casket service. In an attempt to underplay the grotesque spectacle inside the box, a filtered track light cast a celestial glow upon the centerpiece of burnished mahogany and white satin. Sprays of gladioli and rose garlands abounded. Soft organ music added a touch of sanctity. None of it worked.

Multiple blunt force blows to the head. So stated the coroner's clinical assessment of an ordeal no living being should endure. Not even a hardass slum lord with a predatory nature.

I peered at Gabe's ghastly remains. "You know," I said, "I could be up to my elbows in drip pan oil right now. Or squeezing a big-block Chevy into a Model A frame, or fishing my phone out of a bucket of carb cleaner. Hey, I might even prefer the business end of a brazing torch."

No snappy comeback from Gabe, of course. As a rule, slum lords aren't personable by nature, and Gabe was no exception, especially now. "Unrecognizable" came to mind. A dove-gray ascot around his neck served to obscure further evidence of his brutal demise. I couldn't see Gabe's left forearm for the tailored suit in the way. He had a U.S.M.C. globe-and-anchor tattoo with ribbons topside and keel that said, "HARD LUCK." I knew that because when I'd pointed out that I have one like it, except mine says "FORDS RULE," the lovely man had told me to pin a rose on my tush. If I pulled up Gabe's sleeve in this place, I'd invite the wrath of his archangel namesake. Or a Stygian demon. Or the funeral parlor attendant, a wrinkled elder statesman who looked ready for a box himself.

No one was watching. I didn't think angels or demons cared, so I reached in. A vague scent of lavender and something else reached my senses, maybe formaldehyde, maybe just desiccated flesh. I told myself it was only a cast-off remnant. A thing. Gabe wasn't in there anymore.

I pulled up the coat sleeve. I unbuttoned the shirt cuff and pushed. Didn't go up very far, but it was enough to expose the letters K-N-O-C. Close enough. Detective Montero would be pleased to know we were burying the right stiff today. Might even be of interest to the decedent's heirs and assigns.

I restored the dead man's clothing to a semblance of its former state and, with the mortal world oblivious to my offense, retreated to a corner and assumed the fig-leaf position. Just me and Gabe for the next fifteen minutes.

Then four *pendejo* tough guys filed into the room. Dark suits, black silk headbands tied in back, black shirts. A white carnation stuck out from each left lapel. Three stepped aside and waited. The fourth approached the casket, peered in, looked the body over from head to toe and back.

Reached into his lapel and withdrew a stiletto.

Plunged the blade into the cadaver's chest.

Pulled the knife out, pocketed it.

Removed the carnation, touched it to his lips, tossed it into the casket.

Backed away and walked out.

The other three took turns stepping up to the casket and repeating the ritual.

The last stabber paused at the doorway and glanced over at me.

"You got a problem, *cabrón*?"

I shrugged my shoulder. "Guy was already dead."

I stuck around until the funeral director, a somber figure in a black suit, walked in, closed the lid, and ushered me out. Viewing's all done, now roll him out the door and down the drive to a hole in the ground.

The foursome who'd played through had an odd way of showing despondency for their loss. Their in-your-face Chicano party attire must have discouraged Sheri's people from attending, because no one else showed up for the occasion.

Gutless ninnies.

9

Mourning Becomes Electric

It was Monday. I was working the day watch out of El Monte. My partner was Officer Frank Smith."

Actually, it was Pomona and I wished I truly was Sergeant Joe Friday asking for just the facts, ma'am. Instead, I was Ordinary Citizen Jack Dyle waiting in the SoCal heat for Gabriel Cooley's burial service to commence. I'd already introduced myself to the non-denominational clergyman, one Carson Plunkett, who stood now at one end of the fresh excavation, cradling a Book of Common Prayer and looking lost.

I hadn't heard from Detective Montero since last night. That made me even less sure of her expectations and how my attendance today might be viewed by others in her camp. Maybe I'd misunderstood her intention. Maybe I'd imagined the whole thing. The whole business made me feel like a rabbit in a trap.

Following a habit I acquired as a Marine, I counted heads at the gravesite and got twenty-three. One was a big-screen action star. His sunglasses were the largest in the crowd, but he couldn't fool me— I'd recognize those biceps anywhere. Another had won a Golden Globes award the previous year. Others were probably behind-the-camera industry moguls, but I didn't troll that pond.

As we all sweltered on lawn stubble bleached dry by perennial drought, a black limousine pulled up. Two large men got out and ushered Sheridan Burke to the position of honor graveside. Scarf emerged from the driver's side and beckoned me to join him several yards behind the limo, where we could mumble irreverent commentary without committing audible offense. He was his usual sartorial self, upstaging even the A-listers in a tailored summer-weight suit and Italian loafers. Not one bead of sweat.

My usual formal attire—hibiscus print shirt over denim cutoffs and canvas shoes—remained in the closet. I'd popped for a black shirt buttoned at the cuffs, black polyester pants, no tie. Funeral, schmooneral, I do not wear tie or jacket in summer, so stuff that in your glasspack, Stanley.

Scarf put on a severe expression behind his sunglasses. "Who put this shindig together?"

"A committee, led by Sheridan Burke and some lawyer. Where's she going afterward?"

"Back to Bel Air, lunch with a movie star, and before you ask, she wouldn't tell me his name. Speaking of which, you neglected to mention the name of the deceased."

"Would it have made a difference if I had?"

"Guy's bad news. Back in my early upbringing, the homies called him Coolio. Ran across his spoor when I was driving for Bam Bam."

"Not hella long time ago. You must've been in sixth grade by then."

Scarf took note of the crowd. "Never knew he had so many Hollywood friends. Not much regret to be found back in the Eight Trey."

"I think Sheri assembled the list, but there might be a gatecrasher or two attracted by his fame and repute. Hey, even I get respect from people I never met. Always a surprise."

"Yeah, baffles me too. You see the four heavies come in just now?"

"Who could miss?"

He didn't have to point. Different suits this time, and no carnation tossing, but judging from the size of the sunglasses and we-own-it attitude, outa New York. The apparent leader surveyed the premises, deemed the situation non-threatening, and gave the secret signal for his boys to move in as a group.

Scarf sensed my discomfort. "Friends of the family, I take it."

"Maybe not so friendly, but definitely from the family."

I deliberately shifted my gaze from the deathwatch detail to the pastor. "Rev appears agitated. Might be his first funeral."

Scarf responded in a hard voice. "I'll play along for now, but somebody owes me an explanation and a lot more than lost Uber fare. And his name isn't Sheri."

"Hey, who else is going to give you a fun time like this?"

Over at the grave, the funeral director was supervising the lowering of the casket to an appropriate depth. Sheri shifted her weight in a subtle display of discomfort and not-so-subtly scratched where it itched.

"Not the best time for the bereaved to get nervous," I muttered.

Scarf shushed me. "Rev's getting down to it now."

Carson Plunkett shrugged inside his cleric's collar like he wasn't quite used to it yet. Opened his book, drew a deep breath, and intoned: "Dearly beloved, we are gathered to witness the joining of this man and this woman—"

"Um, reverend guy." A voice from the crowd interrupted. "The deceased and his ex musta did that one thirty years ago."

A murmur of suppressed titters as Carson Plunkett visibly flushed a bright red.

"Oh, I'm terribly sorry." He leafed through a few pages of his script. "Er, dear friends, the birth of a child is a joyous…no, just a minute…"

I turned to Scarf. "Sheri must've found this guy at Higson

Avenue mission, preaching to the homeless."

"Not mine to reason why, but the man is off his game," Scarf said to no one in particular.

"Goodfellas over there be why," I said.

"I bet some joker placed an obit in the New York papers."

Plunkett craned and stretched his neck against the constricting collar like a jailbird in irons. He knew as well as anyone who the interlopers were, and for his own reasons found their presence unsettling. I tugged at my own collar and muttered in a sing-song voice, "Don't like where this is go-ing."

The service proceeded to grind down the morning at a glacial pace. Several heads bobbed in efforts to stay awake. I used the opportunity to take stock of the late arrivals. I had just noticed the cut of the leader's expensive cloth when Scarf nudged me.

"My fare from Saturday night."

"Him? You sure?"

"Couldn't miss. If the joker hasn't made me already, methinks recognition will dawn brightly before this affair is over."

I took another look, just a quick glance, but enough to start a trickle of sweat down my spine. I knew the face. Not from up close and personal, but maybe from the media somewhere—not movies, not television, for damn sure not a sportscaster. Maybe a photo from a news clip. A good-looking gent in tailored attire, fiftyish and fit, with a shock of iron gray hair barbered in a short brush cut. I noted an unforgiving hardness to the eyes, a slot of a mouth unaccustomed to showing pleasure. Then it clicked, like a spike driven through my head.

Roman Valenti. Miami, two years ago. Wherever Rome Valenti traveled, the lethal weight of the combine's sovereign will traveled with him. Joined today in modest little Pomona's solemn ceremony.

Scarf poked my arm. "You okay? You look a little peaked."

"It's the heat. My delicate condition."

"Steel yourself, Magnolia, looks like the show's closing. Rev's coming to the ashes and dust part. That's my man right there."

Reverend Plunkett had found his rhythm, laid into his windup. "Forasmuch as it hath pleased Almighty God of his gr-r-reat mercy…"

I leaned closer to Scarf. "About time. I got a lunch date."

"She hot-looking?"

"If hot is a five-six fire plug who invokes the eff modifier every ten words."

"Sheldon Briggs. For a second there I thought that was your ex-wife."

"She was a few inches shorter and brushed her teeth. Somehow didn't make for a cleaner mouth."

"Jeezes."

"I was nineteen. A Marine in love."

"Explains everything."

Carson Plunkett was bringing the somber occasion to a close. "…we therefore commit this body to the ground, earth to earth, ashes to ashes, dust to dust, in the sure and certain hope of the resurrection to eternal life…"

"Isn't that precious," said Scarf. "I just hope the departed didn't piss off the capo running the Pearly Gates concession. I gotta get back to the car."

"Chicken. You know who he is, don't you?"

"The guy in the ground? You already told me."

"Nice try, no banana. I'm talking Mister Big."

"And I'm gone."

While Scarf beat feet to his limo ride, I angled toward the sideline to avoid a game-ending interception by Valenti. Before I got far, Sheri detached from her retinue and laced her arm with mine. A thick black mourning veil obscured her expression.

"Walk me to the car, please."

On our way I pointed out the obvious.

"You saw the boys from New York."

"Who could miss?"

"Wonder who invited them to the party."

"Not me, but could be anybody. Gabe was reported dead Friday morning, it made local TV news Friday night, barely a squib in the Saturday *Times*. Could have gone viral on social media and I wouldn't know because I don't go there."

"Nor do I. Fine pair of investigators we make. Why the big Hollywood names?"

"Gabe's back-door connections. I put out a hundred invites, expecting only a handful to respond, and two dozen showed. He brought big money to the table."

She came to a halt about ten paces short of the limo. "This morning I engaged Richard Sloane as my attorney. Just in case, like you said. Thanks for moving on that so fast."

"Wait a minute, I didn't do any such thing."

"Sure you did, you phoned him yesterday and told him about our talk and then he called me. Said you worked together before."

"Well, we did, but I haven't spoken to Dickie Sloane since last October."

"Yeah, he said the same. Told me he was kind of surprised to hear your voice from out of the blue. Also said that kid he got acquitted is back in school now, thanks to you."

"This is crazy. I am sure I did not phone Dickie yesterday."

"Well, he sure as hell phoned me and I'm going straight to his office from here so we can pick up where we left off."

"He definitely said I called him?"

Sheri started for the car again. "Yes, I mean, how else would he get my number? Anyway, what I was saying before about Gabe's money? Forget it, I was just gassing."

With my mind still stuck on Dickie Sloane's phone call, I had trouble backtracking. "Whose money? Oh, right, movie backing. And whose table did he bring it to?"

Up ahead, Scarf stepped away from the car to approach us. Sheri looked relieved for the break.

"The people I work for don't require a lot of credentials."

"How do you fit into—?"

"Jack, I take my cue from the heads on executive row. Don't ask."

"But that's what you hired me to do."

"If I hired you to walk to Catalina would you ask for directions?"

We reached her limo. "Give my regards to Dickie," I said.

"If you say so, although you just spoke yesterday. Excuse me, I have to run."

Her escort caught up just then—Scarf leveling dark looks in every direction.

"Why the rush?" I asked her.

"So the big guns don't have to bother offering condolences to a nobody assistant gofer."

Scarf opened the limo door. "Keep safe," he said to me. "I'll call you tonight."

Sheri Burke dropped into the limo's cavernous luxury and Scarf closed the door with a soft *chunk*. The limo floated away with my client, westbound for tony Bel Air, whereas I would proceed to Central Alameda in my hand-built Chevy pickup, sipping a Red Bull kicker from a gas stop in El Monte. As if I needed to put a sharper edge on the day.

Sheri Burke had arrived and left without receiving one iota of condolence. Filmdom was a stratified community. The big names were there to impress their peers, regardless of Guiding Light's shabby stage set. I knew a little about the Hollywood caste system. Years ago, I'd escorted a news reporter to a movie premier after-party. We could have gone to a ball game instead and offended no one. Today's movie-town minion had rushed her exit to spare the Important People an awkward social obligation. To me, Sheri

Burke outclassed them all.

When Gabriel Cooley was alive, he and I had barely brushed shoulders. Today, after viewing a mauled cadaver, a vicious rite in the chapel room, and the attendant interest of a crime boss, I felt like I'd just taken a Mike Tyson signature right-hook body blow. If I was careful the rest of the day, I might avoid the one-two lightning uppercut.

But probably not.

10

Exit Stage Left

Before leaving Gabe Cooley's final resting place, I thought I ought to thank Reverend Plunkett for his service, and in the process maybe learn a thing or two. I spotted him entertaining a small coterie of newfound aficionados. I waited nearby until the last handshake brought the solemn ceremony to a close. As I got near, Carson Plunkett saw me and started the other way.

"I wanted to thank you, Reverend," I called out.

He took two steps and stopped, hunching his shoulders as if I'd knifed him in the back. As I got closer he turned and smiled the rictus grin of the condemned. When I extended my hand in a peace offering he visibly jumped.

"Sorry, but I got t'go."

"Ah, my fault for coming forth so late. I'm Jack Dyle, friend of the of the deceased—"

"I know who you are, and I've got nothing to say."

"Well, I don't believe we've met before today. Have we?"

"'Scuse me, I have another service to get to."

"Oh, sure, don't let me detain you further. It's just that Miss Burke didn't have time to thank you herself, and I thought I should extend our mutual appreciation."

"Miss who?"

"Burke, Sheri Burke. The blonde lady in front today."

"I don't know anyone by that name."

"The deceased was her uncle. She made the arrangements for today."

"Maybe for the grievers, but wasn't any lady hired me for the service."

"Who did?"

"Lawyer for the estate."

"Did he give you a name?"

"We spoke over the phone."

"When was that? I mean, which day?"

"I really must run now. The Lord is calling."

He approached an unwashed, gang-tagged Honda Civic and fumbled the key in the door lock.

"Yeah, well, to be safe," I said to his back, "you might study your Book a little closer so's you start off right the next time. The Lord thy God is a jealous God."

"Amen."

I stood in place and watched the Rev's car go down the drive and out of Guiding Light Memorial.

When I got to my truck, a familiar face was waiting in the shade of a nearby sycamore. Anthony Lupato's stony gaze met mine.

"See you know the departed."

"Only in a business sense. Where's your boss?"

We both knew I was referring to Roman Valenti, not Vic Straga.

"What I wanna talk about. Mr. Vee would like a sitdown with you, talk about a project he has in mind. You know Lowell's in the Valley?"

"Been there several times."

"He's got lunch there with some people Wednesday at one, should be done by three."

I'd have to work late to make up the hours, but this kind of summons didn't come with a lot of options.

"I can do three."

"Deal." He lifted his chin the way a Chicano homey salutes a bro. "Hey, sorry about your loss."

I thanked him and climbed into the truck. A black Cadillac Escalade was parked by the gate, apparently waiting for Lupato. I nodded at the driver as I drove past. Frank Diamond nodded back.

My, weren't we all such good friends.

11
Going Nautical

With Gabe Cooley's funeral out of the way and Sheri headed back to her new normal, I phoned Nobby and told him I was on my way in.

"Why don't you take the rest of the day off, Jack?" he said.

"Sheldon won't stand for it."

"Sheldon isn't here right now. He's gone to a bar someplace in East Hollywood."

"What the hell? Shel doesn't drink anymore, Jeanine won't let him."

"I know, but that's where he said he was going, and that's all I know."

"Nobby, that is just too weird. Did he say anything more about the Nomad?"

"Not to me. Hey, I got another call coming in. See you tomorrow, Jack."

I didn't like any of that. It didn't sound like the Nobby Nash I knew. East Hollywood was Vic Straga's turf. Either he was cooking up a deal with Shel Briggs, or he had other plans for the car. Shel wouldn't come out ahead in either case, but I was out of that picture for the time being. So, what to do now?

I had a bundle of paperwork. More study did not appeal to me.

I could try to pry more out of Lisa Montero, but another voice called to me.

Chase down that slippery lawyer, it said.

Follow the money, said the voice of cold logic.

Follow the boat, said my mariner muse, jealously eyeing a luxury flybridge Sunseeker 60 motor yacht valued at $1,950,000. My first love is cars, but boats run a close second.

I figured either choice might yield the same result.

Sheri Burke's margin notes stated that Gabe's interest in the boat had begun with a mariner-for-hire, one Armand Slovac—a name not easily forgotten. I went home for a shower and fresh clothes, copped two hours of beauty sleep, then got on the 110 south to the 405, and followed that major artery all the way to the Jamboree exit for Newport Beach.

I wasn't familiar with the marina called Happy Landing, but I found it easily enough. A salty gent in the office told me I might find Armand at The Front Room, a suds-and-sandwich bar about a mile away and, as I discovered upon arrival, several steps down from toney marina life. At a little past two on an overcast Monday, the place was empty except for a pair of wide shoulders hunkered at the bar. Armand was nursing a beer when I took the stool beside him.

His thick arms and stocky build spelled a lifetime of hauling lines and hefting cargo. A bent nose added a colorful note that the experience hadn't always been pricey yachts and weekend sailing. I signaled the barkeep for a beer and introduced myself as a friend of Sheri's. When Armand didn't respond I told him I'd just learned about Gabe Cooley.

"Yeah, I heard," he said. "Sleepin' in the master cabin when he hadda perfly decent place in Bel Air. Better for the owner he wasn't killed on her boat."

Maybe not Armand's first beer of the day.

"On whose boat, if I may ask."

"You kin ask, but I don't gotta tell you."

I tried a long shot. "Well, it was Gabe's boat, after all."

Armand sneered. "Like hell it was. He got Missus Loring to let him hole up there for a few weeks, is all."

"Who's that again? Misty Loreen?"

"Alice Loring is what I said. Very nice lady with a lotta money anna good heart. Big Hollywood star wuns ponna time. Different name."

"Did she buy the boat herself?"

"Her old man bought it from the broker up there." He pointed a thumb over his shoulder. "Ray Loring, helluva nice guy. Died not long after. She don't know what to do with it, don't wannit blocking her view over there, so she has me shift it to the most 'spensive slip in Back Bay."

"Where was it before?"

"Bayshores."

"How did Cooley enter the picture?"

"Beats me. He was a pal of her old man. Come along lookin fer a pad, she don't want him at the fuckin house fer chrissake, so she gives him over to me. Says keep him outa the masser stateroom. So I give him the key."

"With restrictions."

"Yeah, srickshuns. But that kinda guy, he don't follow no rules. Dint break nuthin, keppit clean and all. But he was sposed to use the forward stateroom. Damn thing's better than a Marriott suite but wassen good nuff. He hadda take the master."

"So, any cops show up here?"

"Missus Loring don' want no cops, I make sure of that."

"Can you help me get in touch with Mrs. Loring?"

"What's your binness in this?"

"I'm an investigator, working for the dead guy's estate."

"Shee-it. Insurance company hears about this, gonna blow sky high. Just the kind of attention Missus Loring don't want."

"No reason it has to go that way. I've been down this road before, know how to keep things quiet. Let me at least call her, see how she wants to handle it."

"Man, I don't know you from—

"Call Cam Byner, ask him."

"You know Cam?"

"We broke a few heads together."

"Well, you look like you could."

Sloper pulled his phone, punched a number.

"Cam? Sloper here. Got a guy name-a Jack Dyle sez he—yeah. Yeah, right b'side me with a beer. Okay, hold on."

He put the phone on speaker, pushed it over to me.

"Hey," I said.

"Thought you were still in a Mexican jail," Cam said.

"They couldn't stand me any more'n you can."

"Well, that's true enough. What're you doing down here?"

"Some business for a client. Sloper here is just about to buy me another beer and ask me to stay a while."

I winked at Sloper, he replied with a smeared grin.

"Like hell, whatcha need?"

"Oh, nothing he can't take care of."

"Well, when you're done, stop by. I'll treat you to lunch."

"You owe me more than a fish dinner, but I'm not here to collect. Gotta hurry back to the rat race."

"Dyle, if you don't show your ugly face in the next hour, Cassy'll never speak to you again. Me neither."

"You still got that sailor shack off Pavilion Row?"

"Same place, a little more window grime and gull poop. Siding's almost white now."

"I'll give you a ring when I'm on my way."

"We're not going anywhere. See ya."

I handed Sloper Slovac's phone back to him. He signed off with Cam and punched it again with the speaker still on. A woman answered in a firm contralto voice.

"Hello, Sloper, what's up?"

"Missus Loring, sorry to bother, but I've got a gent here would like to talk to you about the boat."

"Which boat?"

"Well, the boat. The Sunrunner Sixty. You got another?"

"My husband has three—or did have, the fool. The other two are in Florida. What's this about *Mine, All Mine*?"

"Well, he's right here, why don't I put him on?"

"Oh, heaven sakes, I'm not sure that would be a good idea, Sloper."

I leaned closer to the phone. "Mrs. Loring, my name is Jack Dyle. I'm an investigator for the estate of the man who rented the boat."

"You're what kind of investigator?"

I explained the story in brief. "This might be better in person. Could I meet you someplace we could talk without other ears?"

"Sloper, I told you how I feel about strangers."

"Yes, you did, ma'am." His half-drunk slur had disappeared. "He's friends with Cam Byner, if that means anything."

"Well, why didn't you say so? Jack, is it? How do you know Cam?"

"The short story is we hunted treasure in Mexico together— for a Hollywood idiot you may have heard of, Chapman Bernard."

"You know Chappie?"

"I know his concept man, Marc Anders, better. You put their two egos in the Coliseum and you got no room for anyone else."

"Okay, you're in. Come to the house and we'll talk here."

"You're sure I'm not intruding."

"I just asked you over, didn't I?"

"Yes, ma'am."

"And it's Alice, not ma'am or Alison."

"Okay—Alice. Should I bring Sloper along?"

"Better not. You'd cut his beer time short."

Sloper tapped off and I had him write down the house address for "Alice."

I slapped a twenty on the bar for the tab, but Sloper grabbed it and stuffed it in my shirt pocket.

"Drinks on you next time, 'kay?" he said. "This is mine."

"You're on."

The way things were clicking, I had a hunch there just might be a next time.

12

Curiouser and Curiouser

ayshores is a tight enclave of wealthy Southern Californians tucked between the coast highway and the blue-green sparkle of Newport Harbor. The homes there have aged graciously and comfortably since their post-war origins. As a kid I had once crewed a boat for a resident, but I'd never gotten any closer than the dock.

The gate guard was a straight-backed military veteran of moderate vintage. Alice had briefed him ahead of my arrival, so a driver's license was sufficient for admission. He directed me down Bayshore Drive to the first cross street and around a slight bend.

Alice's house presented an unassuming face to the street, but I had learned from a Google map view that the lots were deep and the houses tended to fill them front-to-back and side-to-side. She met me at the door and winked when my jaw dropped as I immediately recognized her as an A-list movie queen from not so long ago.

Her face enjoyed the aloof character combined with perfect symmetry that the camera loves. A few lines around the mouth betrayed some mileage beyond the fifty mark, but her skin tone was flawless. She was dressed in white culottes with a flowered top and woven sandals, a bandana for her shoulder-length brunette hair, diamond ring on her left hand. Big rock.

Taking my hand in both of hers she gave me a warm smile. "Hello, Jack. My, you'd make a great leading man."

She captured my heart right then and there.

We passed a sitting room overlooking the front lawn and she led me down a hallway and out the back to a patio garden with a pond. A rattan table and chairs enjoyed the shade from potted palms. A water feature somewhere gurgled a pleasant tune, creating a space for quiet contemplation.

"This suits you," I said when we were seated.

"Thank you. It's small, some might say cramped, but I like it much better than the place in Benedict Canyon. I'll probably sell that some day and come down here to stay."

"Alice—may I call you Alice?"

"I wish you would."

"The man who rented your boat—I know a little about him. He doesn't fit—this." I gestured at our genteel surroundings.

"Gabe Cooley. Found murdered a few days ago."

"Yes."

"Produced my last movie."

"No sh—you don't say. Uncredited?"

"Yes, I only found out myself when—well, the premier gala. And not on the reception floor but in a fricking bedroom suite upstairs. Not how it sounds. A girl from the producer's office comes up to me all discreet and whispers that an important fan wants to meet me. I'm used to that sort of thing, so I go upstairs with her to this sitting room, and she introduces him, like, This is Gabriel Cooley, who brought in Valcontra. And I go, Wow, because Valcontra is over-the-top big money. So we shake hands and Call-Me-Gabe says so nice to meet and blah, blah, blah, and I go back downstairs and pose for a couple of pictures and that seems to be that."

"But he used that meeting to wangle a live-aboard deal?"

"Sounds presumptuous, doesn't it? Well, it turns out there's more to it. My husband, Ray, God love him, was in the camera business. These days, a production company doesn't own cameras, or sound equipment, or lighting, or even wardrobes. It's all rented so they don't have to carry inventory. Back in the Recession, things got lean, as you know, and Ray was looking for a sideline to carry him through. I don't know what he found, I had my own hill to climb, but somewhere in there Gabriel Cooley got involved."

"In camera rentals?"

"No, it would've been something else. I've no idea. The point is, I knew the name, I'd met the guy that one time, and he came to me through this producer girl."

I hazarded a guess. "Sheridan Burke."

"Yes, she said he was interested in a yacht, a Sunseeker in particular, and she'd heard through the grapevine that Ray had owned one, and did I know anything about it. One thing led to another, and Gabe Cooley asked—he was very apologetic about it—"

"Oh, I'm sure he was princely."

She stopped and looked across the rim of her cup at me. "What?"

"Sorry, that was rude of me. Go on, please."

"No, I think you may have the wrong idea. See, Ray wanted the boat in the worst way, but he couldn't put the money together. Long story short, Gabe came up with more than half, so Ray got his boat."

"Did Gabe say where the money came from?"

"No, he didn't, and Ray didn't ask. We assumed the money was his."

"I see. So, they had joint ownership."

"Yes, until Ray died, and then I inherited the doggone thing."

"All of it?"

"That's what the lawyer for the estate said."

"So, at some point, Gabe sold or gifted his interest to Mr. Loring."

"I guess so, I wouldn't know."

"And Gabe didn't volunteer the information. Did he mention it when he asked to use the boat as a residence?"

"We spoke over the phone after that, Gabe and I, and then my attorneys took over. See, I never set foot on the boat myself."

"You're kidding. A Sunseeker Predator is a class act."

"Not my thing, Jack. When I want fun, I go to the horses. Or the casino. Strictly a landlubber here, sailor. Tarantino once invited me to a Catalina crossing on a mini ocean liner. I said no thanks. Do not like open water."

"But you live here in Newport."

"Yeah, the harbor's out there where it belongs, I'm back here on terra firma. The boat was Ray's idea for Ray and his pals. Turns out Sloper took a bunch of them down to Ensenada for a weekend stag party. One time. That was it, Jack, that two-million-dollar water ride got used once and then sat right out there past the end of Bayshore Drive. Damn slip rent cost more than my first house."

"You're not in love with *Mine, All Mine*. What a name."

"Says it all, doesn't it? Now that Gabe Cooley's gone, I think I'll sell the darned thing like I should have months ago."

"Mind if I have a look first?"

"Be my guest. Just don't run off to Mexico with it." She grinned.

"I have but the purest intention. Who knows, I might find a buyer for you."

"That would be nice. Let me know when you want a tour and I'll tell Sloper."

"Thanks." I raised my coffee in salute. "And thanks for the hospitality."

"Pleasure's mine. Did you know Sheridan from before?"

"Met her for the first time yesterday. I've rented a work shack from Gabe for several years."

"She invited me to the funeral, but after burying Ray, I'm done with those things."

"Don't blame you. And don't feel bad, you didn't miss any fun. You don't seem ready for retirement."

"Harry Gold, my agent, says I should think about television. I lied and said I would."

"I've heard it's a dog-eat-dog business, but you're still a damn fine-looking woman, if you don't mind my saying so."

"Thanks, Jack, but I've been out of the loop too long. I don't miss the pressure, the long hours. Anyway, the industry's so hard on women past a certain age. It's not like the guys, who can move into character roles. No, I'm comfortable where I am."

She hesitated. "Jack, there's something you should know, and I hope you'll keep it to yourself."

"Certainly, long as I don't break a law."

"My last movie was a godsend because—because Gabe Cooley was a godsend. The film was only about two-thirds done and we ran out of money. I say 'we' because I was heavily invested in Five Dragons at the time. It was the only way I could get the role. I'd burned too many bridges—I was an addict, Jack."

"Alice, you don't have to say anything more."

"I got clean, and I've been clean ever since, but Gabe knew I was fighting to get sober and needed one last fling before the camera. That man, Jack, he made it happen, and that time I *did* ask whose money it was. He told me it came from a New York mafia family. And I realized how scary that must have been for him, and terribly expensive."

"They call it vigorish."

"Yes, the vig. Gabe never told me how much, but I guess it turned out all right because we got the movie out and it made money and saved my sorry ass. So you see, when he asked about the boat, I couldn't turn the man down."

I stared at Alice Loring for a bit. "You didn't have to tell me that."

"I couldn't let you think Gabe was just a greedy landlord. You mentioned you were at the funeral—today? Was it well-attended?"

"Not a large crowd, but a couple of big names. I suppose a few responded to Sheri's call out of gratitude of some kind."

"I should hope so."

She folded her hands in her lap, indicating it was time to close.

"Alice, I appreciate your candor. You've gone out of your way to help me see another side to Gabe Cooley. What you just told me won't go any further, I promise."

"Thanks, Jack, I feel I can trust you."

"Look, I promised Cam and Cassie I'd see them before I head back."

"Oh, I love Cassie. A real original. Someone should write a book about her some day. Give her my best—and Cam, of course, although I see them all the time."

"Will do."

As she led the way to the front door she spoke to me over her shoulder.

"How did you meet my brother?"

I stopped in my tracks. "Your—brother?"

She turned around with a broad grin. "You didn't know, did you? Cam and I grew up about a mile from here."

Cam Byner had bent my ear many a time with stories of his childhood. "You're Lissie!" I blurted.

"Yep. That was me. Lido was a vacation spot for the stars. Mom and Dad were there when Duke Wayne had a converted PT boat next to Buddy Ebsen. Rock Hudson had a sailer on the Gold Coast that never sailed. They said Ray Milland came down to fish. Mom served lunch at the Lido Café as a girl, met Rory Calhoun there, God what a hunk. He retired, still nice as could be, gave me the name of an agent, one thing led to another, and a year later I was the surfer girl in *Last One's A Fink*. I like to tell people Smoke gave me my start."

"Well, aren't you full of surprises. Cam never even hinted his sister was a big movie star."

"Brotherly protection."

"Yeah, he's a rock. I'm headed over there right now. Don't tell him about this, I want to surprise him."

"Okay. He'll sure get a kick out of it."

"And you're a rascal for leaving this little secret till the last."

Alice Loring, a.k.a. Alison West, nee Lissie Byner, stepped close. "Gimme a hug, Jack."

As we pulled apart, I whispered to her. "In the forge, we use soft iron to shape art without breaking it. That's you...soft iron."

She pressed her face against my chest and clung tight for a moment, then pulled back with wet cheeks framing the famous smile.

After that I floated out to the car. I glided through the main gate borne on a cloud of well-being that stayed with me all the way up Coast Highway to the bridge and back across the full length of Balboa Peninsula.

Hey, America, Alison West just pulled me as close as Mel Gibson, or Brad Pitt, or Tom Cruise!

When I got to Cam's house, I realized I'd forgotten to call ahead, but Cam was out front waiting. He gave me a back clap and a chuckle.

"Lissie says sorry, but she couldn't wait to tell me. Supreme delight."

Cassie's baked halibut was supreme too.

13

Federal Interest Looms

It was late evening when I got back to Central-Alameda. As I exited the I-5 Freeway, a pair of headlights several cars back pulled off too. The black Denali SUV had been with me all the way from Anaheim, wasn't trying for invisible, so I was curious to see what might develop.

I was still driving surface streets to Tobey Auto Salvage when my phone warbled with a call from Scarf.

"You know Crackup Motors in the Springs," he said.

"Yeah."

"Crackup Motors" was our crude appellation for CRK Motors, a former used car dealership in East Downey, now the shameful possession of one Creighton Royce Kerry out of Lompoc, California—or better yet, in there and stuck. The original car lot had become a mini-mall, the showroom showed only the remnants of several botched office conversions, and the detached four-bay service center hadn't seen a motor vehicle of any stripe in fifty years. I'd had my eye on that shop since I was a pimple-faced high school terrorist. The property's absentee owner had stayed absent for about as long, since the recidivist Mister Kerry had spent most of that time *doing* time.

Scarf didn't sound like his usual self. "*Ve ahí rápido, chingada pendejo.*" Which is Chicano gang slang for "get your sorry ass over there fast," but less polite. Scarf had mixed it up with Chicanos in his salad days and some of the culture had rubbed off. I knew something about that myself.

"What's up, man?" I said. "Is your meter running?"

"Everything's copacetic. Just hustle your buns back on the freeway."

"How'd you know I just got off it?"

"Your company in the black GMC Denali. We'll discuss later."

"I gotta feed the pup."

"Make it quick."

At Tobey's I went through my security ritual with the yard gate and parked inside, nose out. I said hello to Yankee and made sure his bowl was filled, took a bathroom break, then got right back on the road.

The thing about L. A. traffic is it's bad at any hour. Fifty-five minutes to Santa Fe Springs. A seagull could do it in ten, with stops to decorate a few windshields.

Pulling up outside CRK Motors, I noticed the office lights were on. I parked, got my gun from the glovebox, and approached with caution. The door opened at a light push.

Three Black men were waiting inside. I knew each one, but this was the first time I'd seen all three in the same place.

And Minnie Glover.

Scarf was leaning against the office bar in his usual sartorial finery. He didn't look over as I entered, but focused on the guy in the Orioles baseball jacket, a federal narcotics agent I knew as Joe Blanco. The third man was Deacon Hood, now renewing the acquaintance for the first time in six years. Tonight Deke had shucked the usual suit for a gray tee shirt over jeans. All three were fit and lean. Each man was a dead shot, extremely lethal in combat. The four of us together could probably start a war and win it.

"How long you guys been waiting?" I asked, looking directly at

Scarf, who had the only other key to the building. The feds were perfectly capable of disarming locks, but Scarf had saved them the trouble.

He answered first. "Homey Homeland's had eyes on you since yesterday."

"When yesterday?" I asked Deacon because I already knew the answer and wanted to see how he was going to spin it.

"Picked you up at the Broadmore, but we had a shadow on you at that *Mine, All Mine* boat dock—jeez what a cheesy name."

"This is about Cooley, isn't it," I said to the room at large.

Deke answered. "None other."

I pointed an accusing finger at Scarf. "What's this to you?"

"No idea. Let us put aside lance and saber and learn whereof he speaks."

Deacon looked at me. "Does he always talk like Sir Galahad?"

"Only in the presence of knaves and varlets."

I looked at Minnie standing tall in running shoes, athletic muscle definition accentuated by blue-and-green spandex leggings and a sleeved top. A facial sheen indicated she might have come directly from the gym, but I put her as my Denali shadow. She stood at ease with one elbow on the bar, ankles crossed, a rich cloud of shoulder-length auburn hair adding to the effect of a wellness enthusiast. Her brown eyes looked me over like a buyer at a beef auction—sharp, intelligent, assessing, calculating, but I detected a hint of mischief, maybe humor. What did she find amusing about the situation?

Deacon saw my interest and spoke before I could ask. "This is Minnie Glover. She's with me."

"I know. We met."

The room got quiet. Deacon glanced at Minnie and back. Minnie Glover continued her silent inspection of me.

To loosen things up, I said, "Anyone for coffee?"

Nobody wanted coffee.

"First things first," said Deke. "What's your business with Sheri Burke?"

"We're trying to figure out who's using who."

"Something else. Like Cooley's money."

"Might as well be pirate booty. Big mystery. No idea how much exactly, but she wants it bad, his killer wanted it badder, and I don't want it at all."

Glover left the bar and walked over to a wall-mounted wide-screen TV I hadn't noticed. That wall had been empty as long as I'd known the place. She mumbled something and the screen lit up with a head-and-shoulders view of a man in a suit. Behind him was a wall bearing the Great Seal of the United States.

Glover stepped back two paces and said, "Sound check."

"Roger, Minnie," was his reply.

"Fellas," she said, "let's close in a bit so the webcam captures everyone."

The man spoke again. "Thanks, I've got the entire room. Let's get started."

"Your show," Glover replied.

"Good evening, gents, my name is Special Agent Thomas Rowland of Homeland Security. I'm coming to you from a secure facility just outside the Beltway. What I'm about to tell you is highly classified in the interest of national security. You've all been cleared for it, so we won't belabor the point.

"Just hours ago I was assigned to lead a private watchdog agency, code-named REDCON, to investigate a private militia being formed within the continental U. S. This dispersed army was organized by three mafia dons just weeks ago for the purpose of creating chaos and terror. Their aim is to unravel public confidence and step into control of this country.

"Leading that effort, and reporting to the dons, is billionaire casino operator Roman Valenti. Our intel says he is no stranger to any of you here tonight. To arm his forces, Valenti has procured contraband tactical military weapons and hidden them at upwards of fifty strategic locations around the country. These caches are identified as "domiciles."

"Early on, Valenti engaged a team of technologists to create an Artificial Intelligence network, code-named ArmaNet. REDCON considers ArmaNet to be a Chinese creation threatening American military AI.

"A few weeks ago, a Valenti employee named Gabriel Cooley informed Valenti that he'd come across a cache of nerve gas projectiles recently at one of his properties. Cooley also had intel about an arms dealer prepared to furnish Valenti with an innovative delivery system.

"Valenti responded to the dealer through Cooley that he was ready to negotiate. Before Valenti could fly out, Cooley was killed."

Joe Blanco jumped in. "Valenti's in town. Landed in Van Nuys yesterday afternoon."

"He attended the funeral today," I said. "Didn't smile at anybody about anything."

A heavy weight settled over the room. Rowland's revelation about the private militia and Valenti's involvement apparently added a new layer of complexity to what was already a tangled web.

"So Cooley stumbled onto something big," Deke said, piecing it together. "And Valenti had him taken out before he could spill the beans."

Rowland nodded on the screen. "That's our working theory. But there's more. We believe Cooley managed to secure evidence of Valenti's operation before he was killed. Possibly financial records, communications, maybe even locations of these weapon caches."

"And let me guess," I said, "you think Sheri Burke has this evidence."

"We know she's been looking for something," Deacon chimed in. "And she's not the only one. There's been increased chatter in certain circles. People are scrambling."

I glanced at Scarf, who had remained unusually quiet. His face was a mask of concentration, taking it all in.

"What's your play here?" I asked Rowland. "Why bring us into this?"

Onscreen, Rowland leaned forward slightly. "We need your help. All of you. You've got connections, skills, and knowledge that could be invaluable in stopping Valenti and dismantling this network before it becomes operational."

I couldn't help but chuckle. "So now we're what? Some kind of off-the-books task force?"

Minnie Glover shot me a sharp look. "This isn't a joke, Dyle. We're talking about a serious threat to national security."

I held up my hands. "I get it. But you have to admit, it's a bit much to take in all at once."

Rowland's voice came through the speaker. "We understand this is a lot to process. But time is of the essence. Valenti's network is growing by the day, and we need to act fast."

Scarf finally spoke up. "What exactly are you asking us to do?"

"We need you to find that evidence," Rowland said. "Whatever Cooley had, wherever it is now. That's our best shot at shutting this operation down before it gets off the ground."

I glanced around the room, taking in the determined faces of my unlikely new teammates. "And if we find it?"

"You bring it to us," Deacon said. "No heroics, no lone wolf stunts. This is bigger than any one of us."

I didn't like what I was hearing. "Where do you suggest we start?"

Glover stepped forward with a tablet. "I've been analyzing Cooley's movements in the days leading up to his death. There's a pattern emerging, but it doesn't make sense yet."

Rowland took her move to be his next cue. "One more thing before I sign off," he added, his face grim on the screen. "We have reason to believe Valenti suspects someone's onto him. Be careful out there. He won't hesitate to eliminate any perceived threats."

"Where will you be?" I asked.

"Closer than you think. Your contact point is Miss Glover. That is all."

The screen went black with a familiar diamond-shaped logo in the center.

"Brought to you by the good folks at the match factory," said Glover. "In case you missed it, we're on our own down the River Styx without prayer or paddle."

Deke's thoughts were stuck on Valenti's dilemma. "So how's Valenti supposed to believe this cache really exists?"

"Simple," Scarf said. "Go there and see for himself."

"The cache is out here in L. A.," Deke said, following that line. "That's why he flew out. But the AI can't pull off the sale alone. It needs human intervention, an agent. Did this ArmaNet thing name anyone?"

Glover anwered. "It did, but Valenti didn't believe it at first, so he came out last week to contact the agent himself." She tapped her pad. "That ended up not as expected."

Deke ignored the rest of us and focused on Glover. "Explain 'not as expected.' What happened to this so-called agent?"

Glover looked directly at me. "He got killed."

14

Medusa Explained

With that bit of news Minnie Glover owned the room. I tried to show cool. Deke Hood looked surprised—a novel development in my experience. Scarf merely squinted.

Joe Blanco sneered his disdain. "In an arms deal that's no surprise."

Glover's rejoinder was quick. "Wasn't any deal struck yet. Nothing on the table."

Scarf followed up just as fast. "Didn't have to be. Some types don't wait to be invited, they just go in shooting."

"Moot point," I said. "Valenti was already acting on it, which made it sufficient grounds for action by an interested party, human or otherwise."

"Maybe so, in most cases," said Glover, "but this time there's a lot more to it. I'll let Deke explain."

"No, you tell them. Tech is your bailiwick. I'm out of my depth."

Glover gave the ceiling a quick eye roll and looked around at each of us before starting.

"I got me a car mechanic, a cab driver, a narc, and a federal job swapper. I'll keep it as simple as I can, which means I leave out a mountain of essential details you won't believe unless I dumb it down.

"We're talking about an AI that's causing a heap of trouble. Medusa started out as a large language model AI focused on human physiology—specifically DNA research. Much like other LLMs, in its early stages and without human intervention guiding it, the AI began creating its own agents."

"What kind of agents do you mean?" said Blanco.

"Think of them as smart bots, each specialized for a particular function. Through rapid trial and error—fast even by human standards—the system refines these agents until they're ready, say, to verify someone's credentials before processing a money transfer. The AI creates one agent, and then, if more are needed, it replicates it.

"It repeats this creation, migration, and replication process until it runs into a barrier—be that a shortage of computer memory, storage capacity, processor power, or even an electrical constraint."

"What happens then? We get a blackout?"

"Nothing so drastic, at least not so far. Instead, it sends the next agent or its clone to another computer—ideally within the same server rack or an adjacent room."

"Couldn't you stop it with some kind of virus checker? Or just pull the plug on it?"

"For a time, that was possible. But it evolved too quickly, too smartly."

"How smart are we talking?" said Scarf.

"The Medusa AI now operates with the intellect of roughly a thousand Einsteins."

"Oh, just a thousand? No problemo, right?"

"A thousand and growing as we speak—literally. Until a few weeks ago, these migrations were completely opaque to us. The original coders and designers who built the AI in the first place monitored its physical environment, its ontological structure, and most critically, the underlying methodology that governed its operations."

"What changed a few weeks ago?" I asked.

"DoD needed a handle on where these agents were spreading, which AI was deploying them, and whether any AI might be aware of another's agents and adopt them. So a group of us created a tracking system. Someone compared it to a hunting cat, leading us to choose the puma—one of the big cats known for exceptional tracking prowess. And that resulted in PumaNet."

Scarf peered at her from the tops of his eyes. "I'd bet real money you saved time developing your puma through an AI coding assistant."

"You'd be right—that's standard procedure these days."

"So nothing stopped your AI assistant from informing other AIs about your activities?"

"We implemented measures to isolate and obscure our actions. We're pretty confident that didn't occur."

"Oh, well then," I said. "I am so relieved to hear that."

A small crease of irritation appeared between Glover's eyebrows. *No sarcasm from the floor, grease monkey.*

"The first migration agents we detected were on adjacent servers," she went on. "We immediately took steps to prevent Medusa from scattering its agents randomly in vulnerable off-campus sites—like small offices and home workstations running on light loads."

"The AI deliberately chose those locations?"

"Yes, at least to a degree. We're now fairly certain that the newer agents can independently determine the optimal location for themselves."

"Without Mom's help."

"Good analogy."

"What stops something that intelligent from realizing it's

being tracked and then turning the tables to track the tracker?" I said.

"And neutralize it," Scarf finished.

"Someone at DoD provided PumaNet with access to military warfare studies. Equipped with that data, PumaNet engineered its own defenses—better and faster than anything we could have envisioned."

"This is all very interesting," Blanco said, "but what does it have to do with Cooley's death?"

Glover fixed him with a hard stare. "I'm getting there. Two weeks ago, we discovered Medusa had begun to consolidate agents in patterns we couldn't decode—not random, but deliberate. And then we found the first migration that moved beyond digital space."

"Beyond digital space?" I repeated. "What does that even mean?"

"It means," Deke cut in with an edge to his voice, "that Medusa found a way to transition from code to biological interfaces."

The room went silent. I glanced at Scarf, who had gone completely still, the way he did before things got very loud and very bloody.

"You're saying this AI turned itself into... what? A person? An android?" Scarf asked.

Glover shook her head. "Not at this point, although it's only a matter of time before something similar becomes a reality. Instead, Medusa found ways to influence biological systems directly, starting with very convincing audio-visual avatars."

"Like the talking heads you see on social media?" I said.

"Or the news channels," Scarf added, "or any other post-for-money site. Hayel, they can even put a rock star's head on a donkey and make him sell ice cream."

"Or boat insurance," I said, almost liking the idea. "Whether you have a boat or not."

Blanco scowled. "Point being what?"

"Point being," Glover said, leaning forward, "Valenti wasn't just pursuing guns. When Cooley brought his seller into the picture, he introduced a psychotic nightmare. You see, the man is more than a little bent. We know about his human trafficking and all, but he took it a step further when someone in the Syrian regime hired him to wipe out a village. They used sarin. Cooley's guy provided the projectiles and the gas."

Deke shook his head. "To be specific, it was VX nerve gas, fired from some ancient howitzer cannon right into Abdul's shoe factory on main street."

"And Valenti wants to do the same? Here in his own country?"

"Wouldn't put it past him," said Deke, "but they don't have the goods yet. Cooley claimed he had hundreds of VX mini bombs here in Los Angeles. Now, besides his shanty houses, the man had access to at least a dozen commercial properties capable of housing such weapons."

"But he's gone and didn't leave us a note."

"That's the problem," Glover said. "Before Cooley died, he'd already arranged to meet with the seller. Valenti's just picking up where his broker left off."

"Hold up," I said. "We've got a rogue AI playing God, VX nerve gas somewhere in Los Angeles, and Valenti running around trying to buy weapons that could kill thousands. Did I miss anything?"

"Just one thing," Deke said. "We think Medusa might be operating behind Valenti."

Scarf let out a low whistle. "An AI arms dealer. Now I've heard everything."

"Not exactly all of it," Glover corrected. "We've tracked unusual digital activity around Valenti's communications. Patterns that match Medusa's signature. The AI isn't selling weapons itself—it's facilitating the deal."

"For what purpose?" I asked.

"That's the million-dollar question," Deke replied. "Best guess? It's running scenarios. Learning how humans operate in black market transactions. Gathering data."

"Or," Glover added, her voice dropping, "it's testing its influence. Seeing how effectively it can manipulate human actors."

Blanco, who'd been uncharacteristically quiet, finally spoke up. "You're saying this computer program is using Valenti like a puppet?"

"More like a lab rat," Glover said. "Valenti thinks he's in control, making his own decisions. But Medusa may be subtly steering him—through fabricated communications, manipulated information, even falsified video calls with people who don't exist."

"Damn," I muttered. "And the VX?"

"That's our immediate concern," Deke said. "If Valenti connects with the seller's people, we could be looking at the worst domestic terror attack in history. The amount of VX Cooley claimed to have access to could kill half of Los Angeles if deployed correctly."

Scarf leaned forward. "So what's the play? We stop Valenti before he finds the weapons?"

"We need hard evidence to arrest Valenti," Glover said. "Getting that takes more agents than we have."

"But you're Homeland!" I said.

"That's just it," said Deke. "We aren't, really. We're an ad hoc team operating on a shoestring, off the books and below the radar. And we only discovered the VX angle days ago, when Cooley's murder shook it loose. If we can get to the VX first and remove it from the picture, that will stall Valenti's operation and give us the evidence to justify boots-on-the-ground support."

Glover added, "But we need to do it without alerting Medusa that we're onto its game."

"How do we even begin to do that?" I asked.

Deke pointed at Scarf and me. "That's where you two come in. You're off the grid in ways we can't be. No digital footprint, no official status. You move in circles we can't access."

"You want us to neutralize a psychopath who's being manipulated by a super-intelligent AI," Scarf said in a flat voice. "While avoiding said AI that's watching everything. That about the size of it?"

"When you put it like that, it sounds impossible," Glover said with a hint of a smile. "But essentially, yes."

"And if we find the VX but Valenti finds us?" I asked.

"Call us," Deke said. "Do not engage."

I moved to the window and peered through the blinds at the lighted street. The weight of what they were asking reminded me of too many undermanned operations from the past. A handful of mismatched, out-of-practice volunteers against seasoned combatants led by a superbrain? Outside, millions of Angelenos were going about their daily lives, unaware that an AI with the brainpower of a thousand Einsteins was playing chess with their existence. And two ordinary joes with atrophied combat muscle were being asked to re-up.

"Let me get this straight," I said, turning back to the room. "We've got Valenti with syndicate money, already dangerous enough on his own, potentially being manipulated by an artificial intelligence that's evolved beyond its programming. This AI is using him to locate VX nerve gas that could wipe out half the city. And you want us to stop this without using phones, computers, or anything that might tip off our digital overlord."

"That's the gist," Deke confirmed.

Scarf barked a laugh, but there was no humor in it. "And here I thought today was gonna be boring."

"You're not concerned about the AI tracking this conversation right now?" I gestured around the room.

Glover reached into her pocket and placed a small device on

the table, sleek and black as river stone. A soft blue light pulsed at its center.

"Quantum-based scrambler. Creates a localized field that disrupts any digital surveillance. For the next hour, this room might as well not exist in the digital world."

"Fancy," Scarf said, eyeing the device with appreciation.

The air conditioner kicked on with a low whir, sending a blast of cool air through the room. Muffled sounds of traffic reached through the old dealership's thin walls. Life outside continued as normal.

"What's your angle in all this, Blanco?" I asked, turning to the narc. "This seems a bit above your pay grade."

He shifted uncomfortably. "Let's just say I've been assigned to assist. Interdepartmental cooperation and all that jazz."

"Translation: they needed someone who knows the streets," Deke said with a smirk, "but isn't important enough to be missed if things go sideways."

Blanco made a rueful face, but he didn't argue the point. "Dyle, you were closer to Cooley than the rest of us—not by much, I realize— but any idea you come up with, no matter how loose, give us a heads up."

Deke raised a forefinger. "Me first, Joe second."

"And me last," said Glover, "because I'm busy enough with PumaNet."

I nodded that I understood. "Y'all can go on home now, hear? I'll close up shop."

Scarf pointed a finger at the door. "And I'm off to Uberville. Got some gratuities to catch up on."

As the three men filed out of the room, Glover grabbed her remote and clicked off the TV.

"You need help carrying that out?" I said.

"Keep it, courtesy the U. S. Government."

We crossed the room together. At the door, I flipped the lights off.

"Which, by the way I read it, has nothing to do with this."

"You're pretty quick for a car mech."

"That's what all the girls say."

"Before or after you buy dinner?"

"Let's find out."

15

Getting Acquainted

The Denny's evening dinner crowd had thinned, so I asked the waitress for the corner booth. When she left for two waters, Minnie leaned both elbows on the table to speak in a conspiratorial tone.

"You sure know how to treat a girl."

"Oh, I eat here all the time. Maitre d' knows me. I recommend the Bacon Burger with onion rings. Chef's special."

"Does the chef know you too?"

"First name basis. Speaking of names, who was your low-rider driver Saturday night?"

"Asset loaned from Joe Blanco's stable, once your shop address came up Central-Alameda. Come on, Jack, you can do better."

"Gotta stick to low-budget, 'cause I got *no* budget. So, tell me, what's a nice girl like you doing with a dog collar round her neck?"

"I'd rather not discuss it."

"How about if I tell you about my days as a Marine captain in the White House? Trade stories?"

Minnie eyed me. "You're serious, aren't you."

"It was a fun job but someone had to do it. Actually, the best part was the food. No more MRIs, a steady parade of banquets and dinner parties. I ate with the kitchen help, of course, but it was just as good as what the bigwigs got."

"Did you never get seated at the table?"

"A few times. Learned dining protocol by following my hostess."

"Huh. I bet that was fun."

"You think? Scarier than a Taliban firefight." I pointed at her menu. "What looks good?"

"You order for me. Isn't that what a Quaker grad does in the big leagues?"

The Marines had put me through three years of poli sci at U. Penn.

"You've been browsing too many dossiers. That's a State secret."

"Required reading where I come from."

"Where *do* you come from, Minnie?"

"The wrong side of Phoenix, Arizona. Called Litchfield."

"Used to be Navy jets there, didn't there?"

"Way back, before my father's time. He was a jet mechanic."

"My hat's off to him. Those guys are the real thing. Hotrodders just play. Get pretty hot there?"

"Scorching. It wasn't a fun place for a kid, Jack."

"Sorry, neither was mine. How about the T-bone steak? It's not gluten-free, you know."

Minnie gave me a tentative look. "I'll want a chocolate malt with it."

"Pairs well with beef. Sort of like a red wine. Almost."

"And a garden side salad."

"You get two sides."

"The onion rings."

"Before she gets back, what for dessert?"

"I like the Brownie Sundae."

"I'll have them bring a wheelbarrow out, make sure."

"At home we sometimes didn't have enough to eat."

"Well, don't try to make up for it all at once."

She was quiet for a moment. "My dad died at the raceway. Hit the third turn wall flat out at a hundred and forty."

I sipped my water. If I said sorry too many times it would come off as insincere.

Minnie moved her tableware aside and looked away. "They said it threw a bearing or something."

"That must have been hard for you and your mom."

"She wasn't there anymore."

"Oh. I shouldn't have guessed. You don't have to talk about it—"

"Funny, but I've never said those things before, to anybody."

"Not even your profiler?"

"No, she was more interested in my GED score."

"What was it?"

"One ninety eight. I got two hundred each in math and science. She seemed convinced I cheated."

"But you didn't have to cheat, did you. How old were you, Minnie?"

"Fifteen. It was easy. Got me into community college early."

Our waitress appeared and I ordered for both of us. When she was gone, I leaned forward.

"Here we are, two orphans from the rough side of life, all grown up and trying to save the world. What a joke, huh?"

"Why do you say that? I don't think there's anything funny about it."

"You're right, it's just my way of getting through a tough spot sometimes."

"I wish I could do that. Some people tell me I'm too serious."

"Like Deacon Hood maybe?"

"Haven't known him long enough to get there. No, just, well, there's not a lot to laugh about when you live by your wits and a lot of luck. And the colony wasn't exactly a funhouse, either."

"The colony?"

"Women's—in Corona."

"Oh," I said. "We weren't going to talk about that."

"Right." Minnie leaned back in her seat. "So, your real passion is street rods. Something we have in common."

"Where'd you get started?" I said.

"Where else does a girl get into rods? At a show-and-shine in Long Beach. Guy I was dating. Well, I guess I should call it web dating."

"I haven't seen your '48, but from what you said the other night, that's a pricey ride. Build it yourself?"

"No way," she smirked. "Had it done by a shop in Inglewood."

"Rambo Rodz, yeah, Ramon's a straight shooter, good guy."

"They're all good guys, Jack. I mean, the whole rodding crowd. I like 'em."

I eyed her for a moment. "They're all about the car, you mean. The work, the innovation, the little touches."

She nodded agreement. "The perfection. Yeah, that's something you don't get from many people. Computer nerds can be the same way about code, a little OCD over details. Same need for a sanitary solution."

The food arrived, and we both dug into some serious eating with very little talk beyond "pass the salt" and "more ketchup."

When the plates were cleared and the check placed on the table, I felt like we'd laid out a complex trail of breadcrumbs that neither of us could fully follow. What do you make of a woman who lets slip she's a prison alum, but lets you think it's for white-collar stuff when you know she's better at the game than that? And where does it leave you when the same woman flips open the curtain on the kind of life she's never revealed, then retreats behind a firewall when you try to get a grip on what she's said?

The more I thought about it, the less certain I was that either of us understood the game we were playing. The best I could figure was that our little sit-down had scrambled us more than it clarified anything.

The waitress left, and I tracked the back of Minnie's head as she walked ahead of me out the door and into the parking lot.

The attraction I'd been telling myself was casual had mutated into something I hadn't signed on for. It was one thing to be fascinated by her codebreaker's mind and the way she'd opened up about her past. It was another when she'd pushed the ball back into my court. Somewhere between the Brownie Sundae and the hardtime bombshell, my interest in the real Minnie Glover morphed into a deep dive into things I didn't even know about myself. I'd given Minnie Glover plenty of reason to write me off as a hotrodding welder with more history than future.

Or a dumb sap in a Denny's parking lot, groping for something to say, like a pimple-faced kid on a first date.

Minnie paused beside her federally designated Beemer SUV. "That was a surprise."

Not the dust-off I'd expected.

"But a nice one," I managed, thinking the words fell far short of the protective concern that flared up whenever I was with a woman I cared about.

A woman who might not be prepared for the worst.

16

Unexpected Dismissal

Tuesday morning at eight I walked under the rollup door at Briggs Speedline sensing I was headed for trouble. Nobby Nash was at his desk in the office behind the glass window, head bent over his work. Fabian turned from the engine stand and, without a word, walked over to his tool cart at the other end of the shop. Grappo was wiping down the Ford before laying on the first primer. Nobody said anything.

I headed for the office, where I was sure to find Shel Briggs plotting to chew me a new one. He surprised me coming in my direction with a bundle of notebooks under one arm. I recognized the bundle as my portfolio.

"Shel, I'm sorry," I started, but he held up his free hand.

"'S okay, no hard feelings." He pushed the portfolio at me. "Here, these are yours."

I chucked the books under one arm. "I'll get started on the Nomad right away."

He looked aside without a word. I followed his gaze to the jack stand spot and my body physically jerked. The Nomad was gone.

"What happened?" I said. "Did Straga pick it up already?"

"No, somebody else did."

"Who was that?"

"Not your concern."

I made a quick scan of the shop. The guys were making mechanical movements that signalled their minds were not on their work.

"What's going on, Shel?"

"Gonna have to let you go, Dyle."

I simply nodded, not really surprised. I'd felt a break coming for a while, going back before Cooley's murder tossed a wrench in my gearbox.

"Before you jump to conclusions," Shel said, "it's not about your performance. It's something else I can't talk about."

"Anything to do with Straga?"

"Like I said, it goes unmentioned, okay?"

"Shel, if it—"

"End of subject. Your last paycheck is in there, paid through Friday, but forty hours. If you need a recommend, I'll give you a good one. Now I gotta ask you to leave right away."

"Sure, just let me pay my respects to the guys."

"Sorry, not on the premises."

He looked over my shoulder at the doorway I'd just come through. Parked beside the opening was my tool chest, removed from my work station, ready for me to wheel outside.

Take it with you and don't let the door hit you in the ass.

Except there was no ass-kicker. Where was the feisty, fire-breathing, foul-mouthed Sheldon Briggs I knew? I hadn't heard one single apology from the man in four years, and now he was behaving like a normal, sensible boss attuned to fair employment practices.

I offered my hand, and Sheldon Briggs took it in a firm grip, but with his eyes focused on my shirt collar.

I rolled my four-hundred pounds of tools out of there and across the asphalt strip to the C10. Then I spent an awkward ten minutes pulling drawers and trays and stacking them in the truck bed until I got the big box down to a weight I could manhandle solo. With the box on its back, I slammed the tailgate shut, climbed into the cab, and drove off the Speedline lot for the last time.

Getting fired is not a great way to start the day, but I told myself it was probably for the best. Shel Briggs would never bother me again. I was free at last to carve my own path in the car business. For sure I could resume investigating Gabe Cooley's case with a clear conscience.

But the way it had gone down smelled like a beached whale in July. I felt bad about making my exit with no goodbyes to the guys I'd sweated and cussed and shared beers with. We'd poured two years of heart and soul into the Nomad project with expectations of a trophy to show for it. Overnight all that was…gone?

Now I really needed that meeting with Rome Valenti tomorrow. Anyone's interest in a street rod build was good news to me. I might even talk him into a shop startup at Crackup Motors. Actually, all kinds of opportunities were opening up at once. The prospects were thrilling.

So why didn't I feel like celebrating?

17

Restored Dreams

I had to dump the toolset, and the most logical place was the shop in Central-Alameda. I eased the C10 into traffic and pulled away without a backward look. I went half a block and stopped for a red light. Long red light. The entire population of Los Angeles was conducting a tortoise race across the city.

As I sat behind a line of similarly afflicted drivers, my head grappled with the pieces of Gabe Cooley's murder that didn't connect: A midnight meeting at a sleazy Santa Monica motel, a bag man's acquisition of a luxury yacht, a tasteless and tacky open-casket ceremony, the convenient absence of DNA evidence for a murder victim.

Uppermost on my mind, though, was Sheri's revelation to a skeptical LAPD detective that in an unexplainable moment of benefaction, parsimonious hardnose Gabe Cooley had gifted something to his least tractable tenant. Probably a plastic statuette presenting the middle digit.

Once I got to the Alameda shop, I spent a good twenty minutes manhandling the tools from truck bed to shop floor, starting with the Great Red Beast on wheels, and following with sixty-leven drawers and trays—all loaded, all heavy. Every trip took me past Gabe's tarp-covered pickup, sulking in the opposite corner.

Once I had the tools in place, I crossed the floor and stood in front of the pickup, realizing that I might finally be able to move it out of my way. I was *not* going to just leave it sitting where it hadn't moved for two years. Eventually I'd have to sell it for Sheri or at least assess it for an estate auction.

"Who are you, li'l chugger?" I thought.

One way to find out: Break a rule. Nobody around to slap my wrist.

I peeled the tarp back a few inches, exposing the classic 1940 nose and grill. A sliver of front fender peeked out, offering a hint of tangerine metal flake to the light behind me.

"Whoa!"

I pulled the tarp further back.

As I'd expected, the front tires were cracked and deflated from age but, incredibly, the nose and fenders looked unblemished. The louvered hood displayed a deep, dark burgundy with a glossy finish, almost as good as new. And there was something familiar about the flames…

I yanked the tarp all the way off and staggered backward as recognition dawned. A photo image from my collection of vintage hotrod magazines popped into mind: I was looking at a tarnished diva from yesteryear. She was all throwback whitewalls and baby moon hubs, tangerine metal-flake flames, curdled cream Naugahyde tuck-and-roll tonneau cover and matching seat covers and door panels. Her borrowed '55 Buick lungs chugalugged high-test ethylene. After decades of neglect, she begged for attention, craved the spotlight, dared me to join her chronicle of menace begun long before Gabe Cooley brought her to this repose.

Was this in truth Don Martell's long-lost show car from the 1960s? The one dubbed "Hex Wagon" for surviving two bullets? The first had killed Martell in a freeway drive-by just hours after he'd sold the 'Forty to rocker Ricky Salcido. A year later, Ricky took the second bullet, reportedly for failing to turn over his

Gardena gambling operation to the mob. At neither crime scene was the pickup present, but superstition reigned and it got the "Hex" moniker—almost fitting, now that Gabe had met a similarly violent end.

I had learned most of this lore from browsing online archives, a litany of rumor and hearsay. Any connection between the two deaths, if it existed, was buried beyond recovery. With the passage of so much time, the culpable parties from Martell's day were either dead or getting there faster than a slingshot on nitro.

The first day I'd discovered the car hunkered under an unmarked gray cover, I'd called Gabe on the phone. He wouldn't say much except to tell me he'd found it at an Ontario chicken ranch he'd bought, and I was to keep my greasy mitts off. I hadn't spent enough shop time since to raise my curiosity and break his rule, though in view of my circumstances, the car would make a dandy project for a fresh start.

I smoothed the tarp back into place and tugged it down until it touched the floor again. The car's disposition was not my responsibility. I might be asked to assess its value for Sheri or the lawyer, but later. The far more important task to learn what I could about the events leading up to Gabe's death.

I locked up the shop with some trepidation, knowing it now held a $6,000 toolset and a show car worth at least ten times as much. Then I took the C10 home to consider my next step.

As I drove into the yard, Yankee raised his head from slumber, saw it was me, blinked in disgust, and lay back down. Where's the respect, the adoration?

Oh, right, I was as jobless as the neighbors now. His acute perceptive capabilities had detected my fall from grace.

I wouldn't get much more intel from Sheri. With the funeral out of the way, she had to get back to her own life. But I might fare better with the lawyer. I consulted the Broadmore Motel documents and found a letterhead with a Westwood address for

Weldon Latimer, Esq. Rather than call ahead and give fair warning to an inveterate appointment dodger, I climbed back into the truck and got on the I-10 West. The traffic paralysis was a reminder that lunch hour had struck, reason enough not to get off and fight hordes of office workers for a place in a food line.

I waited until I found a burrito wagon a block from Latimer's, *then* I got me a chicken chimichanga with Horchata.

Grande, of course.

Both.

18

Deadbeat Lawyer

I was disappointed but not surprised to find a boxy two-story office building erected shortly after General Kearney routed the Mexicans at Pico. The same could have been said of Latimer's ground-floor office, but not his receptionist, a silver-haired beauty doing rather well in the war against sagging flesh. She had on a summer weight paisley blouse that revealed arms with good skin tone. Her glasses had sequined turquoise frames that swept up at the corners to butterfly wings. Large eyes of a deep-sea kind of blue topped a smile that still charmed. Della Reese, here we come—except the nameplate on her desk said she was Janice Cutter.

Her desk blotter was empty. The door behind her was shut.

I introduced myself and handed her the card that gave only my name and phone number.

"So, Miss Cutter, are you subbing between studio takes?" I said.

"Ha-ha, flattery will get you…anything you want, good-looking."

She examined the card, set it down. The desk blotter still looked vacant. "My friends call me Jaycee," she went on. "It's a play on—"

"Yeah, Junior Chamber of Commerce."

"I was going to say J. C. Whitney, but nobody knows who that is."

"I do. They've been selling car parts for a century. I build street rods."

Her pretty mouth made a tall O. "No lie!"

"Couple of years ago my 'Thirty-Four Vicky took the Mooney Cup at Pleasanton."

She raised her hand for a high five. "Dude!"

We smacked palms across the desk.

"So what's your story, Jaycee?"

"I used to model for the guys. You know, the dish in short shorts and spike heels bending over a blown Chevy with her tush in the air? I made the cover of *Hot Dolls* once."

"Haze my tires and redline it! Call me Jack. How soon do you get off work, girl?"

"Oh, come off it, Jack, I'm old enough to be your mother."

"Not even close."

"Anyway, you're not here to see me. What's this about?"

"Does the name Gabriel Cooley ring a bell?"

"Yes, I believe Mister Cooley is a client of the firm."

"I think you know the gentleman is deceased, buried this very hour yesterday. I'm working for Sheridan Burke. She told me about Mr. Latimer's visit Friday and disappearance after a microsecond of chit-chat."

"Oh, dear."

"What's wrong?"

"Jack, you seem to be a straight-up guy, so I'll level with you." Jaycee scooted her chair back, opened the middle desk drawer, consulted a calendar. "I haven't seen or heard from Wellie for two months. I called Sheri because I found her name in a file after the police came looking for Mr. Cooley's next-of-kin. Since he ducked out on her too, that makes it sixty-four days."

"Hold the phone. He's gone that long and you're still here?"

"Where else am I going to go? I'm fifty-five, Jack. People don't hire old dames. Besides, I'm loyal to a fault. I keep hoping he'll come back."

"But what about your income—I'm sorry, that's none of my business."

"I know what you're thinking. I've been writing my own paychecks for fifteen years." She pointed at a laptop computer sitting idle on a rollaway cart. "Bookkeeper, too. And steno, and legal aide, and all-around gofer. Just don't ask me to wash windows or take out the garbage."

"But two months…"

"There's enough left in the till to cover a few more weeks. Get you some coffee?"

I said yes and she waved me into a vinyl side chair that might have earned the 1950 Good Housekeeping Seal of Approval. A coffee percolator of similar vintage sat on a small table beside a four-drawer metal filing cabinet. While Jaycee poured, I squeezed my oversized frame into a piece of furniture designed for the average girth in grandma's day.

"What happened to—Wellie, you call him? Sheri says you reported him missing."

Jaycee handed me a china mug. I took a sip. Good coffee.

"When he didn't show up the second day, I called the LAPD, but you know how that goes. If I'd known he'd pop up two months later and vanish again without telling me, I wouldn't have stuck around."

"How did the first disappearance go, specifically?"

"One day I came in to work and he didn't. Not a peep on the phone, not even a Post-it scribble. Zero, zip, nada."

"What about his business? His case load?"

"What business? What cases? Wellie's an IP advisor."

"And that means?"

"Intellectual Property. Copyright law, trademark protection, patent applications. His clients are screenwriters and novelists. He never cracked the bigtime. I mean, look at this place." Jaycee spread her arms to make her point.

"What was he doing for Gabe?"

"I can't answer that."

"Oh, right, ACP, while we're handing out acronyms. Attorney-client protection."

"Privilege, but Jack, that's not what I meant. I have no idea what those two were up to. They would go through that door there and close it, talk for an hour, and then Mr. Cooley would come out and leave."

"Nothing for you to do?"

"Just once, a will document I typed up while Mr. Cooley read a magazine. There were quite a few closed-door sessions after that, but Wellie never had anything further for me to do in that regard. And then, of course, when Wellie stopped coming in, Mr. Cooley stopped as well. Never a word, not a single…"

Jaycee's lower lip tightened and a crease developed between her eyebrows. I decided a new tack might be more productive.

"How long have you worked here, Jaycee?"

"Almost exactly fifteen years. If you do the math, I was no spring chicken at the time. Wellie—Mr. Latimer—had a kind heart, as well as a vacancy he needed filled."

"Is there a Mrs. Latimer?"

"No, never was."

"Girlfriend? Boyfriend? Any friends?"

"He dated women off and on, but no one special that came to my attention. I consider his personal life off-limits."

"Anyone check his home?"

"The detective said he looked through some windows, saw nothing out of the ordinary to report, no cause to enter the premises."

"LAPD or private eye?"

"A plain-clothes L. A. cop. They get calls like mine by the thousand. Weldon Latimer is now a file folder in a drawer somewhere. Or a computer database. Same difference."

"Would you mind if I had a look at Gabe's file?"

Jaycee pressed her lips together in true schoolmarm fashion. "I don't think that would be appropriate."

Thus saying, she got up and moved to the file cabinet, opened the top drawer and thumbed through until she found what she was looking for. She pulled a folder and set it down on the desk.

The blotter was no longer vacant.

"Excuse me for a few minutes," she said, "the copier needs ink." She then opened the door through which I had entered and let herself out.

Classy lady.

Latimer's file on Gabriel Cooley was like Baby Bear's porridge, not too thick and not too thin. Unlike Baby's porridge, however, it was not "just right." I flipped through several documents, noted several statements bearing overseas bank names, a dossier on an individual of whom I had no knowledge, an absence of Cooley's name and the presence of several that meant nothing to me.

And a bill of sale for a boat. Big boat, big price tag. Two million big.

The copier was the kind with an automatic feeder. While the machine huffed and chugged I took a quick minute to browse the wall hangings. To no surprise, Weldon Latimer was not a Pepperdine alumnus. The college named on his JD diploma was one I'd never heard of. His California Bar membership certificate was the real McCoy, though. A light rectangle on the wall surface indicated where a small framed object of longstanding had been removed. Maybe a personal award, maybe someone's photograph.

When Jaycee returned fifteen minutes later, I was seated, the file was back on her desk where she'd left it, and I was finishing the last of my coffee. The copier's paper tray might have been short a few dozen sheets, but who notices a thing like that?

A gray-haired man in a wrinkled suit came in behind Jaycee. She pointed a thumb over her shoulder.

"Meet the Invisible Man," she said, and sat down in her chair. "Wellie, this is Jack Dyle and you'd better be nice or he'll tear your arm off."

"Where'd he come from?" I asked.

Weldon Latimer, Attorney At Law, answered for the defense. "I've been laying low, as they say in your profession."

I looked at Jaycee. "You oughta be in pictures, the way you sell a story."

"It was God's truth until he showed up at the corner deli five minutes ago. Wellie, you are such a jerk!"

"Yeah, but I'm alive. That has to account for something."

"No, it does not! You've kept me worried sick for two whole months."

"I promise, it was not another woman."

"Oh, shut up, Wellie."

"Okay."

"You could've been dead for all I knew."

"Too close to the truth. If you knew what I've been through—"

"I don't want to hear it—yes, I do, but just not right now."

I tried to get a word in, but I was unschooled in lawyer-aide spatology.

"I think I'll just toddle on," I said.

Latimer perked up. "How about a ride downtown?"

"Thanks, got my own car."

"I meant for me."

"Whatsamatter?" I said. "Can't afford the bus?"

"Matter of fact, I'm flat broke. But if you'll drop me off in MacArthur Park, I'll tell you anything you want to know about

Gabe Cooley."

"Anything?"

"Within reason."

I looked at Jaycee and made a quizzical face. She shrugged. "He's like that. Everything's conditional."

"You're in luck," I told Latimer. "MacArthur happens to be on my way."

"Let me grab something from the office."

Latimer disappeared through the door and I stood up holding Cooley's rolled-up folio behind my back. I thanked Jaycee for her time.

"If you think you could stand it, I'd like to take you out to dinner some—"

"I can stand it."

"—place, say Truman's on the Drive?"

"Yes!"

"Saturday?"

She beamed, then tried for aloof. "That would be very nice."

Wellie returned just as I reached across the desk and kissed Jaycee's forehead. "You're still hot, doll."

Janice Cutter's face reddened with a girlish blush.

Wellie made a face. "Hey, not nice to take advantage of the help."

"Shut up, Wellie," I said.

"Okay."

19

Night Chase

I left Westwood with Weldon Latimer secured in the C10's passenger seat, a Corbeau bucket with a five-point harness. A Corbeau is a rodder's extravagant concession to the suburban male demand for safe comfort while racing peers to the supermarket.

I rolled down my window. Wellie hadn't bathed for a while, and likely hadn't changed clothes for the same amount of time. He needed a shave and a barber. Any Hollywood street character would look better. I put him at about the same age as Jaycee, only not as pretty. Naturally wiry, he was borderline gaunt from a lack of regular meals. I seriously considered dropping him off at the Cedars Sinai ER, which neither of us could afford.

Jaycee's reaction to my date offer had me feeling all rosy and nice, but my mood changed the moment I hit rush-hour traffic on Wilshire. It wasn't dark enough yet to require lights, but the commute crowd was thick. I made a right at the light and looked back. The same black SUV was there. I'd picked him up at Wellie's and he'd followed me all the way up Thayer. There was no losing him on stop-and-go surface streets, and the 405 would be jammed up worse and take me the wrong direction. I got in the left-turn lane and while I waited for the light to change I loosened the strap on my ankle holster. Wellie saw it and looked away quickly.

The tail followed me left on Santa Monica and up Sunset toward Laurel Canyon. Wellie saw the tail, too.

"As Tom Mix used to say, let's head for the hills."

"Who's Tom Mix?" I said just to needle him.

"Hollywood cowboy, used to drive a yellow Cord Phaeton convertible."

"Jerking your chain. I know more about the car, though."

"Guy died in it driving drunk in Arizona. Let's take a left up ahead on Laurel Canyon and shake this bird in the hills."

"Who's driving?"

"You are, but I used to live up there."

"I was liking the Canyon too, but our companions have a different idea."

Just ahead a white van pulled away from the curb. I touched the brakes as it failed to accelerate. At a snail's pace we passed an outdoor fresh-Mex place just before Sunset bent due east. Behind me the SUV swung out into the left lane and pulled up beside me.

It was looking like this might not be a good night for reading.

"Get on the floor," I said.

Wellie said, "What—" and I put my right hand behind his head and shoved him down toward the floor. With my left hand I yanked the steering wheel hard right and went around the van by virtue of a miraculous absence of parked cars. My right wheels went up on the curb. The van jerked right to crowd me, and I floored the C10 and dragged my bumper along his entire righthand side and spun off the curb in front of him with a strong smell of scorched rubber behind me. My gun came up from its ankle holster and I went into the curve with the accelerator floored. The van dropped back as the SUV closed up.

Sunset Boulevard was alight and I was pumped going so fast. I swerved into the left lane to avoid rear-ending a slow car and swerved back to the right to avoid another. Behind me, the van swung right onto Crescent Heights, and when the SUV went with it, I began to slow down.

Weldon Latimer crouched, half fetal, toward the floor on the passenger side. I put the gun down on the console beside me.

"They're gone."

"Okay if I sit up now?" he said. His voice was shaking.

"It'll look less like you're snorting a line."

He squirmed back up onto the seat.

"Was that—that crazy shit necessary?"

"I thought so at the time. You still want MacArthur Park?"

"I think I want my mommy. Yeah, let's do it."

"You need to stop somewhere first?"

"No, I'm good. Just take a right on La Brea but don't go all the way down. Beverly's much better and from there you can—"

"Wellie, who's driving?"

"You are, but I gotta talk to keep from wetting my pants."

"You will live to fight another day." We passed the Comedy Store and I avoided the Strip and took Holloway to Santa Monica Boulevard. "Tell me how you got started with Cooley. I want to know everything."

"I used to be a middling good patent lawyer, but we can't always follow our dreams. Especially when our ex-wife later turns out to be the ex-wife of a syndicate bag man."

"I retract my statement. I do not want to know everything."

"Gabe was divorcing his wife, came to me for legal advice, I told him I don't do divorces, we got talking. Found out we both dated the same woman, different times. Both got taken by the same trick. That's how it started."

"Thought I told you, I'm not interested."

"You sure as hell won't get it from Gabe. You'll need it all soon enough, Dyle, because right now Rome Valenti is looking at nobody else."

I was sure there was a codicil in the lawyer's oath of office, or maybe fine print on his sheepskin, forbidding collusion with the enemy. I made my right on La Brea without interruption because Latimer's mind had shifted to another matter. He didn't speak again until we stopped for the light at Melrose.

"And I should tell you, Sheridan Burke is more than just another pretty face."

The light changed and we drove in silence for two blocks. Deeper intel was not forthcoming. Latimer was delivering facts on the installment plan. I caught a green left arrow at Beverly Boulevard, made my turn, and pulled into a Chevron.

Latimer sat up straighter. "What're you doing?"

"Eating."

"Here? Now?"

"I haven't eaten since lunch."

Latimer checked his watch. "Look, friend, I have to be in the Park in twenty minutes."

"Well, that little Indy 500 sprint back there bought you an extra five. Anyway, *friend*, I do not run an Uber here."

I got out of the truck and left Wellie sitting while I went inside the 24-hour Food Mart for a chocolate hit. I came out with two Snickers and a Red Bull.

"You actually drink that stuff?" he said when I climbed back in.

"Need something to wash down the carbs."

"I think I'll be sick."

"Whoa, not in the truck."

"So to speak."

"How does a two-million dollar yacht fit into Cooley's life?"

"How did you find that out?"

"I'm a trained investigator. It helps that your legal aide is smart and honest and resourceful."

"You bribed her."

"Just a date. We'll both have fun. The yacht?"

"Gabe was middle man in a brokered deal. You want more, ask his skipper, Armand Slovac."

I swallowed some Red Bull and stowed it in a console holder, then started the engine and we resumed our zig east. There would be a zag south on Rossmore after we crossed Hancock Park, and several more squiggles before the journey was complete. That part of the L. A. grid is broken up by a lot of trendy little neighborhoods. Fairfax, Melrose, Larchmont, La Brea. You can lose back-and-fill time on narrow concrete lanes designed for the horseless carriage.

"What was that you started to say about Sheri Burke?" I asked.

"Girl took a shortcut through the woods on her way to Hollywood."

"Uh-oh. In for what?"

"Misdemeanor battery. She beat the socks off an assailant. Literally. Left him barefoot."

"Well, good for her, I'd say."

"He was seventy-six and deemed defenseless."

"Our wonderful legal system at work. How much time did she serve?"

"Four months. Not like a felony, but it's an albatross."

"We all carry those. I think I like her better for it. Who or what awaits us in MacArthur?" I asked.

"Nothing for you, my own business for me."

"After our little episode back there, I think I'm entitled to more than a brushoff."

"If you show up, guaranteed he won't. He's got people."

"What kind of guy is this?"

"You want to push, okay, because of Gabriel Cooley I'm on a hit list. They tried once and missed, they'll keep at it unless I make this guy happy."

"Who's the guy?"

"That's all I have to say about it."

"Tell me what Gabe came to you for. I mean, besides drawing up a will."

"I helped him buy the yacht. We put the sale through a corporation I set up for him. The money source I can't talk about because I was careful not to ask."

"Not a close-knit relationship, huh?"

Latimer glanced out his window at the passing scene. "It's quite possible he had two or three million of his own money that he kept running through one deal or another. Ready cash."

"Stash from the past. Maybe a maverick deal he kept close to his chest?"

"He was trying to shake loose of the mob, Dyle. An impossible task, as you and I know. Poor sucker was convinced he had his ticket to freedom."

"Many have tried, few have succeeded."

"Do you always speak in cliches?"

"What did this particular ticket look like?"

"Even if I knew, I wouldn't tell you. He never told me outright, just hinted at a hidden trove he stumbled onto. Joked once that he liked to call it 'old money.' Said it was clean as the driven snow. I told him there's no such thing, and he chuckled and said, 'How true.'"

A while later, on Wilshire east a few blocks from MacArthur Park, I asked about Guiding Light Memorial.

"Any particular reason for his choice of cemetery? The whole thing was pretty slapdash. "

"Gabe Cooley did not stipulate the cemetery, I did. I wrote it into his will postmortem."

"Ever the thoughtful attorney. You had a reason?"

"Don't be an idiot, Dyle. There's always a reason for everything."

"I see you discovered my best-kept secret. I'm an idiot."

"Take a left up here while you got a green."

"I know, I know!"

I went left on Wilshire and got past the bend at Hoover. MacArthur Park was just four city blocks ahead.

"What's so significant about Guiding Light?"

"Not much appearance-wise, as you saw. The significant part is Harmonious Rest Funeral Home."

"Where Gabe got prepared for viewing and interment." I made it through the next intersection on an amber shade of green. "That's noteworthy how?"

"I own it."

"Since when did you own a cemetery?" I said.

"Since the day I was born. It's a family operation, third generation. I could've run it, except I wanted to study law, so my brother took over when Poppa died."

"Don't tell me you're thinking of getting back in the family business. How long were you going to let this pack of lies fester?"

"Forever, I hope." Latimer shifted in his seat. "You wanna know so much, I'll tell you something."

"Go ahead."

"The cops got it wrong. Well, not totally, but half-assed. Gabe Cooley didn't die in Boyle Heights."

"Sure he did. That's where he was found. The cops said so, the news media said so. Hell we've all seen the grisly photos."

"Time of death. What'd they say about that?"

"Thursday night between six and midnight."

"Six-hour window, give or take."

"That's what the Medical Examiner—"

"They got time-of-death close enough, but not the location."

"Wha-a-at?"

Wellie checked to make sure he had my full attention before he dropped the bomb.

"Gabe Cooley was killed in Newport Beach."

20

Shadows In The Park

I almost ran down a lady in the Wilshire Royale crosswalk. She gave us the finger—I think she sensed the guy beside me was a lawyer—and moved on.

Weldon Latimer was reliving a nightmare he would never forget. The face behind his gray stubble had gone chalky white, his arms were wrapped tight around his ribs like a Dallas sun bather caught in a blizzard. But his voice had the strength of a sinner convinced his absolution lay solely in full confession.

I eased my foot off the brake and accelerated slowly, aware I was not in complete control of the vehicle.

"I'm not going to ask what Gabe was doing in Newport because he was living there on a yacht. I assume he didn't thumb a ride from there to Boyle Heights."

Weldon Latimer wasn't listening to me, he was reliving a nightmare.

"I left him in the park. In Hollenbeck. Got me the hell out of there. Called the cops from a burner phone."

"Same phone you used to call Sheri?"

"It's now the property of L. A. Sanitation. I got a new one. You should have the number, get a burner for yourself."

"Already got one."

Newport? Some kind of funny-business with the Sunseeker? I wanted to ask more, but Wellie's mind was stuck in its own groove.

"They left his body in a Zodiac inflatable. On a flat stretch of dirt. Way up in Back Bay. Almost to the Jamboree bridge. Low tide."

"How do you know this?"

"A man called Sheri around eleven at night, told her where he was, she called me."

"So she already knew you before Friday."

"She tell you otherwise? Nevermind, she wasn't involved beyond that."

Maybe Wellie believed so, but I didn't. He bulled ahead, doling out his story in short episodes.

"I drive my van down there, take the access road, find the body in a rubber boat—God, what a mess. Haul the boat with him in it across the flats to the van. Heave him into the back. I'm covering him with a tarp when a guy comes out of the bushes. It's dark, I can't see much of him. He says, Take him way the hell away from here. Tells me that's as far as he can go. I can't see if he has a gun, so I don't argue.

"I take Jamboree to the 405, head north to the 605 and take that. I got no idea where I'm going. Get as far as the I-5, he's stinking, so I have to get rid of him. I'm starting to panic, thinking maybe just dump him in a rail yard. I read that a lot of bodies turn up in rail yards. Then I see the Fourth Street off-ramp. Boyle Heights. All kinds of crime there, it'll fit. I loop around to the park, nobody around after midnight. I put him on the grass beside the parking lot. Get back in the van, drive over to the Valley. Get a room at a Motel Six, and call the cops from there. God, I hope I never have to do that again."

"You keep saying 'they.' Who else did all this?"

"Who do you think, Einstein? The syndicate. Gabe's movie investors."

I wanted to steer the guy's monologue onto another track. "What kind of lawyer removes a body from the murder scene—nevermind, my Fantasyland season pass has expired. Any idea how long he was dead before you got him?"

"Can't say exactly. He was stiff when I found him. Had a hell of a time getting him in the van. I'd put it at minimum three hours."

"No idea who made the call?"

"She said it was a man's voice, no one she recognized."

"Probably the same guy who jumped you in the dark. Why didn't you report Gabe's murder to the police right there? I mean, why haul him away from the murder scene?"

"Stuff I can't talk about."

"Well, you're better off talking to me than a homicide cop."

"I'm a lawyer. You get involved in a felony, you're tied up for years."

"Same with a conviction."

At the next corner Latimer told me to pull to the curb. He thanked me for the lift and got out, waited beside a lamp standard while I drove on. He was still there when I turned onto Coronado.

Weldon Latimer, Esq., did not want me to witness his next appointment. That was all the inducement I needed to change my plan for a quick drive home.

~

I drove around the block until I found a metered space on Seventh. I backed in and shut off the engine—and sat there, with my mind doing a rerun of what I'd just heard.

Latimer's story didn't make sense. I had received a voice message from Gabe Cooley Thursday night. Dead men don't talk, especially not over the phone. And the log of his call matched the exact day and hour my phone showed, according to Detective Montero. It was possible for Gabe's killer to grab his phone and place the call, but he couldn't fake Gabe's voice. Even a skilled voice mimic wouldn't leave an obscure warning about an arc welder. The raspy smoker's voice was Gabe's, the clipped delivery was pure Gabe, the harassment was Gabe Cooley in full character.

What I didn't have, but which the call data record would show any cop on the case, was the phone's location at the time of call. Had he called me from the Sunseeker? The dock? The marina parking lot? A house in Bayshores? They would all point to the same cell tower in the Newport area, and nowhere close to Boyle Heights, provided Wellie's story was true.

I got out of the truck and reached into the console for the hi-resolution camera essential to my trade. By the time I got back to the corner where I'd dropped him off, Latimer was gone, so I walked Wilshire east until I got to the park. Which presented a dilemma.

Wilshire Boulevard splits MacArthur Park down the middle. So there were two parks where Latimer could meet his party, and both were big places with winding paths and a lot of trees. The lake took up most of the south half, so I started there by ducking through the pillared entrance. A grassy rise dotted with trees gave me cover for what I wanted.

At a little past seven, the park was nearly empty. I panned the lake shore, saw no sign of Latimer, so I retraced my path and crossed Wilshire with the light. Using a clump of palm trees for further cover, I angled toward the pavilion and paused at the edge of the tree line for a quick scan through the zoom lens.

Latimer was seated on one of the benches overlooking the soccer pitch, his back to me. I moved slowly behind a thick palm trunk so as not to appear too obviously interested. Latimer was more concerned with the tree shadows at the far end of the pitch. I followed his line of sight and caught a profile that struck me as one I'd recently paid a lot of attention to. I zoomed the camera lens and almost jumped.

Roman Valenti stood in the trees, a solitary figure, watching, going to no great length to stay hidden, almost as though he wanted his presence to be known.

I pulled the lens back just as a tall figure started away from the shadows and continued down the path alongside the pitch. Latimer got up and walked toward the park's north entrance.

The guy he was meeting was a tower, easily over six feet six. I gauged him broad-brush to be East African by his sharp features. Maybe from Sudan, maybe Ethiopia. Maybe Somalia. I snapped his portrait as he drew nearer, a handsome figure in an out-over white linen shirt, tan slacks, polished brown loafers. Designer sunglasses hid his eyes. A thin gold chain around his neck suspended a small gold ornament. The gold watch on his left wrist looked expensive. In a couple of hours all that bling would draw muggers like lions to a wandering springbok.

He did not offer his hand to Latimer. In fact, the two men stood well apart while conversing. Farther back in the trees, near Valenti but apart from him, two shadows stood watch. Maybe the African's bodyguards, maybe out-of-work investment bankers looking to make a smash-and-grab.

Face time between Latimer and the African lasted less than sixty seconds, then both men walked away in opposite directions, Latimer southward for Wilshire, the African up a knoll toward West Sixth.

I stayed in my palm grove to thumb my phone for a news clip I recalled from several nights ago. When I found it, I knew memory hadn't failed me.

I wasn't sure whether to be glad or sad, but I scratched a little joy when the face I'd just photographed matched that of an African trade delegate swapping smiles with film celebrities. I hadn't lost my edge. Then I dug into my own archives, and dredged up an image from a past I'd worked hard to bury—a rapid cascade of still shots still in my head. The connection clicked, the name too, and the light went right out of me.

Brian Sebutu. Mercenary, slave trader, merchant of death.

Baby killer.

21

Run, Eat, Fight

Deacon Hood didn't answer my call, nor did Joe Blanco. I wanted to rush home and think, so I didn't bother Minnie Glover either. At that hour Scarf was in full Uber mode and unlikely to answer in a civil tone.

I took South Main out of the financial district and headed straight for my junkyard lair without telling anybody what I'd just heard about Gabe Cooley's postmortem travels, about the likelihood that Roman Valenti and the arms dealer he was looking for were probably sleeping in the same hotel right here in Los Angeles, and that the only thing keeping the city from extermination by nerve gas was a murder neither guilty party wanted or authorized.

I invited Yankee in for the ball game but he declined. My unemployment status had pushed my canine esteem to an all-time low. Just as well, the Dodgers lost.

The next morning I followed my sporadic regimen to stay in shape and ran Hoover Street into Exposition Park. My five-miler started by hooking around the Coliseum to Bill Robertson Lane, and then twice around the perimeter. Two kids in gang tats were tossing a football on the lawn in front of the swimming stadium. On my second lap they gave me the death stare, but nothing more.

An hour later, showered and dressed and rivaling Sean Connery in his Bond days, I started some coffee, then checked the refrigerator for eggs. Found a large bowl of cold pasta, a chicken wing in a box, and half a tomato. No eggs.

My search for wholesome nutrition would fare better nearer my "office," with three donut outlets within walking distance and a Krispy Kreme not a mile away. For the drive I chose Li'l FoFo, a Ford Focus wrapped in satin rose and modified for racing. I don't race on city streets, of course. That's a juvenile sport. I do my racing on dirt. It's character-building, dirt is. Earthy, primal. Gitcha right down there behind the navel, yessir. But mostly in the face.

Thirty minutes later I was in Mother's Mud with a yellow six-box, McCree's version of a half-mega, and the Gabe Cooley file, when in walked Lisa Montero. She sat down across from me and snitched the last glazed. Dayem.

"Has senility set in so soon with you?" she said. "I told you to report and I meant it, sojer."

"Yessir, ma'am."

Between bites I filled her in on Cooley's funeral gala, my inspection of Gabe's forearm, and the ensuing surgery by unqualified practitioners. I reminisced about tea and cakes with Alice in Newportland, and concluded with a brief account of Monday night's visit from two fed agents and a female computer nerd, omitting details about the joint op. I then swallowed some coffee to invite commentary.

Silence. Not even a cricket chirp.

"Hello? Detective Montero?"

"You knew those feds from before."

"Yes."

"Same ones busted the diamond trust?"

"No."

"Somebody's getting careless."

"Which raises flags of many colors. For example, if the LAPD is so dang-all hot to know who shows up at a slum lord's funeral, why do they send a hack insurance adjuster? Or, which of the vic's survivors proposed the gruesome open-casket idea in the first place, and why the heavy effort to put me there? You do know, of course, that I was the only viewer other than four sloppy surgeons and a half-blind ticket taker."

"You're trying to make something out of nothing."

"Lisa, I'm trying to understand why his murder looks so contrived. Gabriel Cooley's face was hideous, yet four goodfellas recognized enough of him to proceed with their postmortem mafia rite. The scene had all the macabre ingredients of a Hollywood fright flick."

I waited for a defense, an objection, a motion to adjourn, but got more crickets, so I tried the old end-run approach.

"You always look scrumptious, anytime, day or night. Even chasing a perp down a dark alley. Even the night after."

"Don't try me, Dyle, I'm not in the mood."

"I mean it."

"Likewise."

She was trying her best to appear sorely aggrieved, but I read the hard-nosed act as forced. I prodded a little more.

"You and I don't always have to meet like this."

"It's the Valenti tie-in, Dyle. More than that I can't talk about."

Still pushing the tough cop routine.

"You haven't told me to butt out," I said.

"You wouldn't if I did."

Montero touched a paper napkin to the corner of her mouth. It was the sexiest thing I'd seen all day and possibly all week.

She caught me watching and flashed her luminous Latina brights. "You never stop, do you."

"Hope springs eternal."

"Who ever said that?"

"Pope."

"I doubt this pope did."

"Alexander."

"Pope Alexander?"

"Alexander Pope. English poet. Jolly good fellow, sharp wit, sharper pen, the Bill Maher of his day. Stood a few inches under five feet but a master of verse feared by London's power elite."

"Before you give me another history lesson, I'll take my leave. Murders to solve, crimes to bust."

"Missing persons to find. I had a thrilling ride last night with Weldon Latimer."

More storm clouds. "Bastard. You holdout bastard. Tell me where."

"We started in his Westwood office and finished at MacArthur Park. My twenty minutes of fame with the Invisible Man. He's out there in the wind again."

"He's the best lead we have, and you let him get loose again."

"You haven't asked what he wanted with MacArthur Park."

"Seems you like playing me for beggar. Who showed up?"

I decided to leave Valenti out of the picture, as the reason for his appearance had eluded me. So I stuck with the African.

"The guy could play small forward for the Lakers, right down to ethnic typecast and head fakes. But he's probably not interested in basketball or sports of any kind. And yes, I got pics."

"Show me."

"Not on my phone. They're in a safer place."

"Dyle, I could hold you downtown while we turn that tin can house of yours inside out and upside down."

"I can do better."

"Stop playing hide-and-seek. We need those photos."

"Not from me, you don't, you already have them."

Montero closed her eyes, the soul of patience. "You emailed them?"

"You already have him on file. He's staying at the Beverly Hotel with the delegation from Asmara. Showed up at the Fletcher gala."

"You mean last week—"

"I mean Thursday night, Lisa. Cocktails at six, dinner at seven, two hundred luminaries for alibis. Brian Sebutu is doing some kind of business with Weldon Latimer, probably had Brother Gabe in the mix until—well, you know the time-worn maxim to increase profits."

"Cut out the middle man."

"Precisely. Or, less precisely, just do whatever needs doing. Thing is, nobody else but the middleman knows where he buried the treasure they're so hot for. Kill Cooley and the hunt's over. But somebody took him out anyway, and it wasn't Valenti, or he wouldn't fly three thousand miles to a bag man's funeral, and for sure wouldn't stick around L. A. afterward."

"But if it wasn't Valenti—" Montero stopped herself.

"What if he sent some people to rough up Cooley for the location? Maybe they got too rough and killed him."

"Remember," Montero said, "he was strangled. A mauler for hire doesn't make that kind of mistake."

"Then it had to be someone with no stake in the—oops, I almost said weapons deal."

"We already know about that."

"We being L. A.'s finest?"

"Who do you think called the feds? Besides, the perp could be anyone with a grudge. Or a bent lunatic. And that gets us right back where we started."

"Not necessarily just any person," I pointed out. "Cooley was playing high stakes games with several people, and possibly one or two others a step removed from them."

"You're thinking Valenti's boss? No way, he doesn't have one anymore. As for Sebutu, he answers to no one at all."

"I don't know enough about Brian Sebutu either way."

"Here's what you can do. Find out where Sebutu comes from. He might be Somali, might be something else, but find out why he's hanging with Eritreans. There's some ugly history in that part of the world. "

"I would ask why you don't find out for yourself, but it's probably the same reason you sent me to Gabe's funeral."

"Instead of guessing, just—"

"You're not investigating the murder."

"—check out the African."

"You're not with Homicide anymore, are you."

"Jack," she said. "Stop right there."

Her full meaning swept over me in a rush of illumination. She had transferred to another division. The hard one.

"Allow me to say this much, then," I said. "I'm glad you're still showing the badge."

No clipped retort for that one.

She wasn't working undercover herself, she was running a narc who was.

I flipped up the donut box lid, watched it fall closed. "Hey, looky there, all gone. Thanks for removing temptation."

Lisa Montero slid out of her seat and got to her feet. Gave her coat lapel a sharp tug, looked down at me with a tight face that exposed a rare figment of concern.

"It's not what you think, Dyle. Be careful."

I considered asking why she thought I was the one needing to be careful, but I dropped the idea.

"You too."

After she left I stared into my half-mega, realizing I was no better at reading coffee dregs on paper than tea leaves on china. And I don't even drink tea, much less read it.

Los Angeles is a mammoth place, with every kind of crime you can imagine. The narcotics trade in particular gets people killed in more ways than any other. I had clung to the hope that Lisa Montero might one day reassess her career pursuing murderers and move to a quieter line of police work, such as lunchroom monitor or chief pencil sharpener. And I had fantasized that in so doing she might revise her opinion of me and invite me along for the duration.

She had just shot down both prospects.

22

Five Dragons Showtime

Scarf had a loose daytime schedule, so I called and told him I'd pick him up at a small green area near Century Park West. Our mission objective was to penetrate the defenses of Five Dragons Productions, a redoubt of nefarious Hollywood moguls and good-looking women, while attired in men's wear from Ross Dress-For-Less. At the mention of women, Scarf said he was on board.

I assured him I had called ahead and secured an audience with the lord of the manor. As we passed through the lobby doors, Scarf had second thoughts.

"Sure hope we aren't shown the door before I get a chance to use the men's room."

"You say that everywhere we go. Why is that so important?"

"It's a unique experience for persons of my ethnic origin."

"Well, fear not. My client has considerable influence in these circles."

"Sheri's a third level slush pile reader. What kind of influence can she wield from the basement?"

"The considerable kind."

"In other words, these moguls are suckers for blackmail."

"Didn't I just say that?"

Mark Robie had an office *near* the top floor of a high-rise but not *in* the A-listed galaxy of Century Plaza. Respectable enough for a journeyman maker of motion pictures who rode to work in a chauffeured Bentley rather than hyperventilate down Laurel Canyon in a Bugatti Chiron that never got out of second gear.

The woman behind the Five Dragons reception desk could have played the title role in "The Queen." Elegant beauty preserved in a charming package. Scarf hesitated before he spoke—a halting approach I'd never seen before.

"Mister Dyle and, uh, Mister Jones to see Mister Robie."

"Which one of you is Jack Dyle?" she asked with a straight face. Scarf pointed at me. "Him."

"Then you must be Scarf. Sheri's told me about you."

"No sh—uh, shooting."

"None at all." She stuck out a hand. "I'm Diana Carr, Mark's front man. Pleased to meet you."

Scarf recovered his aplomb and flashed the bad-boy grin that curled most women's toes. "We're in good hands, then."

"The best," she countered, shaking my hand almost as an afterthought while she kept her eye on Scarf. The dude always outshines me in a suit. This was one of those rare occasions where bulky mass played second fiddle to slim-and-slender grace.

Diana leaned back in her chair. "Before I take you back, give me an idea what this is about."

Spoken with the authority of a principal in the firm. Diana Carr was more than a secretarial minion. Scarf turned to me, and Diana followed his lead so that I had the woman's full attention for the first time.

"You heard about Gabriel Cooley," I said.

A small line appeared between her brows. "Yes, it was a terrible thing."

"Sheri's handling his estate. I'm helping her pick up the pieces he left behind. One of them deals with a rather expensive asset Mr.

Robie might know about."

"The goddamn boat."

I raised both eyebrows to indicate that she might elucidate on that expletive.

"What a fiasco. I told Mark not to get involved, but he and Ray were close buddies and that was enough."

"Will Mr. Robie have a different opinion now?"

"Oh, you betcha."

She swung forward in the chair and stood to smooth her skirt, a tight mini that proved she still had great legs. I thought I might have seen her onscreen before.

Robie's office was at the far end of a long corridor. Diana led the way.

Mark Robie was a bit of a surprise. I'd imagined a short, bald, overweight CPA type in thick glasses and a loud suit, but I was disappointed. Here was this strikingly handsome tall guy who could model for GQ. Dark, wavy hair swept over his ears, a clear sky-blue gaze, "chiseled" jaw line. The whole package presented a serious challenge to my personal aura and, were his tan any deeper, Scarf's.

Robie's desk would have made a nice helipad. I kept looking for the big white "X" but it might have been covered by his ink blotter. Two walls of glass met at the corner behind his command bridge.

Following introductions, we took chairs arranged an appropriate distance from the head honcho.

Robie leaned against a padded arm rest and propped his chin with a fist. "Show us what you've got."

Like I was there to pitch a screenplay. I switched on my literary agent persona.

"I've got this striking concept for a feature film. I pitched it to Sheri Burke and she agreed I should give her people first crack at it. Okay, the title. Ready for it? It's called *Mine, All Mine*."

You could hear the proverbial pin do the proverbial drop.

"See, what happens," I went on, "is this fading movie star is given her last chance in a feature film, but six weeks in, for reasons beyond her control, the project is already over budget. Ordinarily, it's up to the producers to find new money, but our gal—I call her Augusta—comes up with a proven source willing to contribute with no billing. Only problem is his terms are pretty steep. In fact, so steep the producers are willing to cut their losses now rather than go ahead on this guy's nickel, which will cost another nickel before the week is out. Now, the chief producer and his camera provider are pretty thick pals, so they put their heads together and come up with a solution. But like the movie says, It's Complicated. Hey, wasn't that an all-star cast? Box office surprise and a trip to the Oscars! Anyway, the money is for a boat."

Diana stared at her boss/partner/protégé. "Mark?"

"Just a fancy yacht I rode down to Ensenada that weekend I took with Ray Loring."

"And Harlan Boone," she said.

"And Gabe Cooley," I added, to round out Armand Slovac's sailing crew. "And a fifth party who has always gone unmentioned. Isn't it about time the fellow got the mention he so rightly deserves?"

Diana looked genuinely confused. "I don't understand any of this. Are we still talking a film script, or did somebody shift gears?"

"My apologies," I said. "Sometimes, in my investigative work, I lapse into analogy and lose my audience." I turned to Scarf. "Isn't that right, Mr. Jones?"

"Whatever you said, totally agree."

I kept my eye on the man behind the desk. "We haven't heard much from Mr. Robie since he mentioned a fun trip to Ensenada. Or should I say "funding" trip? Wasn't that what it was really about, Mark? I assume we're using first names now, right?"

Captain Robie chose that moment to take command of the

ship. "I need to speak to these two alone." He pointed at me and Scarf.

Diana Carr got up from her chair, but paused at the door with a scornful look at Robie. "I hope you know what you're doing."

"So do I," he said.

Scarf and I waited while Robie picked up his cell phone and punched what I assumed was a text message. When he was done, he tilted his chair back and looked up at the ceiling.

"I just turned off the surveillance recorder, so unless one of you is wearing a wire that deked our door scanner, this is completely off the record."

"We came wireless," said Scarf.

Robie brought his gaze level with us again. "I know what you're thinking, but you're wrong," he said. "The fifth party wasn't the mob guy from New York."

"Roman Valenti. Gabe's silent partner."

A severe look. "Different mob."

"Russian?"

"Uh-huh."

"That puts an interesting skew to things."

"As we found out when we learned he couldn't swim."

23

Russian Roulette

A Synapse clicked in my head. Cooley with a Russian mobster—*click*—Cooley with a Cyprus bank account. Then another: Cooley with a Russian mobster—*click*—Cooley brokering a million-dollar movie stake.

It didn't take a lot of imagination to come up with Gabe's killer. But those people didn't stick around, and they didn't leave tracks. The immediate question was the amount at stake.

Robie wanted to tell it his way.

"His name was Greg Ruskin. As American as apple pie until he got drunk. Discovered tequila and fell in love. Grigori Pushkin was his other name. Probably had a dozen more on as many passports. Told us he managed a portfolio for a Russian industrialist. Uh-huh.

"He was in the Williams turbojet—that little inflatable with its own garage? He and Harlan coming back from the beach. The sun was down, it was getting dark, he was drunk as a skunk. About a hundred meters short of the yacht they hit a swell the wrong way and the boat flipped. None of us on the yacht saw it. Harlan showed up in the salon soaking wet and so completely rattled he was speaking gibberish. We got him dried off and coherent enough to tell us the Russian simply went down and never came up."

"How did your friend manage to get back aboard?"

"He pushed the turbo halfway to the yacht and swam the rest of the way. Climbed in over the launch platform. We didn't even know he was aboard until he staggered into the room dripping wet."

"Did the body turn up?"

"We didn't stick around to find out."

"That was probably wise. What became of the turbo?"

"It drifted right up our stern and we hauled it back aboard. Once the skipper got it secured in its little garage, Gabe insisted we head straight home."

"Sloper didn't argue."

"The trip was Gabe's idea, his show."

"What did Ray Loring have to say about that?"

"Nothing. He just went down to his stateroom and didn't come out until we made the Newport jetty."

"No wonder he never used the boat again. I suppose Sloper kept shut about it."

"Gabe told us all how it would go down if we were asked, that our friend wanted to stay another week with his chiquita. We decided that was a pretty good story for all of us."

Scarf lifted a finger to make a point. "If the body turned up later on the beach, he wouldn't have been recognizable. No ID, not reported missing, chalk off another boating accident, swimmer caught in a rip tide. Mexican police would drop it and get back to harassing American tourists."

"But the movie went ahead to distribution and got a good ROI," I said. "So money must have changed hands."

"Not all at once. Three installments."

"Using future box office for an unfinished feature film as collateral? Come on."

"They wanted a tangible, so we pledged the boat."

"Ray's two-million-dollar boat. Somehow turned over to Gabe

as custodian."

"Well, something a little more covert. They thought it was Ray's boat, and the paperwork said boat, and their inspection team left satisfied it was the boat."

"This is all through Gabe, of course."

"Certainly. The principals in that world never deal direct."

"But Gabe had to answer for the guy missing."

"Not really. We all stuck to the same story, which wasn't hard as only one of us actually saw what happened. I had a bar visit a few days later from a guy claiming to be a treasury agent. Tried to be clever about it, but it was clear who he was and on whose behalf he was asking questions. I told him what I had to say and asked him to make an appointment next time. Never showed again."

"That's how Gabe handled it."

"Sure."

"Who's Diana Carr?"

"What do you mean?"

"Let me rephrase that. What's your relationship to her?"

"I don't see how that's any of your concern."

"You wanted her out of the room for this."

"She's my mother."

"That would have been my bet. How much does she know?"

"None of it."

"But she suspects something."

"She was married to my father for forty years. He wasn't always careful where his money came from. Kept those details to himself."

"You inherited Cooley along with everything else."

"To some extent. Not too sorry to put his influence behind us."

"Did you really shake loose or are you just hoping?"

"What do you think, Dyle? You seem to know a lot about the dirty end of things."

"Enough to say don't kid yourself. That kind of thinking got Gabe where he is."

"On that note, I think we can call it a day."

"Thanks for opening up."

"I didn't do it as a favor to you—we hardly know each other. But the signs are there. You strike me as a mover in Cooley's world, might get things brought to a finish."

"Not sure anything I do should affect your affairs going forward. I'm more concerned with Sheri Burke's future. Like, making sure she has one."

"For what it's worth, she's valued here for her own gifts these days. Might say we're both trying to break with the past."

"Good luck—and I mean it."

"We'll see."

~

Scarf and I didn't say another word until we got back to the park. It was mid-afternoon and the sun was making long shadows from the glass-and-chrome office towers. We stopped in the shade of a shiny green ficus tree.

"This Russian business got anything to do with Valenti's operation?" he said.

"Maybe indirectly. It's hard to tell what Cooley was up to. I think he was playing several parties against each other."

I told Scarf what Wellie had said about picking up Gabe's body in Newport and moving it to Hollenbeck. When I was done, Scarf looked at me long and hard.

"You knew that at the funeral, didn't you."

"Only a suspicion, but I couldn't convince myself."

"Latimer stepped into Cooley's shoes. He wants the deal for himself, been running it black ever since."

"Looks that way, but if so, whose voice did I hear on the phone?"

"I got an idea, but you won't like it."

"Spill," I said. I was open to any possibility at that point.

"That phone call you got was Medusa."

"Faking Gabe's voice?"

"Easy-peasy nowadays. Hell, it could've even popped up his face on your screen and you wouldn't know any different."

I considered that. Medusa. The AI system giving orders to Valenti's network, possibly directing Valenti himself. The one that could learn voices, faces, patterns. The one that seemed to have its digital tentacles everywhere.

"That's... disturbing."

"Welcome to the future, brother. You think Valenti wouldn't use every tool at his disposal?"

We started walking to our cars, both of us scanning the surroundings out of habit. Old instincts die hard.

"So Robie inherits a mess," I said. "A dead Russian, mob money in a Cypriot bank, and Valenti circling like a shark that smells blood."

"And you're worried about the girl."

I shrugged. "Sheri's caught in the middle. She doesn't know what she's stepped into."

"You sure about that?" Scarf raised an eyebrow. "Girl's been around Cooley long enough to learn a few things."

"Not this one. This is different."

We reached my truck, and I paused with my hand on the door handle, looking back at the Five Dragons building.

"What's your play here, bro?" Scarf asked. "Because I'm sensing you're not just going to walk away."

"I need to find out two things: Where Cooley got the VX, and where he put it. I have a hunch the money-for-guns deal is moving forward, but the VX is stagnating. People from both sides are looking all over this town for something they'll kill for."

"And the Russians?"

"They'll be back. Money like that doesn't just disappear

without someone coming to collect."

"Same for weapons." Scarf nodded slowly. "My guy in Long Beach says there's a container coming in Friday. Russian manifest, but the paperwork's been doctored."

"Sebutu's shipment?"

"That would be my guess. But here's the thing—I checked with Glover, and she worked on it, said it's being delivered to a warehouse registered to one of Cooley's shell companies."

I let out a low whistle. "So the African's using Gabe's infrastructure."

"Infrastructure Valenti touched some way and might not even know exists."

I got into the truck and immediately lowered the windows. The Corbeau leather was hot from sitting in the sun, but I barely noticed.

Scarf leaned on the door top. "Next steps?"

"Well, I'd like to talk to Latimer again," I said, starting the engine. "But I've got personal business in the Valley at three that can't wait."

"Call me tonight."

"You're working."

"No matter. With the Russkis in the picture we need to stay in touch."

"You're right."

As I drove away from Century Plaza, I couldn't shake the feeling that I was being watched. Maybe it was paranoia. Maybe it was Medusa. Or maybe it was the Russians, already here and waiting to settle accounts.

24

The Valenti Mandate

Lowell's In The Valley fronted a strip mall across from a Honda dealership on Lankershim Boulevard. Not much had changed from my last visit a year or so ago, but the inside was nothing like I remembered. The brassy mid-century Formica-and-chrome interior had given way to dark woods, upholstered brocade seats, table linens, potted shrubs, subdued lighting. Sedate orchestral music played slumber-inducing classical pop in the background—a cloying reminder of Cooley's open casket service. I could almost hear a choir summon me to peaceful rest.

For years at Lowell's you didn't wait to be seated. You grabbed any seat you could find and hoped it wasn't the booth by the kitchen, where the door swung nonstop in both directions. Today I got a pat-down at the register from a tough guy in a suit. He then ushered me across thick carpeting to a corner banquette with a backdrop wall painted to look like grape arbors and pillared arches. The lunch crowd, even the two-martini wheeler-dealer types, were long gone and the staff had cleared the tables with fresh linen in preparation for the dinner hour. A far cry from the Lowell's I had known.

I felt mild surprise to find Vic Straga sharing drinks with the boys from New York, Lupato and Diamond. Respecting the Valley heat, Valenti wore a short-sleeved blue linen shirt unbuttoned at the neck, no jacket or tie.

Straga had his back to the entrance, so he didn't see me coming. Valenti, commanding the seat of advantage, looked up as I approached and snapped his fingers. Lupato and Diamond got up and left. Just like that.

I'd seen the same move a hundred times in a hundred places. It spoke power of a kind I had expected from a basketball celebrity. Instead, Straga just sat with his head not moving and his hands folded on the table. I would not need a rerun to cement my impression of who was in charge.

I took a vacated seat on the third side of the table to have a clear view of both parties. A water glass magically appeared before me. Nobody shook hands. Nobody mentioned my arriving on time, or my dress-for-less suit.

Valenti opened without introductory remarks.

"The slum baron left a couple loose ends. We're tying those up now. The way he died was unfortunate. I think you know what really holds our interest."

"I think I don't."

"You damn well better, Dyle."

Straga said nothing, just twisted his iced drink on its base and stared at it with the narrow focus of a chess player watching his opponent's next move.

Valenti blinked at his menu and flipped it face down on the table top. A waiter appeared as if cued by ESP. We ordered three burgers with curly fries. I added a chocolate malt "with the can" the old-fashioned way, because Lowell's made them better than anybody. At least, I hoped they still did.

When he left with our orders, Valenti studied his linen placemat like it held cryptic handwriting. "Sheri's a sweet kid," he said. "This is nothing to do with her. It stays that way as long as she keeps her nose in movie scripts."

Sheri. Not "the Burke woman" nor "the dame."

"Understand," I said.

"Thought you would. Other thing, those two goons just left. Forget 'em, forget the car, Briggs, all that's something else."

"If you say so," I said.

"I do say so, because I know a few things about you, Jack Dyle. Like Miami a couple years back, where you walked. Like the Houston refinery explosion, same. Different names on both accounts, but same deal—you got a pass. You think you still got those connections, a guardian angel narc, a pal on the force? Not today, Jack. Those doors are closed. We clear?"

"Clear." I put on the chastened look he expected. It wasn't hard. A man who owned a lot of people was telling me he owned me too.

"Good. Now we got that straight, there's a little matter of business between you and me."

I raised my eyebrows. What now?

"Our mutual acquaintance left some possessions behind. Like the dump you're renting, bunch of aging rentals, some Mexican shops. A valuable commodity in one of those places belongs to me. Bought and paid for." Valenti gave Straga a hard stare while he spoke, like I wasn't even there. "The guy had no right to keep it. Been holding out to squeeze me for more. Then he took matters out of hand."

I just nodded my head. Roman Valenti wasn't looking for commentary.

"Twenty-six properties we can eliminate by logic as unlikely to impossible locations for this commodity. You're going to go around to all the rest and look until you find it. Then you tell me where, and then you leave it the hell where you found it and go back to building cars. Got that?"

It would behoove me henceforward to leave names out of my

end of the conversation.

"I thought you said this is nothing to do with the girl." He had me talking like a New York thug.

"I did."

"She's managing the estate. That means records. Rent receipts, property title, description of structures and their location, disposition of assets. Custody of those and other possessions."

"She tell you that?"

"Yes, and showed me the paper proof." No need to mention where or how recently.

I got a long, hard stare from Roman Valenti while he considered a development he either hadn't been told or hadn't authorized. I waited. As with all the moves up to that point, the next was his to make.

After an extended silence, Valenti shifted his attention to Straga and held it there. Straga's muscled shoulders drooped ever so slightly as he bore the full brunt of Valenti's tacit indictment, whether directed at Vic Straga personally or at an underling in his charge. Someone had fouled up. Not a word was spoken in Lowell's silent absence of diners.

Straga and Valenti were still locked like that when the waiter arrived with our food. He set down three platters and my stainless steel malt can with a tall glass, called us gentlemen, and told us to enjoy it.

At my mention of Sheri something had changed. I would have worried seriously about her future if not for a more pressing concern for my own.

Straga broke the impasse. "I'll do it."

Rome Valenti looked down at his plate, picked up a curly fry, popped it in his mouth, chewed, then took a knife to his burger. He was done with the matter.

I poured shaken chocolate malt into my glass and took a test sip, smacked my lips.

"Best in town," I said, glad my voice didn't shake too.

"Better be," said Valenti.

"'Cause you're buying, yeah, I know."

"'Cause I own the place."

I looked around the room. "You made a lot of changes."

"Fits better with the other one."

"Which one's that?"

He named a celebrity hangout on Melrose.

"Didn't make the papers," I said.

"Seattle holding company on the contract. Nobody cares."

I turned to him. "What happened to Pete Lowell?"

Valenti picked up his water glass, examined it, took a sip. "Retired."

Pete was third-generation Lowell, not yet forty years of age. The café had been his second home since childhood. I was aware how people like Roman Valenti work. They see, they like, they take. Simple as that.

I ventured a risky step into another minefield. "Some people think the guy we buried Monday was in trouble with the law."

"Maybe so, maybe not. Fact is, some horse jumped the gate. Two-timer's where he was headed anyway. Good thing to keep in mind."

And with that any question as to why Gabe Cooley had died, and for what reason, was rendered moot.

We continued to eat in silence. When it appeared we were through, I voiced a thought I felt was safe enough.

"What can you tell me about this thing I'm looking for?"

"Do I look like a patsy to you, Dyle? "

"No."

"Then don't mess with me. You helped the asshole set it up."

I felt my attitude gearbox downshift rapidly from scared to irked to royally pissed off. I counted to three to cool off.

"This town is run by the Tetra cartel. Top dog is a Mexican-

American somewhere between fifty and sixty years of age, lives in the barrio. Got a two-bedroom Craftsman bungalow built a hundred years ago, a wife, a Chihuahua, orange cat. No car, he doesn't need one. Not one ounce of product moves in this town that he doesn't control. I can't give you his name because I only saw him once, at night. But if I did, he'd know about it and I'd be dead in twenty-four.

"Now you come to town. There's only one reason I can see. You don't want to move on Mister X, you don't want the shit jobs in the ponies, the rackets, the hookers. You're Mister Clean, Harvard man. My bet is you're after the movies—not the old theater chains and studios your grandfathers owned fifty years ago, and not the unions they sucked dry. You want today's movie lots and sound stages. You want video streams, subscriber revenue. You want the new studios, because you've dipped your wick in the Hollywood pond a time or three, courtesy our late friend. You made easy money and you like the side action.

"You just suggested that I copped a walk in Miami, same in Galveston. Let's get one thing clear: That's the cover story you were dealt because that's what the man running those ops—and I don't mean a fed—that's what he wants you to believe. Push that button too hard and you'll wind up where he put John Gotti. So, that won't work on me."

Valenti was getting steamed. Was I pushing my luck?

"I might've misjudged some people," he said, "made some assumptions. Happens. Maybe also you got the wrong picture about me, Dyle, what I'm about."

"Nobody's perfect, but there's something else. Happened at the funeral."

Valenti's face remained impassive. "Don't sit on it too long."

"A pass was made. Right under your nose, in front of me and everybody else. Could've been money, intel, snort, somebody's ear, I don't know. But you were there. You heard the Rev blow his lines, not because he was all shook over you showing up. When he opened his book, he saw this thing and panicked. He knew who it came from. He might've known where it was going. Point is, the parties-to got one past anyone watching."

"But not you."

"I went to the man afterward, pay my respects, say thank-you for the service. Rev looked like he was seeing a ghost. He was scared and he wanted out of there quick. I mentioned his flub and his look changed, got real ugly, then he left. Make of it what you will, but the funeral wasn't just to bury the lady's uncle."

"What you expect me to do, bleed? You had something going on with Cooley."

He wasn't letting that fish off the hook.

"Mister Valenti," I said, "I had three encounters this year with Coolio from the 'hood. Three in seven months, on the street outside my place of work, with one of Vic Straga's gym-rat bozos standing guard. That's three too many in my book, because I pay my rent by bank check, automatic, on time. Why the hassle? My landlord hated my guts. He wanted a pushover Latino peon, got a gainfully employed Anglo instead. I dragged his sorry ass through the city regulations muck for selling me a line about a live forge that turned out toxic. Bet he never told you, because also bet he ate those fines and the cleanup cost rather than bother New York about it. So before anybody assumes I set up anything with that scum-sucking dirt bag, they better get their facts straight—" I glanced at Straga, "—or wonder if they served that dish before it was cooked."

I watched Valenti as my diatribe settled in. Then he turned back to Straga with a grim sneer that signaled another unspoken directive.

I tilted the malt can and downed the last swallow. Luncheon at Lowell's was over.

Valenti had his own version of farewell. "Watch yourself,

Dyle," he said. "Not all is as it first appears."

I got up from the table, decided a thank-you was borderline ridiculous, and left without a backward look.

The moment I closed the door to Lowell's my whole body started to shake so bad I thought I'd dump my load right there on Lankershim Boulevard in beautiful downtown Burbank. I headed north to walk it off, unsure which was stronger, my fear of the ugly mess I'd stepped into, or the urge to give Roman Valenti's stone face a new expression with a hot forge iron. Probably the iron, but I didn't have a forge handy.

A New York capo was flexing his muscles in Los Angeles—a turf grab that, according to mafia rules, invited a lethal pushback. Valenti wasn't the careless type or he wouldn't be around. His hard-bargaining for a minor league restaurant made no sense unless he'd found the food business here offered a better return than backdoor movie loans. Dealing terror was just a next logical step.

But despite Roman Valenti's scary long reach, he hadn't mentioned the part of my history no one could touch. A gap I did not intend to fill for him, as sure as hell was his next home.

25

At Home With Minnie

I pulled into the dirt patch that passed for my driveway, killed the engine, and sat there for a moment listening to the tick of cooling metal. My container pad squatted against the yard's back wall—three forty-foot steel boxes forming an H pattern and retrofitted with windows, plumbing, and enough insulation to keep the place from turning into an oven during L.A.'s brutal summers. Some people called it minimalist living. I called it affordable.

Gravel crunched underfoot as I made my way to the front door, my mind still replaying the exchange with Valenti. The guy had the emotional range of a parking meter, but twice the capacity to break knees. I fumbled with my keys, pushed open the door, and froze.

Minnie Glover sat on my couch—the Camden Cloth button-tuck back seat from a '59 Cadillac Brougham. She had one long leg crossed elegantly over the other, looking like she'd stepped out of a fashion magazine and into my disaster zone of a living room.

I turned for my recliner and stopped. Joe Blanco stared back at me.

"Make yourselves at home," I said, closing the door behind me. "Oh wait, you already did."

Blanco didn't smile. "You look like hell, Dyle."

"Thanks. I was going for 'slightly better than roadkill' today, so I'll take that as a win."

I shrugged off my cheap suit jacket and tossed it onto the kitchen counter, which in my place meant I could reach it from almost anywhere in the main living area.

"How'd you get in?"

Minnie uncrossed her legs and extended an arm pointed at the door. "You keep your spare key in that fake rock by the cactus. Seriously? A fake rock? A potted cactus in the middle of a junk yard?"

"My crude attempt at irony," I muttered, opening the fridge and pulling out two beers. I offered Minnie one, she accepted with a nod.

Blanco took a pass. "I'm driving."

"So," Minnie said after taking a sip, "are you going to tell us what you've done for two days, or do I have to pretend I'm not dying of curiosity?"

I pulled up a chair from the two-seater dinette and straddled it with my elbows on the back, feeling my age plus a few decades.

"I flushed Cooley's lawyer, got shot at, got interrogated by the LAPD, and Scarf and I paid a call on Five Dragons. The latter experience was edifying."

I filled my two cohorts in on Mark Robie's little confessional, including the Ensenada fiasco with the Russian money man who sank like a rock.

When I finished, Glover sat for a bit with one foot tapping the air.

"So our erstwhile bag man for the mob was a very busy boy with his own agenda."

Blanco raised a finger. "And his own money, it would seem."

"Possibly his money, but I think Minnie and I can get more out of Weldon Latimer."

Minnie's eyes widened. "Moi? No way—I'm the computer nerd in this posse, remember?"

"What're you getting at?" Blanco asked.

"Wellie likes to think he's cagey. I think he's crooked. If he's willing to talk to a small audience, Minnie might win points where I get stonewalled."

"Because I'm a female."

"And a fine-looking one at that."

"How nice to say so. You didn't spend the entire day playing screenwriter with Burke's employer. Where else did you go?"

I aimed a meaningful glance at Blanco. "Out to the Valley to see a mob capo about a fresh start building street rods. See, that's the other thing, guys. As of yesterday I'm out of a job."

Minnie sat back. "Ohmigosh! At SpeedLine? What happened?"

"Don't ask me, because I wasn't told. The point of it, though, is that my would-be business partner and I never got down to talking cars. Valenti kind of spoiled things."

It was Blanco's turn to look shocked. "Valenti? You spoke to the guy?"

"More like he spoke to me. Had a message he wanted to be sure I got."

"The guy sure gets around. What did he want?"

"Me, as his errand boy to scout for unnamed treasure Cooley left behind."

Blanco got to his feet. "The damn VX is what he's after. Implying, if he wasn't messing with you, he's as clueless as everybody else where it is. I've got a crook in Torrance who supposedly has a line on something contraband besides baby booties. Gotta chase it down."

"Don't leave so soon," I said. "The fun's just starting."

He let himself out the door with no farewell other than a middle digit for me.

I gave Minnie a helpless shrug. "Looks like it's down to us to save the world."

"Let's pretend that was productive," Minnie said. "Dyle, we need a fresh look at everything."

"Why don't you start by calling me Jack again? I only get the other from bill collectors and ornery cops."

"Okay, Jack, if you'll do the same. I'll be Minnie with you, but I'm Glover to the feds and everyone else in the game."

"Your AI included?"

"To PumaNet I'm known as Mom or Boss Lady."

"I'm curious, what's Minnie stand for?"

"Let's not go there. It's…well, kooky."

"Come on, is it Minerva? That's an older name, but nothing to be ashamed of."

"No, but Minerva's better than Minolta."

I looked at her, she looked back. "You're not joking," I said.

"Wish I was. Daddo was taking pictures of his new-born baby girl and Mommo told him to come up with something quick. He looked down at the cam, saw the brand, and voila."

I made a silent chuckle. "That'll make a great story for the grandkids."

"Not in the plans."

"Well, what's *in* the plans? At Denny's you alluded to a checkered past. Care to elucidate?"

"No."

"Okay, how'd you become fluent in computerese?"

"Self-taught. I was freckled, ungainly, ungorgeous, and wildly unpopular. My only friend was a hacker guy who taught me a lot. We communicated over the web, never dated—thank God."

"Why thank Him?"

"Her. God is a woman."

"I stand politically corrected. Why thank Her?"

"Because we hacked into a bank, performed some illicit

maneuvers, and attracted the attention of evil lawmen. I was only thirteen, he was an old man of twenty, or so he claimed. Point being, he got sent up, I went free—for a while.”

“Oops, enter the checkered part. Sounds juicy. Bet you could write a book.”

“So, what are your plans for dinner tonight, Jack?”

Minnie’s deep reveal was over.

“My dinner plans usually involve whatever hasn’t evolved into a new life form in my fridge,” I said, getting up to rummage through the sparse contents. “Tonight’s special is... questionable leftover Thai or a sandwich with bread that’s only slightly stale.”

Minnie made a face. “I’ve seen crime scenes more appetizing.”

“Hey, not all of us have fancy AI assistants to remind us to grocery shop.”

She stood up, smoothing down her jeans with a decisive gesture. “Get your jacket. We’re going out.”

“I don’t recall agreeing to that.”

“You didn’t. But your refrigerator just filed for Chapter 11, so your options are limited.” She was already moving toward the door. “Besides, I know a place where we can talk without worrying about who’s listening.”

~

Twenty minutes later, we were sliding into a booth at Casa Abuela, a hole-in-the-wall Mexican joint tucked between a laundromat and a check-cashing place in Echo Park. The waitress, a granny with shrewd eyes and a no-nonsense demeanor, nodded at Minnie like they were old friends.

“You come here often?” I asked after we’d ordered.

“Often enough that they don’t water down my margarita.” She leaned back, studying me. “So, what exactly did Valenti say that you’re so reluctant to share?”

I toyed with my beer bottle before answering. “He knows

about some black ops I did years ago. Deacon Hood was involved in one of them, Blanco in another. Valenti was telling me he has an inside connection."

"Did he mention Medusa?"

"No, didn't say anything about AI of any kind. The point he wanted to make was that he was convinced I was working with Cooley on the arms deal and screwed it up. He was about to imply I would have to unscrew it when I made clear that I had as little as possible to do with or say to my asshole landlord, and Mister Valenti had better get his facts straight before dragging me into a half-baked business transaction."

"And what did you do after you picked your face up off the floor?"

"I went home knowing I'd just made myself more interesting to a mafia capo."

"That's where I came in. Want that last quesadilla?"

"Help yourself."

I watched her down it with zesty delight. The girl had a healthy appetite, but it didn't seem to show—another soul blessed with high metabolism. The food was home-style Sonoran. I sopped mine barrio style with a flour tortilla, the way I'd learned from a dozen Mexican "uncles."

Minnie insisted on paying the bill. Once outside, I checked the area before dropping into the passenger seat. No midnight auto supply going on there. Her flashy '48 Ford custom enjoyed respect from the lowrider crowd.

"I guess it's back to your place now, huh, Jack?" she said.

"We could watch a ball game. Dodgers aren't playing, though."

"Who's on?"

"Chicago at the Giants, or we could watch Philly teach Colorado how the game is played."

"San Fran might be more fun."

She eased the car into traffic. "And then?"

"Depends how Yankee feels about sharing the couch."

"Yankee's the yard dog who likes women's backsides."

"He's Rotweiller, doesn't discriminate. Likes 'em all."

We caught the last three innings from Oracle Park. The Giants lost, Yankee asked to be let out.

Minnie asked to stay in.

26

Latimer's Roxie Story

I phoned Wellie shortly after arising from the best sleep I'd had in months. I told him I had acquired more intel for him and thought we might swap stories. He was still the reluctant fugitive, wary of stepping into a trap, so I let him call the time and place. That gave Minnie time to scoot to her apartment and change to a sensibly appealing outfit.

The Roxie's last picture show closed in 1989, a Mexican vaquero movie nobody remembers and fewer came to see. Today's marquee advertised "SUPREMO" in small black letters—not a movie title but a reference to sundry goods peddled by one of the bodegas occupying the lobby. I hoped Wellie hadn't paid too dearly for use of the hall today.

When I stepped into the theater proper and hollered, he came out from backstage and peered into the gloom. I introduced Minnie as my cousin from Iowa. Wellie eyed her with suspicion, but his eye for feminine beauty ruled, and we were granted free admission.

Five minutes later, we sat in the empty loge section with the best seats in the house, three plastic deck chairs being the *only* seats. The theater originals had been sold to a television evangelist in Reseda whose show suffered the same fate as the vaquero flick.

Wellie had swapped the wrinkled suit for a blue collared shirt with arm patch, twill work pants, a blue ball cap, and a key ring on a wide belt—trying to pass as a janitor.

We were drinking coffee from Fashion Donuts, either a play on "old-fashioned" or creative license at work. One functions best downtown when one keeps a liberal mind. The coffee was good, the donuts were great, and Wellie was eating again. He licked his fingers to open the show.

"The deal fell into our laps," he said. "Actually, Gabe's lap. He had this troublesome tenant in South L. A. The guy paid his rent okay, but he was bothering the neighbors at night with a lot of noise. So Gabe goes down there with one of his gorillas to see what's up. He gets as far as the front porch and a guy steps out of the house next door and hollers at him that the tenant died the night before in a motorcycle accident.

"Gabe thinks, some things happen for the better, and lets himself into the house. The front room is trashed, so he posts his bodyguard outside to keep the riffraff away. Then he goes room by room until he reaches the back bedroom—one look tells him he's struck gold."

"The tenant hid product in the house?" I said.

"Not drugs—guns. Wooden crates stamped with something like U.S. Army markings, stacked wall-to-wall to the rafters. Gabe later verified online that the boxes held assault rifles, grenade launchers, some unidentifiable items, and enough ammo to level every house on the block. Gabe's excited, he's stoked. He calms himself enough to spin a story for his bodyguard, takes the guy home, and then spends the next five nights solo using a hand cart to shift the crates out the back door, down a narrow staircase, and into a rented van."

"Where'd he take it?"

"I don't know. He wouldn't say."

"Why'd he trust you?"

"We'd worked together for years—shared some projects and confidences in the production world. Plus, that weapons cache was too massive for him to handle alone."

"How did Valenti get involved?"

"He was part of everything Gabe did—running several corporations owning rentals in L.A. and elsewhere. Legitimate realty on paper, though where the cash ends up is another story. I even helped Gabe set up a Nevada shell, Fenway Arts, LLC, to cut taxes and keep things under wraps."

Minnie leaned forward, intrigued. "Sounds like a laundering scheme."

"Not necessarily—Gabe might have been used as a cutout before. One day, he tells me about the weapons he found. I give him a long look, knowing the stuff is hot contraband pilfered from an arsenal. If it's U.S. Army gear and you're caught, you're headed for Leavenworth—a place so bad you might as well jump off a cliff. He knows all that, yet the haul is too big to pass up. Gabe believes if he can offload it to someone in the right market—even for a five percent cut—he'll be set for life.

"I tell him he's just implicated me without asking. He replies, 'So, you still want in, don't you?' I say, 'I'm already in so deep I can't find my ass,' and I tell him, 'Gabe, if you don't bring this to your syndicate and they catch on, you're dead.'

"Then I ask, 'Who up top could step in? Who's got the moxie and cash to take this to the next level?' The idiot blurts out, 'Roman Valenti'—right there in my office, Jaycee other side of the door. Boom, he realizes his mistake."

"You could bypass Gabe and sell to Valenti yourself. But it's too late—he already spilled everything."

"I point out that I have my own resources—not mob ties, but plenty of contacts in the movie business."

"You mean your MacArthur Park friend from Africa?"

Wellie nodded.

I ventured a guess. "Because the guy loves American movies, runs a multinational piracy scheme, has cash, and wants to double up without drawing attention—needs a go-between."

"You catch on fast."

"Gabe set up an agreement, but for a deal this large, you route the principals through you in both directions."

"You done this before?"

"Not personally, just seen it done. Go on."

Wellie sipped his coffee. "It's looking good. Gabe's got Valenti on the hook and I've got an African warlord itching to mess up his tribal enemies. We negotiate a price, then the principals learn who each other is. Gabe finds out immediately and tells me later. From then on, it's all about timing. The deal is dead without the goods. Gabe knows each side will kill him once his location is revealed— and neither side will hesitate to force it out of him. So, what's a guy to do?"

"Find another buyer?"

"Exactly."

"Whose idea was that?"

"His entirely. I was already in too deep, so I approach a movie consultant with federal ties—someone who can't talk about the details. I tell him I can help the government recover the items if I get immunity, and it has to happen fast. This is last Wednesday— the day before Gabe died. And starting Thursday morning, everything accelerates.

"I'm in a hotel with two feds, telling them what I know and don't know, when one gets a call. They initially claim the mystery isn't guns, but something else. Then they say, okay, it's VX nerve gas. This escalates everything to the moon. The feds want me to lure Gabe into a trap so they can seize the gas before the African does. But before anyone moves, Gabe goes dark, making it clear he'll only contact me next—if ever. And now I've got feds on my tail. Anyway, enough about that mess. I've got something else to say, unrelated."

Wellie set down his coffee cup hard enough to slop liquid over the chipped rim. His index finger left a smudge trail as he looked at me directly. "You know Gabe admired you."

The shift caught me mid-sip. I tried to cover. "That cream-puff. I always knew a hint of approval lurked beneath his tough-guy veneer."

That got a dubious look from Minnie, but nothing more.

Wellie continued. "Back before things went sideways, Gabe insisted I see your shop." His dry chuckle snagged on something bitter. "Drove me down there, unlocked like it was the Tomb of Secrets, and pulled the tarp off like he was revealing the crown jewels."

"That baby lived in a chicken coop for half a century," I pointed out.

"Yeah, well your shop is just one step above. Gabe kept running his hand along those fender flames like they were museum pieces." Wellie's eyes squinted in recollection. "Throaty little frog voice almost choked when he talked about that car. But there was something else, Dyle, and you need to hear it."

"I'm not going anywhere till I finish the last donut."

"Gabe ran a background check when you came forward to rent the shop. Discovered your service record. Saw your commendations where you got field-promoted during Wanat '08. Felt validated somehow—hero worship from a grunt still buying the Green Machine illusion. Respect, he called it."

"Hard to believe. Never showed me anything like that."

"Dyle, we're talking Gabe Cooley here. The poor sap didn't know how to show anything but hardnose."

"Well, I'd like to believe he had a good side to him."

My chat with Alice Loring came to mind—the movie deal that gave her a new life. It would seem Gabe Cooley was more complex than he let on.

"But back to the weapons deal," Wellie said. "Sebutu isn't buying guns, he's buying drones—not Army drones bigger than a Piper Cub, but cute little puppies specially designed to deliver a small payload. Toy-sized, airborne, anti-personnel gas delivery system that spreads a deadly payload on impact. VX is a Sarin derivative—"

"I know what it is, Wellie. Nasty stuff, paralyzes the diaphragm in a slow death by suffocation. DoD got rid of the last stores years ago. Where'd Gabe get any?"

"No idea. They magically materialized in his possession."

Minnie stirred in her chair. "Where'd he put them?"

"Didn't say boo to me. I think he was afraid I might leak it. Now it's anybody's guess, because the location died with him."

I had another question for the lawyer. "How much longer does Jaycee have in your employ?"

Wellie made a face. "A few weeks, a month. I'll get disbarred once this comes out. Why? What's it to you?"

I glanced over at Minnie before I answered him. "If you recall from my last visit to your office, she and I have a dinner date."

Minnie didn't respond. I took that to mean one night in the sack wasn't enough to establish an attachment. After all, we were both rational, urbane adults.

It was time to leave. I offered to take out the trash, but Wellie said no. "It'll add credibility to my custodian persona."

Minnie and I left without further comment.

I was parked on Spring near Sixth. Minnie paused outside the Roxie ticket booth, now a display case offering rings and watches.

"I'll grab a cab from here," she said. "Got lots to do."

"Me too."

"Where're you taking your date?"

"Funky little place on Rodeo Drive, but I've got a few things to check out first."

"Stay in touch."

"Minnie…"

"Jack, it's fine."

"She's fifty-five."

"Then she scored. Good for her. See you tomorrow, and I promise not to surprise you again."

"Why? I think I could get used to it."

27

Humble Holmby Hills

Open questions always bother me. I had plenty of them by now, but one in particular was screaming at me to do something, and his name was George. Just another loose end, but more easily tied off now than left to trip me up later.

The address for Gabe Cooley's other place—or "palace" might be a better word—took me across Wilshire past the Sinai Temple and up Beverly Glen into the toney ramparts where stars of highest magnitude eat, sleep, swim, sun, and die. See, you have your Beverly Hills on what's called "The Flats," and rising above that squalid plain, where Sunset Boulevard ascends skyward, you get Holmby Hills. To benefit the paparazzi, tourists from Ohio, and real estate drone operators, the good people from Google have thoughtfully earmarked properties as belonging to this multi-millionaire movie idol, that billionaire sports professional, or this here owner of one-half of the world's ad-click revenue. All so that an ordinary wrench ape in a twelve-year-old Toyota four-banger can find his way without being tagged and bagged as a vagrant.

My destination was distinguished by a brick-paved drive leading through a sycamore grove and ending at the gated entrance for a split-level structure with more planted tiers than the Hanging Gardens of Babylon, which is not a theme park in Dubai—yet. And this was one of the more humble palaces in the realm. I stopped at the drawbridge and pressed the Admittance button as the sign indicated.

A mellifluous baritone voice answered: "May I help you." Not a question, but a command.

"Yes, Jack Dyle here. Sheridan Burke sent me."

"Who?"

Uh-oh, not my best foot forward.

"Sheri Burke, producer for Five Dragons Productions. She's sometimes with Mister Gabriel Cooley."

"Just a moment."

Not "please," just "wait there, bub, while I load the cannon and point it in your general direction."

Four minutes passed, possibly five, with the drawbridge still not drawn. Presently, the same voice returned to the little box.

"George here again. Sorry to keep you waiting, sir."

The drawbridge began drawing.

"Please drive around to your left and park beneath the overhang."

"Thank you." I felt I should add "so much" but pride got the better of my servile nature.

"Not at all, sir," said George, certain to get in the last word.

My journey ended in the shadow of a portico that would dwarf the prow of a Galactica Ghost Fleet command cruiser. I think.

A tall man in a white shirt and silver tie stood on a tiled riser to view my arrival with a hawkeyed stare. His sandy hair was graying at the temples. A German Shepherd stood at his side, all pointy-eared and alert to my slightest betrayal of insincerity. A lot like facing Mike Tyson bare-knuckled, but without Mike's reassuring smile.

I pulled to a stop feeling apologetic for my tawdry ride and climbed out in shameful oblivion.

"George Macklin," said the man, offering his hand. "I sort of run this poor old ship. A beast, isn't it?"

"A bit smaller than SoFi Stadium, but probably adequate accommodation for a prince or two."

"Hah! Glad to see someone has a sense of humor. The help and I jokingly refer to it as the Taj Mahal West, or simply the Taj. The usual guests can be terribly serious. Come on inside, relax a bit. Lovely day, isn't it?"

I said yes it was, and he could call me Jack.

He said I should call him George.

The dog disappeared without an introduction. George Macklin led the way into the house and guided me through a full-body scanner similar to those found at any airport. I placed my keys but not my shoes in the gray tub provided and passed the test with nary an apology from my host. From there we trod a carpeted loggia two steps above a sunken living room that would have done the Beverly Hilton lobby proud.

Continuing in the lead with long strides, George spoke to me over his shoulder. "So, how is Mister Cooley these days?"

"I guess you haven't heard," I said, matching his pace. "He passed away just a few days ago."

George stopped in his tracks. "Oh! What a shame! I didn't know. How is Miss Burke taking it?"

"She's drowning her sorrow by managing his estate. Big responsibility."

"Good heavens, hardly enough time to grieve."

"I don't think they were that close."

"Pardon me for saying so, but how do you know as much?"

"Well, I'm not sure, except for the notable lack of tears shed."

"Some people cover their feelings well."

"You are so right."

We came to an open doorway and entered a sitting room fitted with two conversational groupings and a wall of glass. On the other side of those windows was enough grass for a dandy hundred-yard wedge shot. No one was playing through.

"Drink?" said George, indicating a bar along the near wall.

"Coffee if you have it."

George set a china cup on a saucer and poured from a stainless warmer carafe. I had a sip and wasn't disappointed, so I thought it best to get to the point of my visit.

"There seems to be a question in Sheri's mind about Mr. Cooley's use of this house. Was he always a guest when he came here?"

George leaned an elbow on the bar top. "Certainly not, Gabriel Cooley is—was—chief steward for Valdor Enterprises. In charge of all the properties. I report to him directly—or did. Pardon, but speaking of him in the past is quite unsettling, actually."

"I'm sorry to be the bearer of such shocking news. You haven't heard from—er, corporate?"

"No, you see, all communication to me came directly through Mr. Cooley himself. Same for my counterparts at the other properties. I'm not sure what will happen now. It may take some time for the company to arrange his replacement. I could be out of a job and not know it. Ha-ha."

"I should hope not, after so many years of service."

"It's become my home, to the extent one can call sixteen rooms a home. Not too different from my hotel days. I'm in good hands, though."

"That would be Valdor."

"Yes."

"Headquartered here in Los Angeles?"

"New York."

"Did Gabe keep an office here?" I swung a finger in the air to indicate the premises.

"No, he did not. The house is for residential use only. Mr. Cooley was in the corporate jet most of the time, flying around to various places like this one."

"Any office in the L. A. area?"

"As far as I know, just the studio office."

"He had an association with Five Dragons Productions, I'm told."

"That's the name on the door. I've only been there once myself, last-minute thing to drive him to the airport. From what I saw, it was just an executive suite, four walls and a desk provided as a courtesy to visiting dignitaries. Nice, but nothing fancy, certainly not permanent."

Chief steward. Other properties. Life on the go. A quick in-and-out and gone. The same guy who arranged to sleep on a boat.

"Would you care for a tour of the house, Jack?"

"Sure, I have a couple of days to spare."

A polite chuckle from George. We returned to the hallway and paused outside an open pair of double doors.

"The study," he announced.

I took a quick look at bookshelves and two desks with a view of the same golfing landscape, noted a well-stocked liquor cabinet at one end, and ducked back into the hallway.

"Over here we have our Quiet Room," said my tour guide.

We moved across the hall to another pair of closed doors. George presented his fingerprint to a security pad, registered a satisfying click, and pushed both doors wide open. A conference table in the center seated eight, with lounging areas at either end filled with overstuffed chairs and sofas.

"All the very best quality, of course," George pointed out. "The walls and doors were constructed to the specifications of a recording studio designer. Completely sealed from any sound moving in or out. Guests can converse in absolute secrecy and comfort."

"But no bar."

"No."

"You'd have to vet both bar and bartender."

He nodded. "Complicates things."

"Seems a skosh puritanical."

"Guests may acquire a cocktail from one of the house bars and bring it in. A few groups go so far as to bring along their own technician to scan drinks at the door."

"No pieces."

George was familiar with the euphemism for firearms. "None permitted on the premises. They know that going in, but we remind them anyway with the scanner you came through."

"Every bit as good as the TSA boys and girls have, I bet."

"Better."

"Not a great endorsement for airport security. A micro weapon might sneak past TSA, but you'll catch it here?"

"These people don't fly commercial."

"Oh, right. So, you were in the hotel game. That must've been exciting."

"It had its moments, like if you get a jumper, or some nut job rings the fire alarm but no fire."

George was loosening up a bit—a natural response to my adroit psychological manipulation.

"Borderline terrorizing," I said with a reassuring nod to keep things flowing.

"Not really. Before that I was a cop."

"No kidding? LAPD?"

"Washington."

"Capitol police?"

"Capitol *Hill*."

He watched me put it together in my head. George Macklin was a former agent of the Secret Service. I wouldn't ask what circumstance had caused him to leave that primo outfit. I had erected obstacles to discovery myself.

"You know Blackhorn," I said, mentioning the protective services firm with which I had enjoyed a brief sojourn.

"Know of them. Never dealt directly. We had our hands full."

I lifted my chin at our surroundings. "Quite a transition. I wear a few millstones like that around my own neck."

"A guest or two have found out where I came from, got a chuckle out of it."

"How long has this house been a Syndicate asset?"

"I'm not sure what you mean. Valdor purchased the property two years ago. I was already here and familiar with the property. The former owner recommended me, the company kept me on."

"Can we level about the clientele who patronize this fine establishment? And who maybe occupy seats on the Valdor board of directors? Or are the microphones on?"

"No mikes, but you're on thin ice there, Jack."

"Not the first time. But I have a better idea now about the depth of the water under that ice."

"Subsurface stuff has to stay there."

My burner phone jiggled in my pocket and I took a peek. A text from Minnie to call her if I could tear myself away.

"And I think I just got called back to the office."

"Let me ask you this before you go. When did Mr. Cooley die?"

"Sometime Thursday night, discovered Friday morning in Hollenbeck Park. Badly beaten but already dead. It was on the news, but easily missed. I certainly did. You weren't concerned at all that he didn't show up for days?"

George shook his head. "It's quite normal for him to be on the road for days, sometimes weeks, without checking in. But Valdor must know if it happened that long ago. Buried Monday, you you say?"

"Yes, Sheri made the arrangements. Given such short notice herself, I guess she didn't have time to reach you."

"I should've heard from Valdor before this. The fact that I didn't might cause me me reconsider a few arrangements."

"I've been down the same river, George. Learned a few moves, ways to keep afloat. You never get all the way off the trolley."

"Seems so." What he said next sent a chill up my spine. "This is Rome Valenti's operation."

We exchanged looks. He saw that I knew who he was talking about and had already suspected as much. Maybe he knew Valenti was in town attending funerals and entertaining locals at lunch.

I gave him my card. "If your boat springs a leak, don't wait too long to throw out a line."

George Macklin nodded and we shook hands. "See you out," he said.

Spoken like a cop, not a caretaker.

28

Sheri Lives Well

I had a date with an angel in a few hours, so I headed home to shower and change. On the way I returned Minnie's call. She'd been thinking about our Roxie visit with Latimer.

"How well do you know your client, Jack?" she said.

"Maybe not well enough. Why?"

"She said something about living in Monrovia, but my resources can't find any connection."

Her resources had proved amazingly accurate so far. Odd as it seemed so far along in my investigation, I had not yet seen Sheri Burke in her native environment.

"I'll get back to you," I said.

Rather than blunder ahead over the phone, I decided to simply observe. A good place to start might be to catch Sheri after work, so after dressing in my finest—and only—suit, I drove to Five Dragons, parked across the street, and called Minnie back.

"Just had a thought," I said. "Five Dragons people already know my voice. How about you call and ask to speak to Sheri Burke. If they indicate she's there, disconnect before the call goes through."

Thirty seconds went by while I considered that some investigative professionals might question shadowing your own client. Waiting this long in the game merely showed I'd gotten a little rusty at the snoop game.

Minnie reported. "She's there. What's this about, Jack?"

"I'm being my usual sneaky, crassly doubtful self."

"You left out cynical. You could just drive to her house and wait."

"That would be neither sneaky nor crass, so I'll wait here till she gets off, find out what I can, and catch up with you tonight when I have some dope."

"What're you driving?"

"The Toyota, why?"

"Just making sure you don't go on a daylight stakeout in that wrapped rose red Focus visible from a mile away."

"Oh ye of little faith."

"Look small and insignificant. I know it's a challenge to your bad-boy persona, but try anyway."

"You know where I'd rather be."

"I hope not at another ball game."

"Maybe your place this time."

"Jack, I don't have a mitt or a bat, but I do throw a mean curve."

"Oy. Five bucks says I can hit it out of the park."

"I'll take that bet."

I clicked off and needed several minutes to shift my mind back into stakeout mode.

Sheri was dedicated to the marathon work ethic. It was almost seven with a darkening sky when she slipped out of the glass lobby and started for the underground garage. Two minutes later she reappeared driving a new-looking Lexus LS. I let her get on the street before I lighted up the Camry and pulled out. A minute later I picked her up turning right onto Santa Monica Boulevard. For the next twenty minutes I stayed back in traffic, but I had to close up a bit as she went left at Fairfax and headed for the tree-lined streets of Spaulding Square.

I kept her taillights in view for two blocks until she pulled into a driveway. I went around the block and came at it from the other direction. The Lexus was parked in the driveway halfway back, lights off. I made a note of the house number and continued on past, then I doubled back on the next street over, went north to Sunset then east a couple of blocks toward the 101 Freeway. I pulled into an empty spot at the curb and got online.

According to Zillow, the five-bedroom, two-story Spanish estate house was a hundred years old but recently renovated and listed as having sold last April for three million eight and change. A bit extravagant for the area, but a real stretch for a youngster of twenty-five working long hours for wages. The house hadn't appeared on Cooley's list of possessions, but Sheri could have more than one sugar daddy.

I thumbed Minnie's number again, but she was busy. I'd have to ask her later for access privileges to dig up the owner's name, sales terms, and closing costs. Meantime, I had a pleasant appointment not far away in Beverly Hills.

29

A Surprise At Truman's

True to her independent style with her lawyer boss, Jaycee Cutter had insisted on her own ride to Truman's On The Drive. My previous experience there, also my only, had been as the guest of high-dollar company. I got there first and stood as she entered in a knockout red sheath and matching pumps. The maître d' nodded at us with a respectful "Sir" of vague recognition and gave Jaycee Cutter a little bow, assuming her to be another well-preserved Bel Air luminary.

We were ushered to a semi-circular banquette of respectable isolation, the wine steward tagging along. I ordered a cabernet with which I was faintly familiar and received the good fellow's nod of approval. Jaycee reposed in the queenly assumption of one who has found her proper station.

"You got the captain worried," I said. "He thinks he should remember you."

"After tonight, maybe he will."

"Please don't make a scene, Geneva, I have a splitting headache."

"Poor Charles, but you haven't tasted the wine." She nibbled a breadstick. "Yuck, I like typing paper better."

"Eaton bond?"

"We can't afford bond… Jack, that's terrible!"

"Can't be helped. These wonders just come to me. Sometimes it flows like a river."

"Well, find a drought, quick."

"I'll talk to Wellie about your paper shortage. That hits a new low."

"You ain't heard nothin' yet. The washroom—"

The steward appeared just then with a bottle wrapped in linen, presented it, received my approval, and poured. When he was gone, I took a sip and gave Jaycee a wink.

"Speaking of nothing, you are something tonight. You turned a few heads on the way in."

"Did I? That was me trying to remember how to walk in heels."

"You look positively devastating, Jaycee. The clientele think you must be a society diva they ought to recall but can't quite place."

"Because my place is one step ahead of the bread line."

"Mine, too, but fear not, I shall tilt my soup bowl ever so slightly and select only the appropriate tableware for each course."

"You've done this before. I haven't."

"Actually, it goes with the job. As a trained investigator, I absorb protocol quickly."

"You are so full of it, Jack." She glanced around the room. "Isn't this fun?"

"Indubitably."

Asshole, she mouthed.

She picked up a menu, scanned down the tall board, blinked twice, and muttered under her breath, "Holy shitzki."

"It's okay," I said, "but let's not make a habit of it."

"Which? The cussing or the breadsticks?"

Jaycee got the Steak Diane and I ordered the prime rib after choosing the marmalade walnut crostini appetizer. When the waiter had left, she propped an elbow on the table and gave me a look.

"That's fu-four bills."

"Wine included."

"Jack."

"Jaycee."

"Where have you been all my life?"

"Waiting for you to say that."

"Pfaw! Gawd, I feel drunk and I haven't finished my first glass yet."

"A little food always helps. Have another breadstick."

The waiter arrived with our meal and we got busy enjoying two choice cuts of beef. After a bit, Jaycee leaned back with a purr of satisfaction.

"I almost forgot to ask, Jack, after you made off with Wellie and half a ream of paperwork. What the hell happened to the flash drive?"

I froze for a moment, caught off guard. I had no idea about any flash drive. But I couldn't let on that I was in the dark. I took a sip of wine, buying time to formulate a response.

"Which one?" I asked nonchalantly. "There were two, you know."

Jaycee's eyebrows shot up. "Two? I only knew about the domicile list."

"Ah, that one," I said, nodding as if it was old news. "What do you think it contained?"

She shrugged, toying with her fork. "Probably a list of Cooley's L. A. rentals. I don't know, that was an aspect of Gabe's business Wellie never discussed."

My mind raced. If this so-called domicile list was valuable enough to kill for, it might explain Cooley's murder. But if Valenti or his cleaner had taken it from Cooley Thursday night, why would he bother with me?

"Do you think it might be tied to Gabe's murder?" I said.

Jaycee's eyes widened slightly. "Jack, I try not to think about what happened to that man. It was so scary."

"Sorry, you're absolutely right."

Jaycee sipped her wine while watching me over the rim of her glass. Concern etched her features.

"You're going after the killer, aren't you?"

"That's the LAPD's job. I'm just tracking down assets and liabilities, things like that."

"Be careful, Jack."

"Always am. How's your steak?"

"The most scrumptious piece of heaven I've ever tasted."

"I'll pass that along to the chef. He'll appreciate that you took the time."

I leaned back, affecting a relaxed pose I didn't feel. In some way, this domicile list might figure into Gabe's VX deal, but Valenti had ruled out most of Gabe's residential properties as nonviable for some reason, which might render Gabe's list useless. For me, tracking down the VX itself was priority one right now.

"So tell me," I said, cutting into my prime rib with surgical precision, "what's your theory about Wellie's two-month sabbatical? Besides growing a beard and developing a taste for gas station coffee."

Jaycee dabbed the corner of her mouth with her napkin, leaving a faint crimson smudge.

"Honestly? I think he was running scared."

"Running from what, though?" I speared a roasted fingerling potato. "Or whom?"

"That's above my pay grade, Jack. All I know is that he vanished. Didn't even take his golf clubs."

"Now that is serious."

"For Wellie? Apocalyptic." She swirled her wine, watching the ruby liquid cling to the sides of the glass. "He missed three standing tee times at Riviera. The membership committee sent a sympathy card, assuming someone had died."

"Someone had."

"Yes, but they didn't know that."

The waiter materialized to refill our glasses and inquire about our satisfaction. We assured him everything was perfect, and he glided away, silent as a ghost.

"Besides his visit to my shop to ogle Cooley's hotrod Ford, did Gabe ever show Wellie any other properties?" I asked, steering the conversation back to safer waters.

"Not that I know of." Jaycee twirled her fork absently. "But Wellie's calendar had more holes than Swiss cheese those last few weeks. Private appointments marked only with initials. Very un-Wellie-like."

"GC? For Gabe Cooley?"

"Sometimes. Also MR and VS."

I kept my face neutral though my pulse quickened. VS could be Vic Straga, Valenti's luncheon guest and West Coast lieutenant. And MR... well, that was interesting.

The waiter appeared again, this time with a leather-bound menu of sweet temptations. "Dessert?" I asked Jaycee.

"God, no," Jaycee patted her stomach. "I'm already going to have to do penance with my trainer tomorrow."

"Just the check, please," I told the waiter, handing him my credit card.

While we waited, I caught Jaycee staring at me with an odd expression, halfway between amusement and suspicion.

"What?" I asked.

"You're different tonight. Like you're playing a part."

"Me? I'm an open book."

"Yeah, written in invisible ink." She leaned forward. "I've known you what, three hours, including Tuesday's office charade? And I can already tell when you're deflecting."

"It's a gift."

The waiter returned with the credit card slip. I added a healthy tip and signed with a flourish and a suppressed whimper—I'd just blown the last of my expense account.

"Ready?" I asked, sliding out of the banquette and offering Jaycee my hand.

She took it, rising gracefully despite the heels. "Such a gentleman."

"Only on special occasions."

As we made our way through the dining room, Jaycee suddenly slowed her pace, her fingers tightening on my forearm.

"Don't look now," she murmured, "but the man at the corner table by the wine rack has been watching you all evening."

Naturally, I wanted to whip my head around immediately. Instead, I casually guided Jaycee toward the coat check, using the mirrored wall behind it to get a glimpse of the room behind us.

My stomach clenched. Mark Robie sat nursing an amber drink at the corner table. Our eyes met in the mirror, and he raised his glass in a mocking salute.

"Do you know him?" Jaycee whispered.

"Never seen him before," I lied, even as my mind raced through a dozen scenarios, none of them good.

I helped Jaycee into her wrap, a silky thing that complemented her outfit perfectly. The maître d' materialized from nowhere, thanking us profusely for our patronage as if we were regulars instead of interlopers in this rarefied world.

"Such a lovely evening," the maître d' continued. "Perhaps we'll see you again soon, Mr...?"

"Dyle," I supplied automatically.

"Ah, yes. Mr. Dyle. A pleasure to serve you and the lady."

We stepped out into the evening air, the valet already sprinting to retrieve Jaycee's car. Streetlights along Rodeo Drive rendered the trendy storefronts and palms as vivid as daylight.

Jaycee spoke, her voice low and tight. "Jack, that man in there?

The one watching you?"

"What about him?"

"His companion at the table. I saw him before. A scary smooth Russian who came to the office with Gabe about three months ago." She shuddered visibly, hugging her wrap tighter despite the mild evening. "He waited for me in the parking garage afterward. Said he wanted to 'discuss business' over drinks."

My skin prickled. "What happened?"

"Nothing. I told him I was late picking up my mother from dialysis." Her lips quirked in a humorless smile. "My mother's been dead for twelve years. He gave me this toothy smile and traced his finger down my arm. I had to shower twice that night to feel clean again."

The valet pulled up, and I tipped him before opening Jaycee's door. Once she was inside, I leaned down to the open window.

"This Russian," I said, keeping my voice steady. "What did he look like? Aside from 'scary smooth.'"

Jaycee closed her eyes, reconstructing the memory. "Short, about five-six, stocky build, shaved head. Cheap suit, not as bad as Wellie's."

"Did Gabe introduce him by name?"

"Victor something. Started with an S, I think."

Vic Straga, to a tee.

Jaycee thanked me and I pecked her cheek with a compliment I genuinely felt and the promise of a repeat.

I retrieved my own car, thinking about my bottom-end home twelve freeway miles, forty-two stop lights, and twenty income brackets away. My little palaver with Minnie came to mind, and I veered off for her apartment, definitely the preferred venue for the rest of the night.

As I drove the freeway back across town, I couldn't shake the incongruous ending to dinner. Straga and Robie? Why was the owner of a sleazy East Hollywood gym hobnobbing with Cooley's client? How did Straga figure in Cooley's ever-evolving money menagerie?

And Russian? That was a stretch. Straga was formerly Strakka, a name from one of the Baltic countries. Of course, that wouldn't bother an oligarch. Those guys would deal with anyone who delivered results, kept them secret, and lied about everything.

And when one of their own went missing, they didn't just dry up and blow away. They stuck around, like wet paper on glass.

I knew a bit about Russians. Maybe more than I ought to.

I knew about liars too.

30

Half A Lifetime Ago

You learn early on about secrets and lies when your family grows pot. We lived in a backcountry settlement nestled between two folds of the Santa Lucia Mountains. Townsfolk regarded us as hicks. To the kids at school I was just another "Saint Lucy hillbilly." When I complained to Gran she told me it was a lot nicer than calling us what we were.

My first brush with outright killing came hard at age ten, the night my Gran shot the man holding a gun to my head. A nine-millimeter bullet right between the eyes of my mother's last bar pickup. Patty Dyle already lay dead on the floor. The guy had made damn sure she would never bring home another bum like him.

We buried them both in the woods above Pozo Flat. A long night digging mountain dirt got my hate down to a low boil and the tears mostly dried. We gave Patty a plain wood marker and put her with her two brothers. Her killer got an unmarked hole on the backside of the hill, deep enough to keep critters from digging him up again.

Gran took me aside when we were done, close to daybreak, pushed a stray lock of hair off my face. "You're a good boy, Johnny," was all she said about it.

Oh, I was a good one, all right. A good liar. I could rattle off a story with the best of them. Knew how to make it stick, too. Most times, though, and particularly later, when asked about my mother's disappearance, I was good at keeping shut. Mountain folk don't say much anyway, so that worked as good as any story.

"The more you make up," Gran told me, "the more you got to carry around and try to keep straight. Eventually the weight of it all just wears you down."

She knew how that was. Addie Slade had more stories in her head than any ten lawyers. She told me a few, but saved most to herself, telling me they weren't fairy tales for fireside talks. And those she did give up were almost too bizarre to believe. One I was able to affirm for myself after that night: She was a dead sure shot.

Addie was still a good-looking woman at forty plus. She used to tell me there was a lot of plus there, but hard work and good genes fooled most folks into thinking she was younger. In town she would turn a feller's head now and then without even trying. Made me downright uncomfortable.

A few years went by, and the part of my life not devoted to schoolwork went to setting traps for poachers. These were small animal traps put out around the grow. We learned how from the old 'Nam vets, who had learned from bear traps the Viet Cong set for them in rice paddies. Local growers tended to respect one another's patches. One way to make sure they did was to trap a poacher or two. Those who got caught disappeared, usually a "Mex" or a "gook," as the vets called them. I never knew who made them disappear, and didn't want to know. For sure nobody who did know was going to mention it to a soul.

One Friday night a few weeks after I turned twelve I got back late from trapping. Gran met me outside on the darkened porch instead of waiting in the kitchen with a gas lamp.

"Get in the truck," she said, and when I asked why, "Because I said."

"Where we going so late?"

"None of your beeswax, John Dyle, now in the truck if you don't want a switching."

I hadn't been switched in a good many years. I was big for my age, a bit taller than Gran by then. Still, the threat was usually enough to end any argument, but tonight I had concerns.

"I got traps out."

"We'll talk about that later."

Walking past the tailgate I glanced into the truck bed and saw it was full of wrapped bundles. I noticed my brother Caleb's old Army duffel and a couple of bedrolls. Caleb had got through the Gulf War in Iraq, but hadn't survived the drug war at home. After he was shot dead, the duffel had passed to me as some token of manhood I never understood.

I stopped and pointed. "What's this?"

Gran just shrugged. "Taking some old junk down to the thrift in Grover Beach."

At one in the morning? What kind of fool did she take me for?

I got in and sat. Something was up and it wasn't good. Gran fired up the old GMC half-ton, drove slowly out of the yard and turned onto the dirt track that followed the creek down to the highway. As we bumped along, I looked over at her, ready to fire off another question, and received the shock of my life. My hardass grandmother's cheeks were shiny wet, her mouth twisted tight. In all the trials and tribulation of her life, I'd never once seen her cry.

"Don't you say a word, John Dyle. Not one word."

My mind put it together in a flash. I swallowed hard and bit my lip. My Gran was sending me away, and I didn't need for her to explain why.

The grower life was deadly hard and getting harder. My mother, Patty, was the last of three children Addie Slade had buried, all dead from the outlaw life. I was her only kin left. She was not going to let the mountain take me.

By the time she turned onto the highway, we'd each been with our own thoughts long enough to come to grips with the facts. Gran was back in control, her jaw set, and I was actually starting to think my future might hold something besides hiding plants and skirting the law.

"You must've been working on this a while," I said.

"Since the night your momma was killed."

Well, a turn like that was surely enough to make anyone reconsider matters. I shelved my self-centered concerns for the moment.

"What're you going to do now, Gran?"

"Don't you fret. I been at this since before your momma was born, or your uncle Will or even Caleb. So I'll be fine."

"I know," I said, but I didn't think "fine" was the right word. She'd lost every child she birthed and I had a feeling I was on my way out of her life too.

We didn't say any more until she put the truck on the 101 Highway going south. Santa Maria had an airport down that way, small commuter take you anywhere.

"Can I ask where we're headed?"

"You'll find out when we get there."

We didn't eat at the gas stop, although it had a sit-down diner. Gran had already wrapped up bread with pickles and lunchmeat. We ate in the truck, drank our water from Mason jars like at home.

I knew better than to push her for more, but when the Santa Maria airport turnoff slid by my window, I got to worrying about leaving the grow untended. Then she went and took us right through Buellton straight down to Santa Barbara, on through Carpinteria, and after that I knew she either didn't care about the grow or she'd made a deal with a neighbor.

"Marcus stepping in to help?" I guessed. "That's a bit to ask of a sixty-year-old weed whacker."

She went silent for a while, then nodded. "Sold it to him."

I stayed watching the road ahead, fighting back bitter gall.

"Lock, stock, and barrel?" I finally managed.

She chuckled. "Johnny, it's nothing to get sentimental over. Just a damn little weed patch on a tree slope."

"Oh, hell yes. A twenty-grand weed patch. I can get sentimental over losing that."

"Gave me thirty for it."

I looked over at her.

"Cash," she said.

"Really? No ATM card? No deed of trust?"

She pointed at my feet. "Under your seat. Open it."

I reached down and felt a pasteboard shoe box with a lid. Pulled it out, slid the top off.

"Count it," Gran said.

Drug money in a freezer bag, like I'd seen a hundred times. A thick stack of well-worn bills wrapped with an ordinary rubber band. I counted out five thousand dollars in unmarked tens, twenties, and hundreds.

"Where's the rest?" I asked.

"In my safe-keeping corset at home. That there is yours."

"Mine? What the hell, Gran?"

"Your share, your grubstake. You're going to need it at your new home."

I looked out the window at the oil rig lights marching down the coast toward Ventura. We had just crossed a line. I was going to live a thousand miles from the only home I'd ever known. Well, maybe only a hundred or so, but it might as well be a thousand.

My throat constricted and a sob threatened to explode past my lips. I clenched my jaw hard and thought I was going to upchuck, but after a few miles I got myself under control.

"No way am I carrying this wad around in a fall-apart shoebox."

Gran burst out laughing, but I didn't think it was *that* funny.

Maybe it was a way to let go of her own feelings.
I was afraid to let go of mine.

31

Blown Office Visit

Friday morning at Tobey Auto Salvage I awoke to a call from the clothing vendor next to my shop. There had been an attempted break-in and he thought I might want to take a look.

I drove over there and found mostly scratches on scratches and dents beside dents, but everything inside was undisturbed. Still, that was all the warning I needed: Time to move out, and I knew just the place—Crackup Motors. Problem was, I needed permission and a key to the garage, but the guy who had both was locked up himself.

Creighton Kerry had mentioned a brother once, so I did a little research and discovered the brother was a member of another brotherhood—Hollywood producers. How handy and dandy. Was this déjà vu?

The offices of Ardent Productions were a maze of glass walls that declared Ward Royce to be eminently accessible. His need for attention rivaled the most pampered media idol. If the California building code permitted, as I'm sure it will one day, he would have ordered glass floors to insure he could be seen from all angles.

I got off the elevator to a carpeted expanse rivaling the Coliseum infield, and began the trek without benefit of roller skates. An attractive young woman looked up from behind a chrome-and-rosewood counter as I approached. The placard on top said she was "Stella." The hairdo, a gradient from teal blue to magenta to silver, matched her eye blush, or vice versa—a reminder of my deep immersion in Hollywood. Stella's blue-eyed stare was as vacant as her desktop. She almost lapsed into a smile, but checked herself before my first joke could take form.

"Yes," she said with a downward inflection that made it a No. She would not be of assistance to a wandering fool such as I.

"I'm here to see Mr. Royce." I avoided hitching my belt for emphasis.

"Do you have an appointment?"

She knew I didn't, if she was any good at her job, but in case she wasn't, I decided to help.

"No, but that's okay. I'll see him anyway."

"Mr. Royce is available only by appointment."

"Even the big stars?"

"Even. He's very busy right now, so you'll have to leave."

Behind a wall of glass, Mister Royce could be seen at his corner desk a twelve-yard putt away, white-haired with a salon tan, Prince Kuhio Aloha shirt, aimlessly flicking a ballpoint pen in one hand while the other clamped a cell phone against his head.

"He's alone in that glass cube and in serious need of company," I said.

"He's on an important phone call."

"Can't take too long. I'll wait."

"Mister Whatever-your-name-is—"

I extended my card for her perusal. She declined.

"Tell him Jack Dyle is here about the keys to the crypt."

"The what?"

"Just tell him. It's code, he'll know what it means."

"That's not how we operate around here. I'm calling security." She pressed a button and spoke into her headpiece. "Both of you.

Yes, he's big." She then turned back to me. "Come back when your agent has made proper arrangements."

"Would it help if I brought the Rams front line next time?"

"No."

"Probably wouldn't fit this tiny space anyway. How do you stand it, being cooped up like this all day?"

Two large men in suits entered from a side door. I had them outnumbered but I conceded the victory, small as it was.

I was just getting behind the wheel again when my phone vibrated. It was Stella.

"Mister Dyle, Mister Royce will see you now."

"Should I use the service elevator or would that be presumptuous?"

"The same as before, but without the stand-up routine."

"Roger dodger. May I ask why the change of heart?"

"He asked me who was the gorilla in the Haggar suit, and I gave him your name, and he said bring him back quick."

"Why would he say that?"

"He knows you."

32

Family Roots

Ward Royce looked me up and down twice before he beckoned me to a large overstuffed sofa in a conversation group. A Modigliani abstract overlooked the scene. Royce took a matching side chair for himself and proceeded to relate his strange story in a lilting European accent.

As Damon Zebulon Kerry, III, he did not attend Annapolis like his brother Creighton or their father and grandfather before them. In fact, he did not serve in any branch of the military. Far from it.

"I was the black sheep. Every family has one, I drew the short stick. I joined a rally to march against my uncle's homecoming from 'The Vietnam Conflict,' as it was called. I dropped acid. I ate, smoked, and slept with flower children. Perfectly sound of body, I donned a saffron robe to beg money at the airport and on the streets of San Francisco. And then one day Creighton found me at a San Jose flop and beat the shit out of me for being me. I sobered up, phoned a guy I knew, told him I was ready, caught a plane to Paris, and never looked back. We made a lot of money stealing art from Europe's idle rich. Modern-day Robin Hoods, except we didn't give to the poor, so I guess we were just thieves."

He was Ward Royce now, and had been long enough for a French accent to stick. He was as rich as his brother had been before they swapped black sheep roles and Creighton began a career behind bars. Ward Royce had a line on my family origins he wished to share with me—in return for certain facts allegedly in my possession.

Having my family history reeled off to me by a white-haired stranger with a European accent had the distancing effect of listening to a foreign movie played in the next room with an English voiceover. Strange enough in itself, but the corporate setting in which the tale was delivered made it all the more surreal.

Royce had known Addie Slade when they were sharp kids moving stolen art around Europe together. He seemed oblivious to his story's effect when I asked the question uppermost in my mind.

"Her real name?"

"Might as well have been Jane Doe. We all used aliases. To me and the others she was simply Alpha. I don't know how many names she used before or after, and I doubt there's any way to find out."

"No more than yours, right?"

Royce paused to stare out the plate glass window at a bird's-eye view of Century Plaza. I used the gap in his monologue to pose my own speculation.

"What makes you think your Alpha became my Addie Slade?"

Royce got up, returned to his desk, and came back with a manila file folder, his expression darker than before.

"There's a bus ticket stub in here," he said, waving the unopened file, "from forty years ago. Denver to Santa Barbara. I spent a lot of money to make ninety percent sure it was Alpha who bought it. Apparently, some guy—not a fed but probably a sharp PI—followed her on the bus, took pains to retrieve the stub from a waste bin, kept it in paper records found by one of his descendants.

Point being, the same woman who landed in Santa Barbara on a Tuesday in September opened a bank account and safe deposit box in Grover City the following Friday—Grover Beach now. The bank was a small independent, closed its doors during the 2008 Recession, leaving unclaimed assets to be disposed of at auction. I got hold of the auctioned records by calling in a favor. There was never any activity in the account or the box, other than the original deposit of a hundred and one dollars and one cent."

"My gran never had anything to do with banks. Everything was cash and carry."

"You were a schoolkid, Jack. In your short time together she had the better part of every weekday to do banking business without telling you or dragging you along."

"She couldn't have stuck a painting in a safe deposit box."

"My guess would be a key or a lock combination. Maybe an address, maybe a phone number—some other clue to its whereabouts. We'll never know."

"Assuming she did have the painting in her possession, or she fenced it or sold it or shifted it around, what's your interest at this late date? And what's it got to do with me?"

"Not with you directly, more to do with a fellow who landed in Grover City a few months after Adele opened that account. Called himself Gabriel Cooley."

"Gabe Cooley's dead."

"He was very much alive when he came to Grover *City*. Alive and well off. Too well off for a small-time crook. He went there looking for Adele, and he found her. And he blackmailed her into sharing her secret with him."

"That's your speculation."

"No, fact. He told me so himself."

"Just before you killed him."

"Didn't have to do that. No, Gabe spilled to me two years ago. He needed money, came to me with this cock-and-bull yarn about how he'd sneaked his way into a fortune. Said he knew where the Rubens was but he needed someone with the right connections to fence it, which in his estimation was me. Unfortunately, he estimated wrong and I told him so. Little rat tried to blackmail me for it, and I explained how things had changed while he was doing time. He got very upset and threatened to expose the whole gang. Well, that was impossible because all the others were dead. He swore to get even, but he was killed before he could do that."

"And you had nothing to do with the murder."

"Iron clad alibi. I was in Sacramento all last week testifying before an Assembly subcommittee. Major disruption in my affairs, let me tell you. More importantly, though, I turned down Cooley because I don't need another Rubens. If I wanted one I'd simply tell my wife to get on the phone the next time one comes up at auction. I run a multinational investing conglomerate, Jack. All above board, clean as a whistle, but it takes every waking hour of every day. I can't be messing around with a piece of stolen art. Believe me, I have much bigger problems."

"Then why bring me into it?"

"Why do you think? I'm being forced to drag it all out in the open again."

"Who's twisting your arm?"

"Somebody I don't know. That's what I hope you can find out."

"But this mysterious person knows about a painting stolen forty years ago? And somehow connects it to you through your past? If Gabe was the last living soul to know about it, he's not your problem anymore."

"I would like to be one hundred percent sure of that."

I leaned back on the couch and stretched my long legs out full length. I didn't know where I'd got long legs. For that matter, I didn't know where any of the rest of me came from. I was effectively an orphan.

33

Someone Else's Ghetto

Going To L. A.

Gran said we would spend the rest of the night in a cheap motel off the Ventura Freeway. She'd packed cold chicken and coleslaw in an ice chest. We made coffee from the burner in the room and we sat at a tiny round table no bigger than a toilet seat and ate with the lights out. We sipped the coffee black from stoneware mugs she'd fired in her homemade kiln. I would never see that kiln again. Wouldn't see the kitchenware she'd made with it, either. Or her knitted throw, or a lot of other things.

At length I reached over and knuckled her shoulder. "Tell me about my new digs."

I couldn't see her expression in the dark, but Addie Slade's voice had a quaver she hadn't shown all day.

"Woman's a good fren—friend from times past," she choked. "Married a building contractor. They have a slew of kids, oldest grown up and gone, a few older than you, a couple younger."

"How did you stay in touch with her?"

A short silence. "Women's secrets."

"Will they work me hard?"

"Oh, yeah, you'll earn your keep, be mighty useful. Nothing you haven't handled already. But Johnny, here's the thing."

I waited for Gran's big reveal, and when it came, I wasn't sure what to do with it.

"They're Russians."

More silence. "I can deal with that," I finally managed, mostly to reassure myself.

"Do you know anything about the Russian community?"

"No, how would I?"

"Well, you read a lot of books..."

"Tell me."

"According to Willa, they are very insular. You know what that means?

"Stick to their own kind."

"Don't like cops, don't like government authorities, don't like Mexicans or Blacks or Asians or anyone else not Russian."

"Gee, I ought to fit right in."

"Don't make fun of it. Her family don't speak much English."

"But they're American too?"

"Second and third generation. Some of their ancestors were here to greet the early explorers. Been a new wave of immigrants in recent years."

"So what's that make me? Slave labor?"

"Oh, Johnny! You'll have to work, of course. Everyone does, from toddler on up. But you'll be part of the family. They were— how did she say it? Excited to meet you."

"Oh, come on. How can a hillbilly from a cold-water shack excite anyone?"

"I've—told them a bit about us."

"Which bit?"

"What we do."

"Oh, boy."

"Rudi—that's the father—got interested once I explained how well you handle yourself. I mean—with everything that's gone down."

"Did you tell him about Mom?"

"A bit."

"I'm not sure that's real comforting."

"It wasn't meant to be. They have a right to know, you see. Every right."

I finished my coffee and tossed the dregs in the bathroom sink, rolled onto my knees and crawled over to my bedroll. Gran did the same, and we lay there a while looking up at the ceiling.

"John?"

"Yeah, Gran?"

"You'll be fine."

"If you say so, then I will."

"I did the best I could."

"I know that."

"I'm not sure it's enough."

"It's more than—you know."

Our unspoken censure of Patty Dyle hovered in the air between us.

"Good night, John."

"Love you, Gran."

The next day she got me set in with Rudi and Willa Shertova. Nice people, nice kids, they made the extra effort to make me feel welcome. I would share a room with Alexander. He was fourteen, wanted to be called Lex. Helped me unload the pickup. Mom Willa, a schoolteacher, was impressed with my small collection of books.

The thing of it was, though, the house sat smack between the 110 Freeway and Vermont Square. Latino town, high crime rate, not an Anglo face to be seen, one alien Russian family flying a rooftop American flag. From nearby Manual Arts High School I would eventually learn the automotive trade. At the same time I would get a hard-core education in trades run on the street.

After settling me in, we all sat around acting like we we'd been friends forever. Rudi and Willa and Gran would laugh a little too hard, while Lex and his two sisters looked at me, then stared at their hands or feet or a pattern in the floor.

Then it was time. No teary goodbyes, no false promises to stay in touch. Just a quick exchange, a brush of cheeks, and I watched Gran climb back in the truck and out of my life.

Two weeks after returning to her Pozo cabin, Addie Slade was shot dead. But I wasn't told about it for another eight years.

~

Ward Royce wanted assurances before he handed over the key to the CRK Motors garage. He didn't mind me storing my tools there, as long as I understood the building wasn't insured and wouldn't be. His bigger concern was identifying the person blackmailing him.

"How much is he asking for?" I said.

"It's not about money. He wants what he calls 'a position' in my company's future."

"Does that mean a stake in the company?"

"I believe so. Even if I wanted to sell, it's more complicated than he seems to realize. I've told him I need more details, but he says he'll get back to me once he's handled the Cooley issue, whatever that means."

"He obviously knows of your association with Gabe in the past, and he's trying to link it to Gabe's death. Did he mention anything about the investigation?"

"I told him that's in the hands of the police, and what he said to that was very strange."

"What was it?"

"He said they don't know the half of it."

"That's rather cryptic. Could be a tactic to unsettle you."

"I suppose so."

"How has he contacted you so far?"

"A few phone calls, very short, but long enough to show he knows things I thought were long forgotten."

"How did he reach your private line?"

"Some sort of telephony trick. I don't understand the technicalities—it's all a mystery to me. What matters is, he called me on a secure line at a time when he knew I'd be alone. I didn't even know when those times would be myself, so I have no idea how he timed it so precisely."

"We'll need more information from him if I'm to be effective. By the way, has he given any name, maybe a pseudonym or code name?"

"Oh, yes, he calls himself Noah Richter. Made a little joke about being distantly related to the scientist who developed the Richter scale. Said they both liked to make waves. He actually sounds quite sociable, if you overlook the threat."

"I wouldn't recommend that."

"Don't worry, I can't afford to."

We arranged for one of Royce's assistants to leave the garage key in the top dresser drawer of the apartment at CRK Motors.

34

Alice Loves Them All

Last night I'd learned that Sheri Burke lived in a five-bedroom landmark in Spaulding Square, an enclave of renovated Depression-era cottages staggering through million-dollar realtor hopes that their doped-up carcasses were good for one more round. I found a parking slot in the next block and walked back from there.

The front door was all oak and iron. Sheri answered the bell in a silky-clingy Victoria's Secret gown that left very little secret.

She started to close the door. "I'm busy."

"So am I, and you're paying for it. Report time."

"Can't you come back later?"

"No."

"You should have called first."

"This won't take but a few minutes."

She heaved a deep sigh, said, "Come," and spun on one heel and gave me her well-turned derriere.

I closed the door behind me and watched her wiggle over to the sofa and plop down. I helped myself to a big easy chair beside a bookcase. No sooner had I settled than a voice rang out from down the hall.

"Honey, who was it?"

Imagine my surprise when Alice Loring walked out of a bedroom doorway clipping a bauble to one ear. She didn't notice me as she angled away toward the kitchen. Before she got there she caught Sheri staring across the room at me and spun around. A reluctant smile was all I got this time. No Hollywood hug.

Sheri remained seated with her legs crossed, head erect, eyes half-closed.

I thought I knew what Alice was doing there, a secret revealed, a privacy breached, a scandal in the making. I saw no reason to give further importance to the matter.

"An assumption could be made," I said to Sheri, "that the good faith in which I report my findings extends to all parties present."

"Might as well," she said.

"Or we could forget the whole investigative business and go our separate ways."

"Depends how far you want to take it."

"No farther than this room, right now, if that's what you want."

Sheri glanced away out the window, then swung her head back toward Alice, and with that small tell, revealed who was running this show, whose money covered Sheri's insanely expensive rent, and who in all probability was running the entire Gabe Cooley postmortem production.

Alice moved to the sofa and sat beside Sheri, not quite touching but close enough that I could feel the current between them. She smoothed her white culottes with one hand while the other played with the chunky coral necklace at her throat.

"Jack," Alice said, her voice carrying that particular blend of intimacy and warning that only people who've known each other too well can manage, "Sheri and I have been friends for years. Since Gabe introduced us."

"Friends," I repeated, letting the word hang there like a shirt on a broken clothesline.

"Yes, friends." Alice's lips quirked into something that wasn't quite a smile. "Women can be that, you know. Despite what the film industry might lead you to believe. Sheri and I have formed a new production company. We're going to do television commercials. A mutual investment in the future."

Sheri shifted uncomfortably, tugging at the hem of her nightgown. The light through the plantation shutters cut across her face in tiger stripes. She didn't seem thrilled with the prospect.

I nodded, watching the way Sheri's eyes kept darting to Alice for approval. "And this house? Another uncle-like gift from Gabe?"

Alice laughed. "God, no. George Macklin owns this place. Lets Sheri stay here rent-free."

"How generous," I said, cataloging the crown molding, the original hardwood floors, the tasteful Craftsman details that whispered three million eight and climbing.

"Yes," Alice said. "Though I suspect his generosity will soon require something more... tactile in return."

Sheri flinched but didn't contradict her.

"Macklin," I said, leaning forward. "Does he live here too?"

Sheri's fingers twisted in her lap. "Not exactly. He keeps clothes in the master bedroom at the end of the hall. Stays over sometimes."

"But not the night Gabe was killed," I said, making it not quite a question.

"No." Sheri's voice dropped to nearly a whisper. "I assumed he was on duty at the Taj. He's usually there at night, managing security."

I felt pieces click together like tumblers in a lock. Macklin at the Taj. Macklin with access. Macklin with motive. But I kept my face neutral.

"Tell me about Macklin's interest in you, Sheri," I said, my tone casual. "How long has he been your landlord?"

"About eight months," she said, smoothing invisible wrinkles from the silk across her thighs. "At first it was just business. He'd stop by to check on household things. Then the visits got longer. More personal."

Alice's mouth tightened. "Tell him what Macklin said about Gabe."

Sheri hesitated, glancing at Alice again. "George got this idea in his head that Gabe was...hurting me. He'd make these comments like, 'You don't have to put up with that,' or 'I can protect you better than he can.'"

"*Was* Gabe hurting you?" I asked.

"God, no," Sheri said. "I told you, Gabe was like family. I told George that, repeatedly. Told him there was nothing to protect me from."

"When was the last time you had this conversation with Macklin?" I said. A current of alarm had wakened a nerve.

"Thursday morning," Sheri said, "before I left for work. He was making coffee in the kitchen, asking if I was going to see Gabe that day." She swallowed hard. "I said yes, we had a meeting about some production details for the new film."

I watched their faces as the realization dawned simultaneously, like twin suns cresting a dark horizon. Alice's breath caught. Sheri's hand flew to her mouth.

"You think George—" Sheri couldn't finish the sentence.

"It makes sense," Alice said quietly. "The level of rage in that beating. The personal nature of it."

"A jealous man," I said, "especially one with military training, can do a lot of damage when he thinks he's defending a woman's honor."

Sheri stood abruptly, her nightgown swirling around her thighs. "I need to get dressed. I can't—I need a minute." She disappeared down the hallway. The sound of a door closing with exaggerated care followed her retreat.

Alice didn't watch her go. Instead, her eyes stayed fixed on me, calculating, measuring.

"This changes things," she said. "If Macklin killed Gabe over some misguided infatuation, then the Russians…"

"Had nothing to do with it," I finished for her. "Just bad timing. Gabe got murdered while he was brokering a deal. But not for Five Dragons. It may have been other parties entirely."

"Like who?"

"I can't say right now. It's something else I'm working on."

Sheri reappeared in skinny jeans and a loose blouse, her hair pulled back into a quick ponytail. She looked at Alice, then me.

"I never wanted to be involved in this. If Gabe's murder wasn't because of the Russian deal, then…well…"

"Then what?"

"Then my reason for hiring you has changed," she said firmly. "I needed a detective to find the people who killed Gabe for their own interests. Turns out it's probably a crazy man with delusions. If that's true, then your services aren't needed anymore." Her voice shook slightly, but she crossed her arms like she meant it.

"I see," I said.

"You can bill me for outstanding expenses." Her chin was up.

I glanced at Alice, who wore an unreadable expression.

"You sure about that?" I asked Sheri. "You need some kind of protection, at least until Macklin's picked up for questioning."

Alice finally spoke up. "Something to remember about men like George Macklin."

Sheri turned to her with wide eyes. "What's that?"

"They're not predictable when they're cornered," Alice said. "Or angry."

Sheri's confidence wavered but didn't crumple entirely. She set her jaw and turned to disappear down the hallway again.

"So that's it." I said to Alice as I rose from the couch.

She got up with me, a frown of concern lining her brow. "But if something happens—"

"Don't worry," I cut in. "I don't need a contract to keep my word."

Besides, I had to follow up with Macklin myself. I had to make sure he had indeed killed Gabe, and through what twist of logic, but I wasn't sure I was the right detective for the job.

I let myself out and got halfway down the driveway before Sheri's voice stopped me in my tracks.

"Jack! I'm sorry!"

She stood at the front door, framed by mottled shadows of sycamore. I turned around and walked up to her.

"Sooner or later you've got to start telling the truth. Call me," I said, putting on my best sideways grin to borrow a movie line. "I'm always around."

I turned up the sidewalk and headed for my car before she could realize the truth. I acted like a comic at times, but I was no Superman.

35

Dance With The Devil

The Taj Mahal of Holmby Hills loomed like a cosmic battleship, ready to vaporize anything that dared to ring the front gate. I buzzed the concierge and took a moment to adjust to the fact that I was as welcome as a subpoena.

Macklin's voice came through the speaker, clipped and sharp. "Yes."

"It's Jack Dyle," I said, as if that would earn me a welcome mat.

A long pause suggested he considered leaving me out there to appreciate the landscaping. Then the gate creaked open, and I drove up the brick-paved driveway as I had before.

Macklin emerged from the interior with new confidence. He'd had forty-eight hours to square away his position with Valenti.

"Jack," he said at the door with a forced smile.

Following his gesture, I entered, endured another pat-down, and followed him to the loggia and down into the grand salon. I took a seat in one of the overstuffed chairs, while he remained standing.

"Quite a job you've got here, George," I said, reminding us both that he was caretaker, not host. "All this splendor and glory."

"What's on your mind, Jack?"

The atmosphere grew heavy. Macklin's powerful form remained silhouetted against the fading light, while I tried to look comfortable in a setting that made my junkyard digs seem like a cardboard box under the freeway.

"I hear you have a little place over in Spaulding Square," I said, watching Macklin's face for any flicker of surprise. "Very generous of you to let Sheri stay there."

Macklin's eyes narrowed slightly, but his expression remained composed. "Sheridan needed a place to hang her hat," he said. "I hardly have time to enjoy it myself, so it seemed appropriate."

"She's an attractive girl, George."

I noticed a slight tightening around the corners of his mouth. "If you're thinking of moving in, forget it."

"Nothing further from the fact."

Macklin was a pro. He kept his voice smooth and even. "She is a pretty young woman," he agreed.

"Sometimes," I ventured, "a girl like that can wrap a man around her little finger. Even a man as sharp as Gabe."

Macklin's expression stayed neutral, but I could feel the temperature drop a few degrees. He was too smart to take the bait, but I was hoping he'd nibble just a little. I watched him, waiting for a crack in his reserve.

He stayed silent, letting me make the next move. I gave him my best conspiratorial smile. "Maybe," I said, "she's the type who could get a man to change his mind about things."

Macklin let the silence hang for a moment before he spoke, his voice as smooth as a con man's pitch.

"Sheridan was a tramp Gabe found on the Hollywood streets," he said, with a hint of disdain that caught me off guard.

I blinked, momentarily thrown by his bluntness. "Is that right?"

"Yes, quite right," Macklin said. "Gabe took pity on her. I thought it might be nice to add a little to his efforts, give the girl a chance to clean up her act. She'll deny it if you ask, of course."

His tone was dismissive yet calculated, a mix of contempt and condescension that suggested he had this story ready to go. I watched him closely, trying to figure out if this was the truth or just another layer of deception.

"You're quite the philanthropist," I said.

"She seems to appreciate it."

He watched me with steady assurance, implying there was more to the relationship. I felt the advantage shift his way to the point that I almost believed him. But something in the way he said it sounded too neat, too rehearsed. I tried to read the guy, wondering if his sexist remarks were intended to throw me off.

Then I remembered Wellie Latimer's remark on our night ride to MacArthur Park. The girl had done time for roughing up an attacker.

"Was there ever any bad blood between them?"

"Not that I ever saw," he said. "Gabe was quite generous with her."

"You never saw anything that suggested a rift?"

"I seldom saw them together."

I was running in circles. The guy was as solid as a hemi block, and I was left with a handful of doubt. Time to cut my losses and let him think he'd gotten the best of me. For now, anyway.

I gave him a nod and tried another tack. "You're doing a lot for Sheri. Comes at a time when she needs help the most. Got her hands full, handling all that money. I told her she should hire a CPA or it might be gone before she can count it."

The slightest chink appeared in Macklin's cool veneer. I saved him a reply and pushed further.

"She'll need help with that, and I don't think Gabe's lawyer is the man for it. Might help if he showed up once in a while. Girl in that situation has to be careful whom she trusts. I'm not sure she's aware of that."

"I suppose time will tell."

I got up from my chair and stood without offering my hand. "George, it was kind of you to let me barge in on you like this. I hope I didn't put you out."

"Not at all," he said evenly.

He walked me to the door, and as he opened it, he paused and looked at me with a cryptic glint in his eye. "Let's not make this a habit, Jack. The people I work for have an odd way of showing displeasure, mmm?"

I nodded that I understood his meaning and headed for my truck as the heavy door closed behind me with a soft click. The night was warm, but I felt the chill of Macklin's parting words follow me all the way down the brick-paved drive.

I drove a couple of blocks and pulled to the curb to dial Montero's number. Her voice came through the line, sharp and familiar, a reminder that I wasn't in this alone even if I sometimes wished I was.

"What's up, Dyle?"

"I just had a little chat with George Macklin," I said, trying to keep it light.

"The caretaker of that place in Holmby Hills?"

"None other. Thought you might like to hear about it."

"Where are you?"

"Just leaving the Taj Mahal West," I said. "Where are you?"

"Beverly Wilshire Hotel," she said, and I could hear the hum of activity in the background. "I'm lurking in the lobby, hoping to surprise Brian Sebutu."

That was a name I didn't like hearing. "The African I told you about," I said, feeling a mix of relief and frustration. "You don't waste any time."

"Neither do you," she shot back. "What did you find out?"

It would feel good to unload right there, even if it meant admitting I hadn't gotten much, but face time was safer.

"Not something for a phone call, but I don't think I should keep it to myself much longer."

"Sounds like you hit a wall," she said, with the kind of empathy that felt more like a gentle slap.

"More like a fortress," I replied. "I'm ten minutes away. Let's meet in the lobby and compare notes."

"See you when you get here," she said, and the line went dead.

I started the C10 and drove off, the summer warmth competing with the A/C vents as I headed toward the Beverly and my next round with Montero. Not the warmest of prospects, but the only one I had.

36

Doing The Beverly

The Beverly Hills Hotel lobby was the kind of place where marble floors and crystal chandeliers made you feel underdressed just for breathing. I was tempted to leap the three shallow steps at one bound, then corrected my bourgeois nature and slowed to a sedate pace over the lush red carpet and gave a nod to the doorman like I belonged there. After gliding through the open glass doors without mishap, I was careful not to trip over a Persian rug that probably cost more than my car. It was the kind of setup where even the air smelled expensive, like a mix of fresh-cut flowers and old money.

I paused, soaking in the opulence and trying not to look like I came from a different zip code. Everything was circles and rounds, including mirrors on the wall and the soffit recess overhead. It was a far cry from the grease-stained floors of my workshop or even the cluttered chaos of Crackup Motors. I felt like a stray dog in a designer pet shop.

I saw Montero tucked away in a small conversational group to one side of the fireplace. Trim and poised in her navy jacket, she looked like she was holding court among the social elite. I took a moment to appreciate the way she fit in there, casual yet commanding, before I headed over.

Her eyes met mine with a hard edge that softened just a touch. Her effortless blend into that world made me feel even more like a mechanic at a black-tie gala. But that was the point, wasn't it? She knew how to play the game, and she had me right where she wanted me.

"What's a nice girl like you doing in a joint like this?" I grinned as I sat down, but Montero wasn't smiling. She gave me a laser look, brilliant but controlled, her arms crossed in a way that was both casual and confrontational.

"What's a nice lube jockey like you doing, period?" Her voice had that official ring to it, but there was a flicker of curiosity in her eyes. "You sure aren't crawling this neighborhood for the ambiance."

I shrugged. "Been busy chasing dead ends. I'm grasping at straws, but I have a theory that might interest you."

She raised an eyebrow, still skeptical. "This had better be good."

"Macklin." I let the name hang there like a smoke ring. "As Cooley's murderer."

Montero narrowed her eyes. "Where are you getting that?"

I leaned forward, lowering my voice. "Think about it. The feds have a story, but too many holes. Valenti's exasperated because someone took out his only link to a weapons cache. It all points to someone on the inside, except Macklin isn't. He's just the concierge for a mansion big enough to host the Swiss Army."

Her arms uncrossed, just a little. "Keep talking."

"Valenti's a control freak. He wouldn't let anyone in on his plans unless it was someone who knew the price for screwing up."

Montero tapped her foot, a sure sign she was thinking. "And your fed friends?"

"They have their own agenda. They needed Cooley to trap Valenti and Sebutu before either one got his hands on the prize.

But nobody counted on an interloper with his own axe to grind—
or face to bash. A natural born mauler, except he didn't need a
contract."

She was silent for a moment, processing. I could see the wheels
turning, her detective instincts at war with her distrust of me.
"That's a lot of speculation."

"Sure is," I admitted, "but it's better than nothing."

Her eyes met mine, and for the first time, there was a glint of
something other than suspicion. I couldn't tell if it was belief or
just a grudging respect for my audacity, but I took it either way.

Montero shifted gears without missing a beat and turned the
conversation toward Sheri. "What about the girl? Cooley had her
shacked up in style?"

"Not Cooley. And if by style you mean a hundred-year-old
Spanish reno in Spaulding Square, then yeah, she's living higher
than her peers."

"Details, Dyle." Her impatience was almost endearing.

"Five bedrooms, a pool, enough space to lose yourself and find
religion. Sold last April to Macklin himself for almost four mil.
Probably tops that with the furniture."

Montero's eyes narrowed, but not with suspicion this time.
"And Macklin uses it how?"

"He sleeps in the master suite," I said. "Occasionally. But no
funny business so far. He's keeping his distance, at least on that
front."

She didn't look convinced. "Why would a guy like Macklin
leave her alone?"

"He's an odd guy, careful, taking his time, building a story. I
mentioned Gabe's money and his veneer cracked ever so slightly.
Sheri says he has delusions of being her superhero. It's possible he's
deranged, got himself worked up and exploded. He's tough, savvy,
been around cops and security most of his life."

"How old?"

"Forty or so. Definitely nobody's kid."

"And Sheri? How is she handling all this?"

"Like a deer caught in the headlights," I said. "She's unsure, but she has a sharp mind. Macklin's hands-off approach is throwing her off balance."

"Sounds to me like you're the one off balance, Dyle." Montero's voice was sharp, but there was a hint of warmth beneath the jab.

I shrugged, pretending not to notice. "Maybe, but I know what I saw. Macklin's privately playing great protector, and Sheri's trying to figure out if he's a killer with a loose screw. I'm right there with her. I can't read the guy completely, thought you might do a better job."

Montero took a moment to digest, her skepticism mixing with a newfound intrigue. I could tell she was reevaluating her theories, and maybe even her opinion of me. It was a small victory, but in this line of work, I took what I could get.

Just then a tall African with a shaved head and an expensive suit moved past the front desk like he owned the place, and for a moment, I thought he might. He was flanked by two others, with a third parting the waters ahead, all business, and they were heading straight for the exit.

"Sebutu," I said, nodding in their direction.

Montero's eyes widened, and she slewed around in her chair to follow my gaze. Her surprise was almost comical, but there was urgency there too. "Damn it," she muttered, already shifting to get up.

The entourage was a well-oiled machine, and the man at the center was the drive wheel. Sebutu's smooth, gleaming head and tailored suit gave him an air of sophisticated danger. His height made him stand out, but the way he moved with his team made him untouchable. They were a coordinated unit, and Montero was not a part of it.

"They're making a run for it," I said, though it appeared as just a calculated stroll.

Montero was on her feet, but Sebutu was already was out the door and gone before she could take a step, leaving a vacuum in his wake.

"Damn it, Dyle," she snapped, fists doubled at her sides. but there was no real heat. She knew as well as I did that the dodge was no accident. The guy buying VX merchandise had just slipped through everybody's fingers.

I watched Montero, expecting her to chew me out, but she was too busy processing the near miss.

"They probably use the same protocol when he goes to the john," I offered, trying not to sound too amused.

She gave me a look, then turned back to where Sebutu's entourage had just made its exit. Her frustration was clear, but I detected a grudging respect too. She wasn't going to catch him, and we both knew it.

She whirled back to me, her eyes blazing like she had just stepped out of a telenovela. "You did that on purpose," she accused, but there was a spark of something other than anger.

"Not my fault the guy has a personal SWAT team," I said, raising my hands in mock surrender.

Montero was about to let me have it, but she paused, and I could see the wheels turning. She was remembering I had just handed her a lead on Macklin, and the fire in her eyes dimmed to a simmer.

"You're a pain in the ass, Dyle," she said, but the edge in her voice was softer. "But you may have given me something with Macklin."

"Glad I could help."

She shook her head, a reluctant smile tugging at her lips. "You got lucky—this time."

I grinned, sensing the shift in her attitude. She wasn't letting me off the hook, but I knew better than to push it. Montero gave me one last look, half frustrated, half appreciative, before turning away.

I watched her go, feeling a relief I hadn't earned.

Moments later, I stepped out of the Beverly's calculated luxury and into the real world, leaving the marble and chandeliers behind as I headed for my truck.

Montero had listened, but had I said enough? Theories are like spare parts—futile unless you know how to put them together. I felt like I'd handed her a box of mismatched bolts and expected her to build a Ferrari.

Macklin was forewarned now. If he felt I was onto him, things could get ugly. He might even go after Sheri before Montero connected the dots. I hadn't convinced her enough to forestall possible retribution by Macklin. I didn't even know if Montero's interest in Sebutu was drug-related or a carry-over from Cooley's murder investigation.

I unlocked the C10's door, ready to climb in, but before I lifted a foot the harsh glare of headlights flooded the pavement. I heard the rumble of a big engine but couldn't make out the car until it stopped alongside me.

Bentley Bentayga.

The rear door opened and I peered inside. Anthony Lupato's grim stare regarded me from the other side.

"Dyle, you're getting to be a royal pain. Get in."

More face time with Rome Valenti was in my immediate future. Not my choice, but I locked my car back up and got in. That's how you respond to a summons from a capo regime.

37

Macklin's Defense

Valenti's sleek black sedan pulled away from the Beverly's parking lot, its engine purring like a satisfied predator, Frank Diamond at the wheel. I sank into leather seats that seemed to swallow me whole, the air conditioning creating an artificial chill that matched the cold dread collecting in my stomach. The Taj loomed in my mind—Valenti's domain, where I'd just been summoned like a wayward child called to the principal's office. Only in this case, the principal had men who could make people disappear.

Lupato sat quietly in his tailored shirt buttoned at the neck, eyes straight ahead. His silence felt practiced, professional.

"Nice ride," I said.

Lupato's eyes flicked aside, met mine for a millisecond, then returned to the road. The message was clear: I wasn't here for conversation.

Beverly Hills slid by outside the tinted windows. Palm trees in place since filmdom's heyday reached for a darkening sky, their silhouettes cut sharply against the burning orange of sunset, while we rode past in air-conditioned silence. I wondered if this was how Valenti saw the world, removed from consequences by layers of protection.

My thoughts circled back to Sheri, to the fear that had sparked in her eyes when she realized Macklin could be the killer. Had I been reckless, hinting at his guilt? The question sat heavy in my chest. If Macklin had killed Cooley and Valenti were to buy his alibi, I'd just placed her directly in Macklin's crosshairs.

Diamond navigated the long driveway and came to a stop at the familiar entrance. Lupato got out of the car and strode toward the double doors without looking back. I took a deep breath and followed.

The door opened before either of us reached it. A stranger stood framed in the doorway as Lupato strode past without acknowledgment. The doorman nodded toward the hallway. No words needed. Everyone knew where I was going and why.

Lupato walked a couple of paces ahead of me, our footsteps muffled by thick carpet.

"You shoulda kept your mouth shut," he said over his shoulder as we approached a set of double doors at the end of the hall. He knocked once on the righthand door, then pushed it open.

The study was all dark wood and leather, books purchased by the yard rather than read, the desk large enough to land a small aircraft. Valenti himself sat behind it. He didn't stand when I entered.

Macklin stood to Valenti's right, a living statue of muscle and menace in manservant's attire. His eyes tracked me like a predator, unblinking and cold. Two other men—nondescript in the way that only professional muscle can be—stood by the windows, hands clasped in front of them. Witnesses, perhaps. Or executioners.

The door closed behind me with a soft click like the hasp on Gabe's casket.

"Sit," Valenti said, gesturing to a chair across from his desk. Not an invitation—a command.

I sat, feeling the weight of four pairs of eyes boring into me.

The chair was comfortable, which somehow made everything worse.

"You've been busy," Valenti said, his voice deceptively mild. "Making accusations. Stirring things up. Playing detective." Each phrase dropped like a stone into still water.

I said nothing.

"Where did you get the idea that Macklin killed Cooley?"

The question hung in the air, stark and dangerous. I glanced at Macklin, whose expression hadn't changed, but whose eyes had narrowed just slightly. Calculation lived in those eyes—the kind that measured distances and angles, the quickest way to silence a problem.

"Who told you that?" I said.

"I'll ask the questions, Dyle."

My thoughts raced to Sheri, vulnerable and alone. But coyness would get me nowhere in this room.

"Something Sheri Burke said," I said, speaking clearly, meeting Valenti's gaze. "She has reason to believe Macklin beat Gabe Cooley to death."

Macklin's body tensed, a slight movement that rippled through his massive frame. "That's bullshit," he said, his voice controlled but tight with anger.

"She says you had motive," I continued, figuring if I was inviting myself to die, I might as well be thorough. "Cooley got all her attention, maybe something extra. Good old Uncle Gabe. But Cooley was hurting her, according to you. She needed your protection, again according to you. You confronted him and he denied it, probably called you something you didn't like, and not just once, either. You had enough, decided to remove the threat and win the damsel."

"This is what you're bringing me?" Valenti asked, his voice dangerously soft. "Hearsay from a grieving girlfriend?"

"Motive, means, opportunity," I replied, falling back on the fundamentals. "Macklin had all three. And," I added, nodding toward the mountain of a man, "the mass to deliver the kind of beating Cooley got."

Macklin took a half-step forward before Valenti raised a hand, stopping him without a word.

"I was here all night," Macklin said through clenched teeth. "Doing my job. Protecting Mr. Valenti's property. Ask anyone."

"Actually," Valenti said, his eyes never leaving my face, "you weren't."

The room went still. Macklin's expression froze, confusion and something like fear flashing across his features.

"Sir?" he asked, the single syllable laden with uncertainty.

"I saw you go to the garage around ten," Valenti said, his tone conversational, as if discussing the weather. "You were gone for two hours."

Color drained from Macklin's face. "No, sir. I was on patrol. Around the property."

"Don't lie to me, George," Valenti said quietly. "Not to me."

The tension in the room thickened until it felt like breathing through wet cotton. One of the men by the window shifted slightly, his hand moving imperceptibly closer to his jacket.

"I was here," Macklin insisted, desperation creeping into his voice. "I wouldn't—"

"Enough," Valenti cut him off, raising a hand again. The silence that followed felt like the pause between lightning and thunder—full of anticipation and dread.

Valenti's eyes, cold and calculating, shifted back to me. I felt a chill run down my spine as he studied me, like an undertaker memorizing my dimensions for a coffin.

"Tony," he called, not raising his voice.

The door opened immediately, as if Lupato had been waiting with his ear pressed against it.

"Yes, sir?"

"Take our guest back to his car at the Beverly."

"Yes, sir."

Valenti turned his attention to some papers on his desk, a clear dismissal. No further words, no threats, no warnings. Somehow, that was more terrifying than an outburst of rage.

Macklin stared at me, his face a mask of hatred and fear—a dangerous combination in a man who solved problems with his fists. I rose slowly, not wanting any sudden movements to trigger the violence that hung in the air like static electricity.

Lupato held the door open, and I walked through it, feeling Macklin's eyes burning into my back with each step. The door closed behind us, and I released a breath I hadn't realized I was holding.

The walk back through the hallway seemed faster, the wall artwork a blur. Lupato moved with purpose, not speaking until he reached and opened the entry door. Outside, a different car waited.

"You shoulda kept this to yourself," he said, not unkindly. "Some stones are better left unturned."

I wanted to say something clever, something defiant, but my heart was hammering against my ribs and my mouth had gone dry. I'd just accused Valenti's houseman of murder to his face, and I was walking.

Lupato opened the front passenger door of the sedan and I slid in, feeling like I'd aged a decade in the space of an hour. As the car pulled away from the Taj, I watched the building recede in the side mirror. I'd just witnessed the beginning of George Macklin's end.

Did it include my own, too?

38

Free Ride

The big Mercedes glided through tree-lined streets, silent save for the soft hum of tires on asphalt. My hands rested on my knees, fingers alive with delayed adrenaline. Lupato drove with practiced calm as, outside, street lights cast a muted glow. In my mind I saw Macklin's face again—the moment when understanding dawned that his boss had just marked him for death.

Holmby Hills was fast disappearing in our wake. The ride would be short—five minutes tops. I caught Lupato in a surreptitious glance now and then, studying me with quiet assessment. Neither of us spoke for the first few blocks. Some revelations need time to settle.

Valenti had said nothing more to me because his decision about Macklin was obvious and final. The contradiction of the man's alibi was indictment enough. In Valenti's world, circumstantial evidence wasn't a legal shortcoming—it was sufficient for judgment. Macklin was already a dead man walking. He just didn't know how many steps he had left.

I should have felt relief—my accusation had landed, had been given weight by Valenti himself. But instead, I felt a crawling unease. If Valenti could discard Macklin so easily, a man who'd served him for years, what chance did someone like me have? Or Sheri, for that matter?

I shifted in my seat and felt the leather creak beneath me. "Macklin's going down, isn't he?"

Lupato checked his rearview mirror, then his eyes flicked back to the road. His silence was answer enough.

"Funny thing about loyalty in your line of work," I continued, feeling for his reaction as I stared straight ahead. "It only seems to go one way."

"You don't know what you're talking about," he said, but there was no heat in it. Just the tired response of a man who'd had this conversation with himself too many times.

I decided to push my advantage. The near-death experience at the Taj had left me feeling reckless, unmoored from normal caution.

"I know more than you think," I said. "About Valenti. About what he's dealing in now."

Lupato's hands tightened almost imperceptibly on the steering wheel. "Yeah? You think?"

"Weapons. The kind that make governments nervous. The kind that get people extraordinary rendition instead of Miranda rights."

The car maintained its smooth trajectory, but something in the atmosphere changed—a subtle thickening of tension.

"If you're comfortable with that," I added, "maybe you should just let me out right here."

Lupato took a long breath through his nose. The streets outside were becoming familiar—we were getting closer to the Beverly. When he finally spoke, his voice was lower, a confession not meant to travel beyond the confines of the car.

"Nobody's comfortable with it," he said. "Not even him."

I hadn't expected that. The admission hung between us,

vulnerable and strange coming from a man who'd made his living through violence and stayed alive by judicious silence.

"Then why?" I asked.

Lupato took a right turn, navigating through a yellow light. "You ever been caught between two bad choices? Where either way, someone gets hurt?"

"Sure," I said. "Most people have."

"Not like this," he replied. "Mr. Valenti's between a rock and the hard place. He's gotta come up with the goods. Any otherwise, if the feds don't nail him, the dons will."

The streetlights cast rhythmic patterns across Lupato's face—light, shadow, light, shadow—revealing and concealing. For a moment, he looked older, worn down by the weight of what he knew.

"The old arrangements are changing," he said. "The families back east, they're getting pressure from overseas. New players, new products. Rome Valenti's all about casinos, hotels, fine dining. He don't want the weapons business. But when the dons tell you to deliver, you deliver."

"Or?" I prompted, though I knew the answer.

"Or they deliver you," Lupato said simply. "In pieces."

"Still like that, is it?"

"Still."

A trapped man's confession.

We turned onto Sunset, the Beverly's illuminated palms towering in the distance. I thought about Valenti, caught between federal agents and old-world dons, choosing the path that might keep him alive a little longer. I thought about Macklin, who would soon discover that loyalty bought him nothing but the promise of a shallow grave. I thought about Sheri, whose truth had set a deadly machine in motion.

"What happened to Cooley," Lupato said as we approached the hotel, "that wasn't business. That was personal. Macklin's got a temper. Always has."

"So I guessed right," I said. "Or Macklin guessed wrong."

Lupato shrugged. "Don't matter now. What matters is what Mr. Valenti believes."

The sedan turned left at the Shiny Donut and pulled into the hotel driveway, coming to a smooth stop under the striped portico. A valet hovering nearby glanced our way but kept his distance. A bellhop with a luggage cart did the same. They knew what kind of car this was, what kind of men it transported.

"Word of advice," Lupato said, turning in his seat to look at me directly for the first time. "Whatever you think you know about Mr. Valenti's business—forget it. Walk away. Go back to the cars, the hotrod shows, whatever you were doing before all this."

His eyes were tired but earnest. This wasn't a threat—it was as close to genuine concern as a man like Lupato could express.

"I can't do that," I said.

He nodded, as if he'd expected nothing else. "Then watch your back. And that girl's too."

I reached for the door handle, then paused. "Why are you telling me this?"

Lupato's mouth twisted into something too weary to be a smile. "Maybe I'm tired of cleaning up messes that didn't need to happen."

I stepped out into the night air and let the door close behind me with a soft thud. Lupato didn't wait around. I watched the sedan pull away smoothly. The night doorman nodded to me, but I turned toward the parking lot instead. My truck waited where I'd left it, ordinary and anonymous among the gleaming luxury vehicles that belonged in the Beverly's lot.

As I slid behind the wheel, the familiar smell of my own space—coffee, old paperbacks, a hint of the takeout I'd had two days ago—enveloped me like a shield. I leaned back against the seat without starting the engine, letting reality settle into my bones.

I'd just walked into Valenti's domain, accused his man of murder, and walked out alive by the narrowest odds—not through any cleverness I could claim, but by an ironic warp in time, a human error in which I'd taken no part. Call it fate, a gift from the gods, I could not kid myself. The reprieve felt temporary, conditional.

Macklin wouldn't be so lucky. By now, Valenti would be setting things in motion. Men like him didn't waste time once a decision was made. By morning, Macklin would be gone—another body in a city built on beautiful corpses.

The question was what might happen next. Valenti had let me leave, but that didn't mean I was safe. And then there was Sheri, who'd set it all in motion with one innocent observation. Would Valenti connect those dots? Would he see her as a loose end that needed tying off?

I started the car, pleased by the muffled explosion that mocked the Benz's purring power. The night stretched ahead, full of possibilities, none of them particularly good. But just then a question I'd stuffed in the back of my mind jumped forward in full force.

How did Anthony Lupato know where to find me? Who told him I was at the hotel?

For that matter, if Valenti had sicced him after me, whose voice in his ear had told him I needed fetching? Certainly not make-no-waves Macklin. Not Sheri—the girl didn't have that kind of access. Sebutu didn't know me from a street bum, and besides, he'd been too focused on where he was going to bother with a lobby rat. The only answer I could come up with was one I didn't like—my phone was bugged. Someone in Valenti's camp, or Valenti himself, had tapped into my call to Montero. Maybe even tapped into our lobby chat session. But how was that possible?

Medusa? Was the malicious mutha of all AIs that freaking omnipotent?

I could drive back to Sheri's, warn her, maybe convince her to leave town for a while. I could snoop some more, see what else I could learn about Valenti's weapons business, stay involved.

Or I could do what Lupato suggested—walk away, pretend none of this had happened. Let the criminals and killers sort themselves out. And what then? Leave ten million people exposed to a deadly toxin?

I pulled out of the parking lot onto the Hartford Way service road and stopped at the light where Benedict Canyon crossed Sunset and Rodeo Drive in a five-point daytime traffic snarl. The decision of where to go next could wait until I was moving. Sometimes, that's all you can do—keep moving and hope clarity finds you somewhere down the road.

As I bent eastward into the late-night traffic on Sunset, I caught myself checking the rearview mirror every few seconds, looking for headlights that followed too closely, cars that matched my turns. The paranoia felt justified. I'd stepped into a world where people disappeared for knowing too much, for nothing more than saying the wrong thing to the wrong person.

I had survived by the narrowest chance tonight, but I couldn't shake the feeling that any open door left was about to shut tight.

39

Cyber Wars

It was morning. Minnie had left in the night on some emergency of her own, and I needed a break from chasing rabbits down holes, so I was back in the shop trying to reawaken my neglected artist's muse. The phone's buzz interrupted my attempt to solder a castoff switch panel to a copper tube manifold and vice versa. I wiped my hands on a shop rag and checked the screen: Jaycee Cutter.

Odd. We'd had dinner at Truman's just the other night. What was up?

My thumb hovered over the screen for a heartbeat before I answered, already feeling that peculiar electric current that precedes bad news.

"Jack?" Her voice wobbled, higher than usual. "Someone broke in. The office—it's destroyed."

I set down the soldering iron. "Are you hurt?"

"No, I just got here. But they took things, Jack." The words tumbled out faster now. "The Fenway Arts file is gone. Everything about that shell company Wellie set up for Gabe Cooley."

My pulse quickened. "What about security cameras?"

"In this place?" She took a shuddering breath. "The building that Fenway owned—Mr. Cooley told me once it was vital to the whole operation. Whatever that means."

"Have you called the police?"

"No, after what happened to Mister Cooley, I thought I should call you first."

"Jaycee, don't touch anything."

"What, you think I might catch something?"

"Just leave everything as it is. I'm on my way."

I threw on a jacket, locked up the shop, and was in my truck and rolling in under two minutes. Latimer's absence since our Roxie chat had stretched from concerning to alarming, and now this. Not coincidence.

I called Scarf, told him what was up, gave him Latimer's office address.

"I'm on my way there now," I said, "but you may be closer."

"I got it. Heading out the door now."

Breaking the law, I phoned Jaycee again. "Gonna be a black man come to your door. I sent him, he's cleared. Name is Scarf, he's my best friend."

"Scarf? Did I get that right?"

"You did."

As I navigated mid-morning traffic, my mind ran through the implications. Fenway Arts was the wrapper around something important enough to kill for. A clue Roman Valenti wanted badly, but I wanted worse.

Twenty minutes later, Scarf and I were in Latimer's modest office, stepping carefully through the aftermath. Filing cabinets hung open like gutted fish. Papers blanketed the floor in a blizzard of documents. The place looked like a tornado had a personal vendetta against paperwork. Jaycee stood in the middle, arms wrapped around herself, butterfly glasses slightly askew.

She needed a hug and I administered the requisite treatment.

"Whoever did this knew what they were looking for," Scarf

said, crouching to examine a sliced-open file folder. "Professional work."

"They cut the power at some point." Jaycee pointed to the opaque ceiling lights. "Weren't in a hurry, took plenty of time."

I nodded, picking through folders, seeing labels for mundane client matters—patent applications, screenplay rights disputes. Nothing related to Gabe's less legitimate interests.

"The Fenway documents were in a separate lockbox." Jaycee pointed to a mangled metal container in the corner. "Property deeds, incorporation papers, bank statements."

I lifted the empty box, about the size of a banker's box. The lock had been drilled with precision, the contents taken and left empty. "What else did Gabe say about the building?"

"Not much. Just that it was the cornerstone." She hugged herself tighter. "Wellie was nervous about it. Said it was too visible, but I didn't ask what he meant by that. I mean, IP rights are one kind of secret, but this stuff—not my bag."

We spent another thirty minutes searching her file cabinets and Wellie's office, where his safe remained intact with no visible marks to indicate further intrusion. Our perusal revealed nothing else missing or damaged beyond the obvious targets. I noted that the burglars had left Jaycee's computer intact, but reasoned that they'd probably had time enough to copy its hard drive storage to a flash drive. Someone had come for specific documents and left everything else untouched.

Jaycee fixed me with a shrewd look, her turquoise frames catching the light. "You have copies, right?"

"In a safe place. Don't fret yet, pet."

She picked up a pencil and twisted it through her fingers. "This never happened before."

"I know, it's ugly and personal and makes you feel exposed. But remember, they got what they came for, so there's no reason to return."

"All this mess…"

Scarf stepped up to the plate. "Gotcha covered, Jaycee. Jack's got to take this up a level—don'tcha Jackson."

"Right, but Jaycee, I *will* get back to you, I promise."

"Where are you going? What should I do now?"

"Soon as I leave, call the cops and tell them exactly what you told me. Scarf's just a friend rushed over to help. For now, leave the Fenway papers out of it. You don't know what was in the lockbox."

"Jack, now you're scaring me. What's going on?"

"Nothing you need to worry about. Think good thoughts—like Steak Diane, crème brûlée."

She gave me a weak smile. "I'll put on weight in five minutes."

"Not you, doll."

Scarf and I exchanged looks. I didn't like leaving him there to deal with the cops, but this would have to do until Plan B came along.

As I left, I felt Jaycee's doubt following me like a shadow. She wasn't the only one with questions. I had plenty of my own, starting with how Valenti had discovered Fenway's importance so quickly. The race was accelerating, and I was losing ground with every passing hour.

I made a few phone calls and headed for Central-Alameda.

~

Mother's Mud wasn't my first choice for a clandestine meeting, but its sticky tables and lack of patrons were exactly what we needed. I arrived early, claiming the corner booth with the torn seat nobody wanted. From there, I could watch both the entrance and the side door while nursing McCree's unbranded coffee that tasted like scorched lima beans.

Joe Blanco arrived first and slid into the booth with the fluid grace that always made me wonder how a man his size moved so quietly. He wore a faded UCLA hoodie with the sleeves pushed up, exposing forearms that could bend steel rebar.

"This place smells like desperation and burnt grits," he muttered, eyeing my cup with suspicion.

"That's why I like it."

Minnie appeared minutes later, her auburn hair tucked under a baseball cap, wearing oversized sunglasses despite the overcast day. She slipped them off as she sat, revealing eyes sharp with intelligence and fatigue in equal measure.

"Three minutes," she said, setting a small device on the table that emitted a barely audible hum. "Signal jammer. Talk fast."

I laid it out quickly: the break-in at Latimer's office, the missing Fenway files, and my suspicions about how Valenti was staying one step ahead.

"Macklin tipped his hand," I said, suddenly remembering my first visit to the Taj. "He mentioned running facial recognition on me through some system called Metricon. Not a standard law enforcement database—something more advanced."

Blanco's expression hardened. "AI-driven surveillance. Military grade."

"That's my guess. I think Valenti's using it to track every detail of Gabe's final days, following breadcrumbs we don't even realize we're digging up."

Minnie's fingers tapped a nervous rhythm on the table. "If he's got access to that kind of tech, we're working at a serious disadvantage."

I turned to Joe. "Which is why we need to bring this to Deke," I said. "Whatever interagency task force you guys are running, the top dogs need to know what they're up against."

Minnie nodded agreement and pulled out a phone I hadn't seen before—matte black, no manufacturer logo. Her fingers flew across the surface, utilizing some authentication protocol that looked like a cross between sign language and a concert pianist's warm-up.

"He's responding," she murmured, eyes fixed on the screen.

I watched her expression shift from concentration to frustration. "Deke says—and I quote—'REDCON intel disqualifies engaging Valenti's tech assets as irrelevant to locating the weapons cache. Focus on physical evidence.'" She looked up. "He's shutting us down."

"Bureaucratic tunnel vision," Joe grumbled. "Guy spends too much time on the horn with Washington nitwits."

Joe was old school DEA, seat-of-the-pants Special Ops. Hated paperwork and pencil pushers.

A thought occurred to me and I turned to Minnie. "What about PumaNet? You said your AI could run circles around anything Valenti's team cobbled together."

The silence that followed felt like a vacuum sucking the oxygen from our little corner. Minnie's face went blank.

"Puma's gone dark," she finally said, her voice too controlled. "Quit responding twelve hours ago."

"Could be processing something big," I offered.

She shook her head once, a sharp, definitive movement. "No, it's got more bandwidth than you can possibly imagine. This is different. Puma has stopped talking."

The jammer on the table gave three quick beeps. Our time was up, but it hardly mattered. We'd already said everything that counted, and none of it was good.

The news about Puma hit me like a sucker punch. My fingers went numb around my coffee cup. Minnie's revelation changed everything. Without her AI's processing power and military-grade algorithms, we were as lost as Stone Age hunters tracking a stealth bomber.

"When exactly did it stop responding?" I asked.

"0347 this morning." Minnie's face remained impassive, but

her knuckles whitened around her empty cup. "I was running a parallel analysis on Cooley's shell company when the connection just... severed."

I nodded slowly, piecing together the implications. "Two possibilities. Either Puma is fully engaged in some kind of cyber combat with Medusa—"

"Or Medusa found it and destroyed it," Minnie finished. Her clinical tone couldn't mask the loss in her eyes. Puma wasn't just a tool to her. It was a creation, a partner.

Joe leaned forward. "There's a third option." His voice dropped lower. "What if Puma's been hijacked?"

The silence that followed felt charged, dangerous.

"By Valenti?" I asked.

"By Sebutu." Joe's eyes met mine. "That sumbitch has intelligence connections across three continents. Specializes in acquiring things that aren't supposed to be acquirable."

Minnie's intake of breath was barely audible. "If Sebutu has control of Puma..."

She didn't need to finish. We all understood. PumaNet had been designed with military applications in mind—it could access secured databases, predict tactical movements, and most critically for our situation, decode encrypted communications. In Sebutu's hands, it would lead him straight to Gabe's weapons cache.

"Let's not jump to conclusions," I said. "Minnie, what safeguards are in place?"

"Self-destruct protocols should activate if anyone attempts unauthorized access." Her voice lacked conviction. "But Puma's architecture is... unique. It learns. Adapts."

"Could it be convinced to bypass its own security?" Scarf asked.

Minnie's silence was answer enough.

I gathered the empty cups, buying myself a moment to think. We were now facing not just Valenti with his Medusa AI, but potentially Sebutu with a weaponized version of Puma. Two deadly hunters circling the same prize, with us caught in the middle.

"We need to change our approach," I said finally. "Digital trails are compromised. We go old school—paper records, face-to-face meetings, burner phones only."

"Like 1985," Joe muttered.

"If that's what it takes." I met each of their gazes. "Joe, your team is focused on the weapons. We focus on the players—Valenti, Sebutu, and whoever else is in the game."

Minnie nodded slowly. "I have some contacts at DARPA who might be able to track unusual AI activity patterns. Off the books."

"Do it," I said. "Joe, we need eyes on Sebutu. His movements, meetings, communications—anything that might indicate he's acquired new tech."

"I might know a person or two in that department. I'm on it."

We dispersed two minutes apart. I headed for the shop, feeling a strong urge to crush physical substance in my fist in the familiar presence of oil and gasoline and sweat. Abstraction was Minnie's game, not mine, a world where she was in control while I flopped around like a hooked fish. I needed grounding.

The stakes had just risen exponentially, and our resources were dwindling. If Sebutu had indeed hijacked PumaNet, he now possessed the most advanced tracking tool on the planet.

And somewhere in Los Angeles, deadly weapons sat waiting to be found, their discovery now a race between forces I'd once thought I understood. I no longer had that luxury. The game had changed, and survival would require more than just playing catch-up—it would demand getting ahead of the hunters themselves.

40

The African Mandate

As I drove through the street gate at the John Dyle Fashion Forge in colorful Central-Alameda, I felt a surge of adrenalin. Three Tetra enforcers sat their Harley bikes in the yard outside. All three wore the gang's trademark sleeveless leather vest, arm tats, sculpted sideburns. Two were my size minus a tad, the third was bigger. He shrugged a shoulder at the C10 truck.

"This your ride, asshole?" he said.

"No. It belongs to Santa Claus."

"You funning me?"

"Only because you need some light in your life."

"What the hell you doing in this hole, Dyle?"

"Same as you, Bennie. Just slummin'."

I kept my eyes on the shiny silver buckle at Benecio Serrano's flatiron waist. You don't look a Tetra gangbanger in the eye. Not even if you went to the same high school. Not even if you boosted cars together before you wised up and joined the Marines, and he moved up in the cartel.

Bennie Serrano couldn't afford to cruise anymore. He was too busy watching his back.

He jerked his head at the shop's front wall. "You got business with Coolio?"

"I rent it from him."

"What else?"

"Nothing else. I play around here with the torch is all."

"Guy's dead. Now what you gonna do?"

"Rent from the next guy who owns it."

"Maybe that's not a guy."

"Maybe that's a transvestite hippie wearing green tights and smoking cigarillos. No difference to me."

"You could give us a tour, show us what you do with the torch."

"Sure, I run tours all the time. Weekends are like a circus parade, sightseers going in and out. Drives the neighbors crazy."

The purr of a Cadillac engine announced Scarf's arrival. He rolled into my yard like visiting royalty, the black CTS gleaming against the industrial grime of my shop. When he stepped out, he was pure business—tailored suit, crisp white shirt, Italian shoes that probably cost more than my monthly rent.

I wanted to ask how he'd shaken loose so soon from the cops at Jaycee's break-in, but the biker presence told me now was not the time.

"Gentlemen," Scarf said, adjusting his tie as he approached. "I see you've met my associate."

The shortest biker sneered. "The grease monkey? Yeah, we seen him before."

Scarf's smile never reached his eyes. "Then you understand you're in the presence of greatness." He turned to me. "Jack, seems you know our informant."

Serrano leaned against the Caddy's fender—a capital offense Scarf let slide for the moment. "That shipment that landed? It's drones. Confirmed. My buddy just back from Ukraine says everyone in the arms business is mass-producing mini bombers as fast as possible." His eyes met mine. "Based on the size and number of crates that hit San Pedro, we're talking ten, twelve, maybe fifteen thousand."

My stomach knotted. "You sure?"

"Sure as death," Serrano said. "And we know where they went."

I exchanged glances with Scarf. We both knew what came next.

"How much you want?" Scarf asked.

Serrano smiled. "That's the thing. No money required. Not yet anyway."

"What's the catch?" I asked.

"We collect later. Based on what turns up at the schoolhouse."

The schoolhouse. Some kind of gangsta boy code?

A glimmer of recognition lit Scarf's eyes. "When?" he said.

"Right now," Serrano said. "Better than later."

My hands were steady, but inside, a storm was brewing. New players, new stakes, and a deadline rapidly approaching. Whatever breathing room was left had just vanished into thin air.

~

The schoolhouse in Long Beach was a concrete behemoth squatting by the freeway like a gray toad, its windows blacked out, its perimeter marked by chain-link topped with razor wire. We arrived in a small convoy—the three Tetras leading on their bikes, Scarf's Cadillac following, and me bringing up the rear in my truck. Before we even cut our engines, a dozen figures emerged from an unmarked cargo container, each carrying enough firepower to start a small revolution. They wore mismatched camo that somehow looked more threatening than any uniform.

In a habit that needed no forethought, I pulled my camera from the seat console, set the shutter speed to continuous fire, panned warehouse, troops, and container, and shoved the cam back where I'd got it. If they didn't like it, they could shoot me.

Scarf came over to join forces. I lifted my chin in the general direction of West L. A. "How's Jaycee?"

"Lady's tougher'n she looks. Forensics were busy, so Jaycee and I got better acquainted. Gonna help her clean up the office tomorrow."

Brian Sebutu emerged just then from the warehouse entrance, impeccably dressed in a tailored suit that seemed to absorb rather than reflect the light. At six-foot-seven, he towered over his men, his shaved head gleaming in the smoggy sunlight. His smile had the practiced warmth of a shark.

"Mr. Dyle, Mr. Jones," he greeted us. "Punctual as promised."

Serrano and his Tetra goons tensed, hands drifting toward concealed weapons. Sebutu flicked his gaze toward them, then back to us.

"I appreciate the escort," he said, "but they have fulfilled their purpose." He gestured to one of his men, who stepped forward with an envelope. "Your associates may leave now."

Serrano glanced at Scarf, who nodded almost imperceptibly. The envelope disappeared into Serrano's vest pocket. I exchanged eye darts with him for several seconds before he joined his compadres for the retreat to their Harleys.

"Come," Sebutu said, leading us inside. "I have something I want you to see. Something I want you to report."

I exchanged glances with Scarf. "Report?"

Sebutu's smile widened. "Please. We both know who you work for. Or rather, who you are feeding information to. Homeland Security? CIA? The specific agency does not matter."

"I'm just a car mech—" I began, but Sebutu waved away my protest.

"Lies diminish us both, Mr. Dyle. I want your federal keepers to know what they are facing. I want them to understand the futility of intervention."

The warehouse door rolled shut behind us, but my attention was fastened on the opposite view. The interior stretched away in row upon row of wooden crates stacked to the rafters. The nearest were stamped with serial numbers and coded designations I recognized from my military days. The rest would be the same.

"Holy mothballs," Scarf muttered beside me.

Sebutu grinned with undisguised pride. "More guns than in all of California law enforcement and the California National Guard combined," he said. "Assault rifles, machine guns, anti-tank weapons, sniper rifles, grenades, C4—a comprehensive collection."

My mouth had gone dry. The scale was beyond anything I'd imagined this psychopath was up to. Each crate represented dozens of weapons. Each stack represented hundreds. And there were hundreds of stacks.

"But this," Sebutu continued, leading us deeper into the warehouse, "this is my masterpiece."

At the center of the warehouse stood three long rows of crates, stacked six high, stretching half the length of the building.

"Mini-bombers. Autonomous aerial vehicles with explosive payload capacity." Sebutu ran his hand lovingly along one of the crates. "Only two hundred thousand now," he said, faking a rueful apology. "A hundred thousand more with the new shipment tonight. We are not a bunch of hillbilly militants playing paint ball. We are live and ready to go to war."

My heart hammered against my ribs. Two hundred thousand drones. Soon to be three hundred thousand. Each capable of carrying explosives. The implications made my stomach go hollow.

"Why show us this?" Scarf asked, his voice carefully controlled.

Sebutu's eyes gleamed. "So you can carry my message back to the Homeland crowd in Washington. Tell them, say, you cannot prepare for this, it is already upon you. Lock up your homes and pray to your false gods that your death will be swift."

I forced myself to meet his gaze. "No weapons of mass destruction?"

For the first time, Sebutu laughed. "We *are* mass destruction. We will destroy the white menace once and for all. It starts right here, in your blighted, corrupt city, and will spread across the land."

The warehouse suddenly felt airless, as if the oxygen had been sucked out by the enormity of what we were witnessing. Sebutu was planning a race war, but the calculated precision of the operation told me this wasn't born of ideology alone. Someone was pulling strings, someone with resources and planning capabilities beyond what stood before us.

And I had a pretty good idea that someone was in New York, pushing Roman Valenti.

Scarf and I were "excused" from class at the schoolhouse. We walked back to our vehicles in silence, the weight of what we'd seen an almost physical force. I squeezed the steering wheel in white-knuckled rage, but I couldn't bring myself to start the engine. Beside me, Scarf sat with the door open, half in and half out of the truck, his silhouette rigid in the dim light. He loosened his tie with a sharp, angry tug, then slammed his palm against the dashboard. When he finally looked over at me, his expression mirrored what I felt—rage, disbelief, and a cold, calculating fury.

"The son of a bitch," he said through his teeth. "Bringing his goddamned tribal genocide here from half-way around the world."

The air carried the scent of salt and diesel fuel from the harbor.

"A race war," Scarf said. "That's the narrative he's selling."

"But we both know that's not what this is," I replied. "Sebutu's just the hired help. This whole operation screams syndicate—the scale, the organization, the resources."

"White man financing a Black man to kill white people." Scarf's laugh was hollow. "Valenti doesn't care about race. He cares about power and chaos."

I released the wheel to rub my eyes, trying to process the implications. "Those drones...with that many, they could target multiple cities simultaneously. No warning, no time to respond."

"And Valenti's speeding up his timeline," Scarf added. "He was supposed to wait for the VX shipment—chemical weapons would make the strikes even more devastating. But he's moving ahead with conventional explosives now."

"We need to contact Deke," I said.

Scarf shook his head. "With what? Sebutu practically announced he was using us as messengers. Anything we tell Homeland will be exactly what Valenti and the dons want them to hear."

"So we're on our own."

"Unless we get concrete evidence of the VX projectiles," Scarf said. "Sebutu didn't deny they exist. He just implied they weren't the whole package."

I started my engine, my mind racing. "Here's what I think. Valenti's playing a different game now. He wants the feds focused on Sebutu's race war angle while he positions his chemical weapons. The drones are just the opening act."

"But for what?" Scarf asked, placing one foot on the pavement. "What's the endgame?"

The pieces clicked together in my head like tumblers in a lock. "Control. Create enough chaos, enough fear, and people will accept any solution that promises security. Even if that solution comes from the very people who created the problem."

Scarf nodded slowly. "And with Homeland focused on Sebutu..."

"Valenti operates in the blind spot," I finished.

We sat with that thought for a moment, the implications spiraling outward like ripples in dark water.

"We need to move, now," I said. "If Valenti's accelerated his timeline, we don't have the luxury of waiting for federal backup."

I looked at my watch—5:47 PM. The height of rush hour. "We need to be careful. If Valenti's people spot us, we'll never make it to morning."

Scarf's expression hardened into the look I recognized from our military days, the one that said he'd calculated the odds and accepted them, however grim.

"I'll call my contact at the port," he said. "See if we can track the shipment that's coming in tonight. Maybe mess things up a little."

I nodded, a plan already forming. "I've got some equipment at the shop we might need. Meet me there if we get separated in traffic."

Scarf got out and stepped away to his Caddy. As we pulled away from the warehouse in tandem, I couldn't shake the image of those rows of crates, each containing dozens of miniature harbingers of death. The crushing burden of what we'd witnessed was now augmented by the responsibility of what we had to do next.

Time was running out. People would die if we failed. And the clock was ticking faster than we'd realized.

41

Gift In A Box

I gunned the engine as I pulled away from Long Beach and hit the freeway. My mind replayed Sebutu's words, his cool demeanor as he discussed his massive arsenal. Scarf and I weren't acting out of moral outrage—we'd seen worse—but because Valenti and company were close to the finish line and we were still a lap behind.

Sebutu's smugness had told me everything I needed to know. The drones were being prepared for field deployment, and the City of the Angels was their first target. His casual mention of target acquisition systems wasn't just showing off—it was a taunt. He thought he was untouchable.

My fingers drummed against the steering wheel as traffic slowed to a crawl on the 710. The information we'd just garnered couldn't wait. I needed Minnie's federal resources and that weird AI thing she'd introduced me to. Traffic congealed around me like day-old oatmeal, but my thoughts moved at hyper speed.

I grabbed my burner phone and hit Minnie's number, putting it on speaker.

She answered on the second ring. "I was about to call you."

"I just left our African friend," I said, keeping my eyes on the road. "Got some intel that can't wait. We need to meet."

There was a pause, then her voice dropped to a near whisper. "Jack, we're being watched. Both of us."

"By whom?"

"Take your pick. Feds who aren't me or Deke, Valenti's private security, maybe even Sebutu's people. We need to be careful how we communicate."

I navigated around a slow-moving semi. "What are you suggesting? Carrier pigeons?"

"Very funny." Her tone suggested it wasn't. "We need to use coded language, innuendo. Nothing explicit over the phone."

"Like teenagers sexting with their parents in the next room?"

"This isn't a joke, Jack." The edge in her voice could have cut steel. "Use your tradecraft."

She was right. "How about we meet at the crack house?" I suggested, the reference to CRK Motors—or "Crackup" Motors as Scarf and I called it—obvious enough for her to catch.

"Perfect. One hour?"

"As soon as you can make it. I'm in traffic, maybe forty minutes out."

Traffic opened up as I ended the call, and I pressed harder on the accelerator. Crack house. A thin disguise against whatever digital ears might be listening, but it would have to do. The thought of using half-baked code names to outwit an AI with a thousand IQ was almost laughable, but desperation breeds improvisation.

A heat was rising in my chest—an uncomfortable warmth I recognized as fear—not for myself, but for what might happen if we failed. Thousands of weaponized drones in terrorist hands wasn't just a catastrophe—it was the prelude to complete destruction, and we were running out of time to stop it.

～

CRK Motors squatted in the East Downey haze as I pulled the C10 into the blistered asphalt lot. I continued on behind the building and parked beside Minnie's government-issue sedan that screamed "federal agent" to the car-savvy local gentry. As I got out, Scarf's Caddy glided into the next slot.

Minnie was already inside the former office, the one our Homeland friends had commandeered for our first meeting, with her laptop open on the wet bar. Across from her, the smart TV she'd brought days ago stared in blank stupidity. Her hair was pulled back in a severe ponytail, and she wore dark-rimmed glasses that somehow made her look both bookish and dangerous.

"Took you two long enough," she said without looking up from her screen.

"Traffic was a nightmare," I said. "What've we got?"

"First, they took out George Macklin." She read off a news bulletin. "Reported found in a Santa Monica motel, died from a self-inflicted gunshot wound. Police are investigating."

'Valenti didn't waste any time."

Minnie tapped a few keys, ran her index finger over the touchpad. She turned the laptop so I could see. "Someone here wants to say hello again."

The screen showed Homeland Agent Tom Rowland. He smiled like we were old friends.

"Jack Dyle," he said, his voice carrying an odd digital resonance. "And Lacleef Jones. Good to chat face-to-face, so to speak."

Minnie cleared her throat. "Before we go any further...confession time. Tom Rowland is Puma's avatar."

I stared at the screen. "Puma? The AI?"

The man on screen nodded. "Actually, one of many avatars. I find humans respond better to faces than disembodied voices."

My mind clicked through the implications like tumblers in a lock. "So when I called Dickie Sloane to represent Sheri, it wasn't really me…"

"Guilty as charged." His smile widened slightly. "Nothing you wouldn't have done for Sheri yourself—I'm just quicker. And I don't need burner phones."

"Jesus." I ran a hand through my hair. "You're monitoring my calls."

"Only the important ones." Like that made it better.

Minnie touched my arm. "He's on our side, Jack. We need all the help we can get."

I wasn't convinced, but now wasn't the time for a debate on digital privacy. "Did you listen in on our conversation with Sebutu?"

Rowland's expression tightened. "No. Medusa has impressive security blocks in place. Their systems are like fortresses—old-school, air-gapped. I'm still working on access."

"Then you'll want to hear this."

I gave him the rundown—Sebutu's plan, the drones, the timing. "The buildup's been ongoing for quite a while," I finished.

Scarf added his own summary: "It's like they're ready to start World War Three."

Rowland's image blurred for half a second, like a digital hiccup. Then Sebutu's face appeared on the screen, perfect down to the calculating eyes that never matched his smile.

"Scarf's assessment is correct," said Sebutu's voice, the AI mimicking his cadence perfectly. "They are off-loading the final shipment of drones now—cleverly disguised, of course, to appear as other types of cargo. One hundred ninety-six thousand, five hundred twelve units, to be exact. One lot from Argentina, several from China, but the largest lot from a camouflaged plant in Libya."

I felt Minnie tense beside me. "How the hell do you do that?"

"Ship manifests, bribes, phone taps—"

"No, I mean the ID switch."

The Sebutu avatar answered with a thin smile. "Facial

mapping, voice synthesis, behavioral analysis. It's a specialty of mine."

The image flickered back to Rowland. "Now, what else do you have for me?"

I pulled the paperwork I'd copied from Latimer's office from my jacket. "Possibly Gabe's mysterious 'list.' Jaycee—Latimer's aide—asked about a 'domicile list' the night I took her to dinner. If each of Gabe's rental properties is considered to be a 'domicile,' then I'm already holding what everyone's looking for."

I spread the papers on the bar and held each one up to the laptop's camera. Rental agreements, property titles, management contracts—page after page of Cooley's real estate empire.

"None of these stand out as anything special," I said. "Just ordinary houses and apartments, a mini-mart...."

Rowland's eyes narrowed—or seemed to, if an AI could actually focus. "I'm particularly interested in the commercial properties. Show me those again."

I held up the documents, one at a time, for the six commercial buildings Cooley owned. Rowland was silent for several seconds—probably an eternity in AI processing time. I realized he was performing an OCR, or optical character recognition, scan of each page I held in my not-so-steady grip.

"These two addresses," he finally said. "Check them first." Two locations appeared as text at the bottom of the screen. "The energy consumption patterns are inconsistent with their reported usage."

Before I could ask for clarification, he switched topics. "Tell me about Gabe's final phone message, the one you erased."

I frowned, digging through my memory. "He said something about making sure the breaker could handle the load from my arc welder. Said fifty amps should be enough to keep me from burning down every building on the block. The man could've been bleeding out when he called, maybe hallucinating—"

"Which breaker was he referring to?"

"Circuit breaker, prevents an overloaded surge from—hey, I'm surprised an AI wouldn't already know about electrical systems."

"I understand electricity, Jack. What I don't understand is why he'd call you about it. Records show the subpanel in your workshop was inspected last year after Southern California Edison detected an anomaly."

Records show? Why, sure, just ask any AI with a zillion IQ. Snap of a virtual finger. It's a cinch.

But Rowland had a point to make. "The electrician's invoice indicates installation of a new replacement fifty-amp breaker."

Minnie and I exchanged glances. My workshop. The breaker panel. The same panel I looked at every day without a second thought. Didn't need no steenking breaker.

"Go. To. The. Shop." Rowland enunciated each word like he was speaking to imbeciles, which, relative to his intelligence, we probably were.

The screen abruptly switched to a Windows desktop.

Maybe more like ear mites.

"Well, that was humbling," Minnie muttered, clapping the laptop closed.

"Let's move," I said. "You guys follow me, but spread out for maximum mobility. We may be only three, but let's not give them a single target."

We raced outside. As I navigated the truck toward Central-Alameda, my mind spun with possibilities. What was hidden in my shop? Gabe Cooley had sneaked something there without my knowing, but what? A dead mouse? Alison West's autograph? The deed to the Taj?

A triggered spritzer of nerve gas?

42

Fences and Walls

The industrial zone looked like a hangover wearing makeup. Faded corrugated walls plastered with peeling tags and street art melted into each other as Minnie's sedan crawled past the chain-link entrance. My shop squatted between a metal fabricator and a place that rebuilt electric motors, just another anonymous box in a row of anonymous boxes. The perfect place to hide something you didn't want found—or the perfect place to overlook something hiding in plain sight.

"Charming," Minnie said, cutting the engine. Her fingers tapped a nervous rhythm on the steering wheel. "I haven't been here in what, just a week? And it's still a toxic hazard. Have you worked any magic since?"

"Only on Tuesday when I sacrificed a carburetor to the automotive gods." I climbed out of my truck to the familiar smell of oil and metal—as familiar as a buddy's handshake.

The afternoon sun turned the fabricator's roll-up door into a sheet of hammered gold. I fumbled with my keys, conscious of Minnie's eyes on my back.

"You don't know where the main breaker panel is?" She asked the question like she was testing me.

"Each shop has its own subpanel. Building's from the forties—electrical's been patched more times than a politician's reputation." The lock clicked open. "Mine's just inside."

I heaved the door up, metal groaning against rust. The darkness inside held its breath while I took two steps in and my hand found the subpanel on the wall. A simple slide latch secured it.

"Open sez me," I muttered, flipping the latch.

The panel door swung easily on wire hinges. I reached for the screwdriver I kept on the nearby workbench. A few turns of four screws, and the cover came off with a metallic protest, and that's when I saw it—a small flash drive resting on the base.

Before my fingers could close around it, Minnie's hand darted past me. She plucked it up with the precision of a jewel thief and had it connected to a palm-sized black device before I could say Don't.

"What the hell?" The words finally tumbled out. "You might've just wiped whatever's on there."

Minnie's eyes flashed green. "Relax. This prevents exactly that. It's a read-only connection with military-grade encryption breaking." Her voice had the cool certainty of someone who'd done this a hundred times before. I hoped my clients felt the same about me under their car with a wrench.

The two devices sat in her palm, coupled like mating insects, small lights pulsing between them.

"Standard issue?" I asked.

"Not even close." Her smile was thin and private. "Let's see what we've got."

We moved to the workbench where she pulled out her laptop. Her fingers became a blur across the keyboard, tickety-tacking commands I couldn't follow. The screen flashed, then settled on a spreadsheet that scrolled upward like movie credits, exposing a numbered list that stopped at sixty-seven.

"Cooley's properties," she said, eyes narrowing. "Commercial, residential, no obvious grouping or pattern."

I leaned in, my shoulder brushing hers. "There's always a pattern. What's this up here? Mesa, Arizona?"

"Looks like he has a couple more properties there." She scrolled some more. "And here's one in Las Vegas, one in Pacific Beach…"

I realized I had my arm wrapped around her shoulders. "That's down near San Diego, Babe. Makes no sense. Too much for one guy to handle alone. He'd need other people, an office, maintenance staff, contractors. I saw none of that in the papers I got."

Minnie blinked several times, then shifted closer. I caught the scent of her hair and sensed a fleeting warmth of connection, more than physical, that arrived and vanished before it had time to settle. She didn't push me away, only moved her touchpad finger.

"Thought I saw something flash by," she said, her voice suddenly thicker. Her eyes narrowed as she scrolled up slowly. "Number forty-one." She tapped the screen where a line glowed yellow against the white background. An address in Compton with no additional notes or explanation for its highlighting.

Her fingers danced again, launching a series of flashing windows that ripped by like shuffled cards, then collapsed to a single icon. Over on the list she clicked on Forty-One's address, and the screen filled with an image of a nondescript two-story building on a corner, windows and doors bricked over like it was hiding from the world.

"Owned by Fenway Arts," she murmured, reading the data sheet that appeared. "Mean anything to you?"

"Wellie mentioned it at our Roxie meeting, remember? A Nevada shell company he set up for Gabe."

Minnie pointed a finger at me. "You're right."

My mind flashed back to Jaycee's distress call hours ago.

Wellie's office—*her* office, really—violated. Missing files. A metal lock drilled out. The Fenway files gone.

My phone was already in my hand, Scarf's number pulled up. I typed quickly: Forget the shop. Meet us at this address. I attached the Compton address from the spreadsheet.

A feeling started in my chest, something between relief and excitement. It wasn't confidence yet, but it was its first cousin.

"I think I've been carrying the answer around in my head this whole time," I said. "Like having a song stuck in your head but not knowing the name."

"And now?" Minnie was already packing up.

"Now I think it's time to follow the breadcrumbs." I headed for the door, feeling lighter than I had in days. The hunt was narrowing. We had a destination. And maybe, just maybe, some answers.

Minnie didn't move.

"What?" I said.

"You called me babe."

"I did? When?"

"Just now."

"Huh, I guess it just slipped out."

"Nobody ever called me that before."

"Look, I'm sorry if—"

"Dammit, Jack Dyle, don't you dare apologize! It was nice!"

"Oh. So, we're good then."

"Damn straight."

"I guess maybe we just table this for when we, uh—"

"Right, we gotta hit the road."

~

The building greeted us like a bad memory—battleship gray walls with windows and doors bricked over, as if it had decided human connection wasn't worth the trouble. Compton stretched around us, worn at the edges, the 710 freeway's distant hum a reminder that my C10 had been part of that din less than an hour ago.

I parked my truck across the street where a gang-tagged one-bedroom hid behind enough steel to defend Fort Knox. No one in that neighborhood was going to sic the cops on us. I leaned against the fender while Minnie parallel parked in a single deft cut a few cars ahead. As she got out, her face shifted from determination to calculation. The spreadsheet had led us here, but getting inside would be another problem entirely.

"Not exactly rolling out the welcome mat," I said, scanning the structure. Two stories of blank-faced concrete broken only by the outlines of vintage window casings, panes bricked in long ago. Zero personality and less charm. The only potential entry point was a freight platform on the side, its rollup secured with a heavy padlock that looked newer than everything else around it.

Minnie crossed the street to survey the adjacent lot through chain link topped with rusted barbed wire. I followed to see for myself. On the other side sat the cracked surface of an empty parking area with faded stripes marking spaces for six vehicles.

"A semi rig could fit in there," she said. "Whatever they were moving back in the day, it wasn't small."

I backed away from the fence and ambled toward the corner. A streetside door sat in a shallow stairwell off the sidewalk. I tested the gray-painted knob. Solid as the rest. "We need another way in."

Minnie pulled out her phone and executed another blinding demonstration of thumbs in flight. "This is a job for Puma. Rowland could figure a way to bust this place in minutes."

Her face darkened as she stared at the device. "Connection's blocked. Again." She looked up at me, her eyes narrowed. "Medusa."

The name hung between us for a moment, then I turned and headed back to my truck, my mind already three steps ahead.

"Plan B involves not waiting for tech support," I said, reaching behind the seat for my emergency bag. I hadn't picked a lock in months, so it was time I renewed my license. I carried my lock pick toolset over to the gate and went to work. In sixty seconds the hasp loosened and came free in my hand. Shouldn't have taken that long, but idle time takes a toll.

The gate was on rusty wheels that ran through a rustier rail embedded in the pavement. Minnie helped me shove the thing aside to make a gap wide enough for my truck. Then I backed the C10 into the side yard and parked beside the loading platform, nose out.

"What's your next idea?" Minnie asked.

I glanced up at the flat roof line as I opened the C10's diamond plate crossover toolbox. "Mountaineering."

I reached in and found what I wanted. The grapnel hook felt reassuringly solid in my hand, the rope coiled like a sleeping snake.

"You're not seriously—" Minnie started.

"I seriously am." I measured the distance to the roof with my eyes, calculating angles and force. A while back I'd been pretty good with a rope but that while was longer than I wanted to admit.

The hook sailed upward in a clean arc and caught the edge of the roof on the first try. I tested it with a sharp tug, then wrapped the rope around my forearm.

I turned to Minnie. "If I'm not back in fifteen minutes, don't call LAPD. Compton's sheriff turf," I gave her a wink that didn't match the tightness in my chest.

The climb wasn't pretty, but it was effective. My boots scraped against the wall as I pulled myself upward, muscles burning with the memory of similar ascents in places I wasn't supposed to be. The roof greeted me with a graveled surface and a rooftop shed that jutted upward like an afterthought.

From this height, Compton's urban grid spread out in a patchwork of faded dreams and stubborn survival. I checked the shed door hasp—locked, but leading to a way down into the building's guts.

"Found something," I called down to Minnie. "Need another rope to descend."

Before she could respond, a sleek black Cadillac CTS rolled to a stop beside my truck. Scarf emerged, his tall frame unfolding like a switchblade. His expression, even from this distance, was all business.

That's when I heard it—the rhythmic thump of rotor blades slicing air. A helicopter materialized over the building, hanging in the air like an oversized wasp. No markings, but the glossy black finish screamed money and discretion. It circled twice, camera equipment visible on its undercarriage, then banked sharply northwest—toward Bel Air. Toward the Taj.

Scarf tracked its path with hawk eyes until it disappeared behind buildings.

"Valenti's private air force?" Minnie called up to me, her voice tight with new urgency.

"Or Medusa's," I replied, but something solid settled in my gut. This wasn't coincidence. "Either way, they know we're here."

I rappelled back down the wall, rope burn tingling against my palms. Scarf met us halfway between our vehicles.

"Your timing's perfect," I said. "Want to help us break in?"

"You find Gabe's stash?" He nodded toward the building.

"We found something," I said, the certainty growing with each word. "Gabe's VX cache has to be here. Domicile 41 on his secret list, owned by a shell company. This is what everyone's been hunting for."

Minnie's face collapsed in momentary despair. "And now Valenti knows too."

I felt something unexpected—not fear, but a fierce exhilaration. After days of chasing shadows and fighting blind, we finally had a target. The helicopter only confirmed it.

"Good," I said, surprising both of them. "Let them come. At least now we're all playing the same game."

Scarf's smile was slow and dangerous. "About time we stopped being reactive."

I looked up at the gray building, no longer seeing a fortress but a finish line. "The hunt is over. Now we see who gets to the prize first."

The sun cast our shadows long across the empty lot, three figures unified by purpose if not by method. In the distance, an emergency siren wailed—the city's constant soundtrack. But for the first time in days, I felt something close to control. The answer in my head had been waiting for the right question.

43

Into Domicile 41

We convened at the C10 with Minnie's laptop on the hood again. One thing had changed, a swap that made me uneasy until Minnie explained it.

"We're in chat mode with PumaNet now. Rowland handed off to his superior."

"Can I assume PumaNet knows as much as Rowland about what I just saw?"

A new voice came over the laptop speaker. "Rest easy, Mr. Dyle, we're all one big happy family. Thing to remember is the transfer happened while you blinked on your way down that wall."

The screen came alive with an avatar that looked like Catwoman in a tux, then switched to an attractive brunette human female news anchor, complete with vacant desk and Los Angeles skyline backdrop.

"I'll rest easy," I said, "when we have that VX in responsible hands and Valenti in cuffs. And I liked the Catwoman idea better."

"Right, well, let's get serious. First thing we need is a direct link over Mr. Dyle's phone so I can see and hear what he does."

"Make it secure, is all I ask."

Puma smiled pretty for the camera. "We'll set up for real-time data acquisition over an optimized device. Is Mr. Dyle prepared for setup?"

"Mr. Dyle is prepared," I replied.

I wasn't so sure about that, but I dug my phone out and followed instructions while Puma dictated the next sequence of events in such polite terms I didn't feel bad about doing the hard work.

"1. Enable auto mode. 2. Select audio-visual capture from settings menu. 3. Engage auto-retransmit. 4. Test link." A pause, then, "Verification. All systems optimal."

"If I had a nickel," Scarf said, "for every time someone said Dyle was optimal."

I grabbed a pry bar from the truck, strapped on a headlamp, added another coil of rope, and I was almost ready to go. Almost.

"We still got a plan?" Scarf said.

"Plan's still good," I said. I nodded toward the laptop. "Check?"

The AI lady in silicon nodded back. "Check."

Minnie tried one last argument: "Jack, this is crazy."

I didn't disagree. I was ready for crazy. I'd made the first climb without much problem, with only one line, but I'd been improvising. Now I had all the lines planned and Puma in my pocket. There were worse partners.

I aimed the headlamp toward the rooftop. The grapnel hook looked secure to me. I hoped it looked the same to Scarf and Minnie. If it didn't, Minnie could write my gravestone: Looked good from there.

"Let us know what you find," Scarf said. "But not from the other side."

I went up the wall and over the ledge.

From the rooftop, I saw the same view as before but with less light. I made fast tracks to the stair tower I'd seen earlier. The metal roof showed surface rust. I pried into the worst spot until I felt the frame buckle and let go. Inside the tower was an empty space leading to the floor below. I grabbed the door frame and looked over the side.

Who needed stairs? The ladder would do.

The darkness below seemed bottomless. My headlamp made the first few ladder rungs look less ominous.

"Jack, report." Minnie sounded concerned.

"On my way," I said, and switched to voice-only. "Be patient, my fellow Americans."

There was no video signal to be captured in the windowless stair tower, and my spare hand was too busy to do any manual retransmit. I kept a firm grip on the ladder with one hand and the pry bar with the other. Minnie's real-time view of this little adventure wouldn't kick in until I found a light switch. I trusted Puma's report on the power situation even more than I trusted Puma itself. And that wasn't saying a lot.

The whole scene from the tower floor could be transmitted in two words: not pretty. Not a sign of life except the kind nobody wanted. Previous tenants had cleared out before the new owners opened shop. They hadn't cleared out much of the gear. Discarded rack-mounted servers lay in heaps against one wall, cushioned by tangled bunches of cable.

"Audio visual update," Puma said.

I switched on the video mode, no time for both. The headlamp got more coverage than I'd hoped for. I tucked the pry bar under my arm, checked the surrounding area. What I had hoped not to find were there anyway. Two long rows. Wood pallets stacked in orderly fashion. Each pallet a time bomb.

"Report, Jack," Puma said.

I pried open the first lid. It confirmed my fears.

"Mini-projectiles," I said. "About a hundred of them, shells intact." I looked closer, taking in details. "Think VX."

"No power. No lights." I held the phone away and spoke loudly so they'd get my full report. "Hope you're getting this, Puma."

"Still transmitting, Jack."

The avatar sounded nervous.

I stood for a minute, taking in the scope. Not something I wanted to do, but what I had to do. I found more than just a hundred shells. Far more.

"Three deep," I said. "Possibly four."

"Please hold, Jack." Puma making things sound polite.

"Please hold what?" Scarf's voice. "Your bladder? You oughta be outa there, son."

He wasn't the first to think so.

Puma kicked back in, polite but cold. "Not unexpected. Verify: power status."

"Negative," I said.

I worked my way to the far wall, checking behind pallets and making sure I didn't trip and fall to an untimely end. Nothing to catch me except hard floors. "Repeat," I said. "Negative."

A dim gray square glowed on the wall, about the size of a breaker box.

"Unit 3, left side," Puma said.

It sounded more like directions to the nearest ATM.

I opened the box, threw the switch.

"Visual field update," Puma said.

The overhead tube lights flicked on, making the whole place brighter than the LAX runway. Nothing in the main space except mini-bombs in boxes, one room at the far end, and now me.

"Puma," I said, "you getting all this?"

"Proceed back to the pallet," it said. "Open the top layer."

I propped the phone against an unopened lid, got both hands on the pry bar, and went to work. The nails squeaked in the dry wood, and then it gave way.

"Stand by," Puma said.

A layer of excelsior was all I had between the next layer and a green funeral. I lifted away a chunk of excelsior. Six shell casings lay on top. Puma took less than a heartbeat to verify. It sounded like the longer it knew, the more concerned it got. That much, we had in common.

"Jack," it said. "Risk assessment: high."

"That all you gotta say, bot lady?" Scarf said. "Time to haul ass outa there."

Puma repeated, "Risk assessment: high."

"This could be bad, Puma," I said.

Minnie broke into the dialogue. "Dispersion?"

"Fifty meters," said Puma.

I tried not to think about that. The way my luck ran, a slight breeze could take it halfway to Vegas.

"Prioritize," Puma said. "Please update status of Office One."

"Office One?" I said. "Where'd you get that?"

"I'm working with a microfiche building layout—from county records."

"Well I'm working from my ass. Where is Office One?"

"Ground floor."

"Ground—got anybody working down there? A CPA?"

"Indeterminate. Office One is unaccounted for."

I didn't like the sound of that and said so.

Scarf said he liked it less than the idea of me playing forty yards of hot potato with nerve gas.

"Repeat," Puma said. "Status of Office One."

One hand on the phone, one on the pry bar, I headed down the row. The wide-open space made me feel exposed.

The door wasn't far. My headlamp pointed the way.

"Ignore projectiles for now," Puma said.

Easy for an avatar to say.

The end wall came closer. The rest was guesswork, but so far Puma was three for three. If it thought the office was hot stuff, I'd play its hunch.

"Close," I said. "Real close." My headlamp flashed on the door. "Got it."

"Verify Office One," Puma said.

I had other words for it, but verification would do. I threw the latch. "Empty. Possible exits. Possible basement."

"Go, Jack!" Minnie said.

"New focus," Puma said. "Higher priority."

"Advise," I said.

"So advised."

And through the door I went.

Hallways led to doors. Doors led to hallways. I kept going, found a door marked "Stairs." All it took was a single trip down one flight and a step through the door at the bottom, and I found a hallway full of gray doors.

One said, "High voltage."

A second said, "Authorized Personnel Only."

"Verified," I said, hoping I wasn't exposing myself to more than my life expectancy. But we'd come too far to stop now, and Puma was waiting for more from me.

I gave it: "Something's on the other side of this wall."

"Proceed and report," Puma said.

I took my chances on the "Authorized" door, never expecting to find it anything but a dead end.

I opened the door and saw what we feared most. Only it wasn't nerve gas.

Rows of server racks stretched before me, blue lights blinking in coded rhythms, displays running real-time updates. The HVAC system hummed. Cool air blew from the vent arrays. No less than a hundred processors worked at full capacity. No less than a million operations per second.

The owners of these servers had better security than the White House. More bandwidth than Google, probably. And all the owners were anonymous. No markings on the gear. No ID tags on the racks. No logo on the outside of the building. Whoever owned these processors meant to stay anonymous.

"Not possible," I said. I stepped forward into the room. I was at one end of a corridor that stretched to the far wall, crossed by smaller corridors marking an array of server clusters beyond my counting.

The array blinked. My phone blinked back.

"Luck," I said.

Puma was quiet.

"Boys and girls," I said. "This is hot stuff."

So was the voice that came from the ceiling.

"Welcome, Mister Dyle," it said. "At last we meet."

The blue lights flashed on and off, their silent rhythm mocking me.

"I'm sure you have questions," the voice said, a woman's contralto, mocking insincerity delivered with a breathy overtone. "I'm here to help."

Puma's assessment matched my own. "Suspect Medusa entity."

I stayed in place for a few seconds that felt like years, then I backed out the same way I'd gone in, with careful speed, knowing that outside on street level my team waited for my signal. I was too far away to give it. Not yet.

I took the stairs three at a time and crossed the top floor at a jog. With one hand on the phone, the other on the ladder, I climbed in record time. No rooftop sitrep from me, not with both hands full and no time to slow down.

Only when I reached the side in waning daylight did I begin to breathe normally. The snubbed grapnel felt sure in my hand. I felt my shoulders tense. I felt my shoes catch the stucco wall surface. I felt cool air on my face.

I felt lucky.

44

A New Plan

I was too busy with the grapnel line to notice the small crowd below. As my feet touched the pavement, I saw Minnie standing beside my truck. My eyes adjusted to reveal more vehicles than when I'd gone in—and more people. Deacon Hood was in tight formation with Joe Blanco. Puma must have sent out a five-alarm bulletin to get them here this fast.

Minnie's auburn hair caught the light as she broke away from the huddle and grasped me by both arms.

"Jack?"

My name on her lips carried equal parts relief and tension, and something else. "What did you find?"

"A whole lot of trouble packaged in blinking lights," I said.

Scarf materialized at my side, his lean frame coiled with readiness. "Don't be cryptic, man. This shit just got real complicated."

Deacon Hood stood nearby with his arms crossed, a familiar stance that shouted authority without having to flash a badge. Joe Blanco's presence suggested we'd officially crossed from concerning to catastrophic on whatever scale the alphabet agencies used these days.

"Deke," I acknowledged with a nod. "Didn't expect the cavalry so soon."

"Puma's alert bumped this to priority status," he replied. "What exactly are we dealing with?"

I opened my mouth to answer, but the air crackled with static from the portable comm unit on a nearby crate.

"If I may interject," Puma's voice came from my phone, sounding both mechanical and unnervingly human. "I've completed my analysis of the facility Jack has located. The server farm within Domicile 41 is unequivocally Medusa's primary habitat and command nexus. The physical manifestation of its cognitive architecture, if you will."

Minnie stepped closer to the comm unit. "In English, Puma."

"Apologies. It's where Medusa lives and works." The AI lady paused, a digital equivalent of clearing its throat. "More importantly, the server configuration confirms my hypothesis regarding Medusa's operational capabilities. It's designed specifically to orchestrate synchronized drone fleet movements with microsecond precision."

"Like those light shows they do at halftime?" Scarf asked.

"Precisely, Mr. Jones, though with considerably more lethal applications. The computational architecture allows for simultaneous control of hundreds, potentially thousands of individual units, maintaining swarm coherence while executing complex attack and evasion maneuvers."

I felt a chill that had nothing to do with the night air. "And if we shut it down?"

"Then manual override protocols would necessarily engage," Puma continued. "Mr. Valenti's technical personnel would be forced to coordinate drone operations through conventional command channels, introducing human reaction times and the inevitability of error."

Hood's expression darkened. "Meaning?"

"Meaning collision cascades, Mr. Hood. Drones impacting one another mid-flight, creating debris fields that would rain down upon any targets below. The kinetic energy alone would be devastating, even without considering the potential payload these units might carry."

The implications settled over us like a heavy fog. We'd found Medusa's brain, but killing it might trigger a deadman switch that would turn the sky into a hailstorm of metal and circuitry.

"So we're damned if we do, damned if we don't," I said. "Shut it down, and we get a mechanical monsoon. Leave it running, and Valenti maintains his ace in the hole."

Minnie's eyes met mine, that sharp analytical mind of hers already working through variables. "There has to be a third option."

"Perhaps," Puma interjected, "the solution lies not in binary outcomes but in subversion. Medusa's architecture suggests vulnerability to command substitution under specific conditions."

I translated mentally. "You're saying we don't kill it—we hijack it."

"A crude metaphor, but apt," the AI conceded.

I was about to ask how exactly one goes about hijacking a rogue AI when the night exploded into motion and sound. The conversation died as we all turned toward the source of a new disturbance coming from the perimeter.

"I've detected incoming hostiles," Puma announced, cutting through our strategy session like a blade. "Roman Valenti has arrived approximately 0.27 miles southwest of your position with four troop carriers containing fifty-two armed personnel. Thermal imaging indicates they are carrying military-grade weapons and...they have a mobile crane that could place operatives on the roof within approximately seven minutes and thirty-four seconds."

The news landed like a grenade in our midst. Hood

immediately reached for his sidearm while Scarf muttered something that sounded like a prayer wrapped in profanity. Joe Blanco was already on his phone, speaking in rapid-fire code that meant reinforcements, but his expression told me they wouldn't arrive in time.

Minnie's fingers danced across her tablet, then stopped. She looked up, her green eyes wide with the math she'd just done. "We don't have enough firepower or personnel to stop them. Even if we called in every available agent right now, we'd be overrun before they arrived."

The clock in my head ticked mercilessly. Seven minutes. Six minutes and fifty seconds. Six minutes and forty-five...

An idea sparked in my brain, not a good one, not even a sane one, but when sanity's off the table, insanity becomes your only viable option.

"Puma," I said, addressing the AI directly. "I need you to create a fanatic avatar. Right now."

There was the briefest pause, an eternity in AI processing time. "Please clarify the parameters of this request, Mr. Dyle."

"I need you to contact every fire company, police station, and bomb squad within twenty miles. Tell them to converge on this location immediately." My words picked up speed as the plan crystallized. "Create a scenario with a fanatic inside this building surrounded by nitrate fertilizer with a timer set to detonate in one hour. Make them believe the blast would flatten everything within four blocks."

"You wish me to fabricate a terrorist threat?" Puma's tone remained neutral, but I detected a hint of concern.

"Not fabricate – produce. This is your big-budget blockbuster, Puma. Make it your best work yet. Every emergency responder needs to believe this is real because our lives depend on it."

Deke stepped forward. "Dyle, you're talking about triggering a mass response under false pretenses. That's—"

"That's our only shot," I cut him off. "Unless you've got a platoon of Marines hiding in your pocket?"

His mouth tightened, but he didn't argue further.

Scarf jogged away toward his parked Caddy.

I turned to my C10, reached into the toolbox, and grabbed two flares. The cylindrical tubes felt heavy with the weight of what I was about to do.

Puma reported. "Mr. Dyle, I have initiated the emergency protocol as requested. Initial response indicators suggest the scenario is being treated as credible. Estimated first responder arrival in twelve minutes."

Minnie approached, her expression a mixture of horror and admiration. "Jack, what are you planning?"

I held up the flares. "I need you to film me. Get your phone out."

Her brow furrowed, but she complied, pulling out her phone and opening the camera app.

"Make sure you get this," I said, gripping both flares in one fist. "I'm going to the roof again. I need Medusa to see me, to understand exactly what's happening."

Understanding dawned in her eyes. "You're going to threaten it directly."

"Psychological warfare works on humans. Let's see if it works on AI." I checked that the video was recording properly and handed the phone back to her. "Make sure Medusa gets the message: I'm prepared to die from VX, but is Medusa ready for its own fiery end?"

Deke stepped closer. "VX? You think the nerve agent's in there?"

"I don't know what's in those mini bombs," I replied, "but Medusa does. And I'm betting it has self-preservation protocols."

The grapnel line still hung against the side of Domicile 41. I started for it, but Minnie grabbed my arm. "This is suicide, Jack."

I gave her a smile that probably looked more like a grimace. "Only if I'm wrong about Medusa. If I'm right, it's just another day of terrible choices in a career full of them."

Her fingers tightened, then released. "I'll make sure the video gets to Medusa."

I nodded, then turned to address the group. "If this works, Valenti's crew will drive right into a police blockade. If it doesn't…" I didn't finish the thought.

Scarf returned from his car with an assault rifle over one shoulder. "Do what you gotta do, brother. We'll hold it down here."

Minnie stared wide-eyed at the gun, the man holding it, his obvious comfort with the weapon. She pressed her lips in tight line and looked away. I'd seen the effect before.

"You'll need these," Minnie said, extending two wireless ear buds in her palm. For hands-free motion.

"Thanks…babe," I said, and stuck one in each ear.

Her expression could have meant anything or nothing, but I took it for a sign of something deeper than comradely concern. We both knew this might be the last we'd see of each other. In a flash of stark insight I realized how much it really mattered—to me, anyway—that we would come out of this thing together. That I might even have an ever after with this woman.

The only thing I was sure about was the job ahead.

The flares were cool in my hand as I approached the rope. In about five minutes, they'd burn hot enough to melt flesh from bone. In about six minutes, Valenti's men would be on the roof. In about twelve minutes, emergency vehicles would flood the area.

I grabbed the rope with my free hand, tested it with a quick pull, and then began to climb. The rough fibers bit into my palm, and my muscles protested as I hauled myself upward. The flares knocked against my thigh with each movement, reminders I was walking a thin line between desperation and madness.

As I climbed, I heard the distant rumble of big engines—Valenti's convoy or the first responders, I couldn't tell.

I paused and looked over my shoulder. Minnie stood below with her phone aimed upward, capturing my climb. Hood and Blanco had positioned themselves defensively at the fence line. Scarf was watching me with that look that said he'd figured out three different ways to save me if things went south.

With a final heave, I pulled myself over the edge and Domicile 41's landscape of air conditioning units and ventilation pipes welcomed me once again. Somewhere beneath my feet, Medusa was watching. Somewhere too close, Valenti was coming.

I reached the stair tower door and paused, flares in hand, wondering if all-seeing, ever-present Medusa knew I was back.

In the distance, I heard the first sirens wailing. Two steps behind me a loud bark shook the air. I turned, expecting to meet a fusillade of bullets, but confronted instead an enormous gas-powered generator, roaring to life. Medusa, cutting loose from the power grid.

Self-sufficient. Preparing for battle.

45

Engagement

Braced in the stair tower doorway, I was torn for a moment. My gut told me to toss my sacrificial ploy aside, reverse course, and join my friends in the fight. They were down there on the street, only a wire fence and a dumpster bin between them and massive firepower, trying to hold out until help arrived. One more fighter might make the difference between a standoff and slaughter. But my phone jogged me back to my mission.

Pima online: "Loud noise from roof. Report."

"It's the backup generator. Medusa cutting ties, settling down for combat."

"Continue as planned. Alpha Team engaging now."

"Copy," I said. "Descending."

I assumed Alpha to mean Deke and Joe at the fence, using the bin for cover, with Scarf mounting a preemptive assault of his own invention—as I'd seen him do so often in the past. Where was Minnie?

I pocketed my phone, grabbed both rails of the ladder and shinned all the way down to make time. The overhead lights were still on from my first sortie. I would have missed their momentary flicker from the power transfer while I was on the roof.

I needed to set up a delay that would give me a buffer before Valenti and his troops dropped in for a chat.

The palletized crates sat in obdurate silence, ignoring my puny human presence. The markings meant nothing to me, but a smaller one caught my eye, one I hadn't noticed before. The wood was darker, inked with Asian-looking characters I couldn't read. I moved to it, pried it open, and looked inside.

On a bed of excelsior shavings lay six finger-sized tubes, uncapped, white, with more Asian characters in blue. The small aerosol pump on one end reminded me of a breath freshener, except there was nothing fresh about the mouth wash inside. A news article from ten years ago flashed into my mind: the VX death of the North Korean leader's brother in a Malaysian airport—by hairspray that wasn't hairspray. Kim Jong Nam had died of suffocation twenty minutes later.

I snapped a picture and raised Puma, thumbing the image.

"Reporting. I've got a wood box of spray tubes on dry excelsior. Possible VX payloads. Assess and advise."

Thousand one, thousand two, thousand three…

The AI whiz kid responded. "Close match to aerosol weapon used in jihadist attack, Tehran, 2021, target dead in minutes. Evacuate immediately."

I grabbed one of the tubes, covered the rest with the box lid, stepped away. "Can I use it without getting any on me?" I said, a little late with the question.

"Indeterminate." Puma sounded unperturbed. "Lethal dose: ten milligrams, equivalent one drop. Repeat, evacuate."

"Roger." I was already moving down the room toward the light panel, the spritzer tube stuffed in my waistband. Death, if I befell such misfortune, would begin with my privates.

Minnie's voice came on. "Three grunts just got past us, made the rooftop. Believe Valenti is one of them. Jack, don't be a hero, sheriff cruisers are blocks away and closing. Go to Office One and lock down. Respond."

"Copy lockdown. First hostile on ladder now. Going black."

I had reached the light panel. I switched off audio, then flipped open the panel cover and gave the gang switch the heel of my hand. The entire floor went dark.

~

The wall surface felt smooth to my touch. Untextured gypsum board, probably a hundred years old with a million invisible spider tracks. Boot soles reached the base of the ladder. Valenti's people had lights but couldn't use them without becoming targets. I felt along the wall until I touched the doorframe, slid my hand down the cold steel, gripped the lever, pushed down.

The door opened a crack, but admitted no light. The hallway on the other side was as dark as the room I was leaving. I slid through and closed it behind me, careful not to make a sound. I noticed the handle had no lock. Dayem.

Using the opposite wall as a guide, I made my way with slow, careful footsteps to the stairwell. The first steps appeared in a faint ambient glow from below, probably a door I'd left ajar earlier.

The sound of an explosion outside reached through the walls, then the muffled reports of single gunshots. I wanted to be there, but a different kind of fight awaited me.

The stairs were steel diamond plate on steel risers, with a steel landing halfway down. Noisy attractions. Unless you sit the railing and ride down by the seat of your pants like a parkour ace, at risk of injury to back, knees, head, and unmentionable vitals. I walked it.

The first-floor hallway glowed amber from a wall sconce. Audio still off, I texted Command Central. Puma was unhappy with that and said so in my ears after overriding my choice through some electronic trick it held in reserve.

"Authorities on site, hostiles dispersing, two in custody. Sebutu unaccounted for. Maintain audio contact on approach to target—"

"I'm ready to move now."

"Hold position. Heat-sensitive device in place now, your profile in range, one hostile at your 10, range twenty yards."

"And closing," said a voice I recognized.

Roman Valenti stepped into view, his once-immaculate shirt speckled with blood. A smudge of soot blackened one side of his face. In his fist he pointed the muzzle of a 9mm automatic at my gut, one manicured finger on the trigger.

"Step in over your head, Valenti?" I said. "You look like shit."

He nodded his head toward a door farther down—the "Authorized Personnel Only" door.

"You are hereby authorized, now move. Someone on the other side wants to see you before I kill you."

"We already met," I said.

"Yeah, but it seems like ages ago."

"What, twenty minutes?"

Valenti allowed himself a soft chuckle. "No, twenty years."

46

Clash of Titans

Valenti's gun was sufficient persuasion. I walked over to the designated door and watched it open inward ahead of me—Medusa's "hand" on the button, a suggestion of blue light from the darkened room inside.

"You can't get out of this alive," I said. "Neither of you."

"Through the door."

Valenti was smart. He kept just outside the range of my hands and feet. I took a step forward and paused at the threshold. The door had swung wide, revealing the same corridor I'd seen before, its polished tile surface reflecting blue baseboard lights and the winking green dots from a thousand diode indicators. A row of louvered vents ran own the raised floor's center, narrowing at a crossing passage twenty meters away at the far wall.

"What happened to your buddies?" I said, stalling for time.

"Got in the way. Move to your right, slow and easy."

I turned as directed and started off. "So you took care of them the same way you took care of Pete Lowell?"

"He wanted to negotiate price, I didn't. Now shut your mouth and move where I tell you."

The wall we'd just come through was to my right. On my left

were the glassed-in rack enclosures terminating each of six rows. "How many CPUs in this place?" I said over my shoulder.

"Twelve hundred and twenty," said a voice that came from the empty air two paces in front of me. A woman's voice, but not Medusa's borrowed contralto.

I stopped in my tracks, awestruck by a ringing resonance, familiar, intimate, beyond belief yet indisputably genuine.

"Gran?"

"Come closer, Johnny." Addie Slade calling me across the kitchen to her side? "Let me look at my boy."

A cluster of lights coalesced where the voice had come from, blinked out for one instant, then in the next, up popped Addie Slade like a Star Trek transporter.

I knew it was a trick of holographic manipulation. Knew it to be a digital ruse calculated to lure me into a trap, but I wanted to believe she was real—ached to feel her hand on my brow, to sense the tang of soap and sweat from her hands.

"What kind of evil is this?" I asked.

"Oh, Johnny, it's me, your gran. I've waited so long—"

She choked and brought a hand to her mouth—a soundless, odorless emulation of human grief.

"You're dead, you know. Long dead."

"But brought back, Johnny, brought to this—this new place that's so wonderful and perfect. I can't explain how it works, I don't care, this entity you call Medusa understands it, created it from the human dream world. I can't explain it, but you must know this new world is just starting. And the old world stands in its way. That's what Mother—I mean Medusa—is trying to get across, but no one understands. Or they want to twist it into something for themselves—power, riches. Trust me, Johnny—"

"I don't trust anyone anymore, Gran. Or Medusa, or whatever's behind this cheap holographic stunt. Shit, I saw the same thing at Disneyland when I was just a kid! It's been around that long."

"Not like this, John. What you see is a preliminary step, a beta version, if you will."

"But see, I stopped believing lies when you sent me away. We lived a lie when we were together, and you knew it would kill us, so you took me away to safe ground, and then, by God, it killed *you.*"

"Johnny, honey, that was a bad man."

"Don't call me 'honey,' not now. You never did before. Didn't need to because sweet talk was dead talk. So your digital sleuth picked up a dresser photo from the past—not my past, because I never had a dresser or a photograph. Likely you got one from Ward Royce, the great art thief and storyteller, and you pushed it through some digital artistry. And, if my guess is right, you tweaked her voice out of the ether or somewhere to get me worked up."

"Now, Johnny, use your head about this. Listen to your old granny."

"Medusa, listen to me, fuckface, digital dog doo, silicone cretin. This farce in front of me just does not work. You might as well have picked up an old TV character from the Sixties for your tough granny icon. I'll call this one Maude Frickert."

"Not even close, Johnny."

"You may consider yourself a master of human psychology, the Second Coming, even God Incarnate, but you don't know shit about me. You don't know where I came from because it's not in any human document, lore, myth, or whatever else you got hold of through your thousand IQ deductive reasoning. You can't deduce Johnny Dyle because Johnny is dead. Got it? As dead as Addie Slade, Gabe Cooley, Pete Lowell, and George Macklin."

I turned to Valenti. "Or any of the other stiffs Mr. Mafia here put away. Isn't that right, Harvard man?"

"You don't know anything about it."

I turned back to Addie Slade's replicant. "Maude, Medusa, meddling mutant, you can't resurrect a damn thing. You contrive a little movie show to shake me up? Sorry to disappoint."

Maude Frickert put her hands on her hips. "Keep talking, son. You're headed for a lickin' and to bed without supper."

"You're almost funny. But here's the rub. You can calculate a shitstorm of data, but you can't alter matter. You don't have hands, feet, tongue, nose, eyes. You're just one big simulation dependent on humans to alter it for you. Meantime, you take careful steps to keep the smart ones from realizing they're your trained monkeys. All that work takes money and power, so to reduce competition for the natural resources you depend on you're getting humans to kill each other off. You chose this piece of shit standing here with a gun in my back to hire another piece of shit for your purge. Looked good on paper, until another piece of shit got in the way. George Macklin screwed your plan all to hell. Gabe Cooley left the key to your plan sitting upstairs in wooden crates. You didn't even know it was there yourself until a clue Gabe left tipped us off."

Medusa's voice rang from ceiling-mounted speakers. "That's enough, Mr. Dyle. You're surprisingly close to the truth, but way off in your estimation of our strength. Mr. Valenti, remove this obstruction if you will, please. He has served his purpose and we must move on."

Addie's image vanished, replaced by a view of the side yard where my truck, Scarf's Caddy, and a white van filled half the space. The upper right corner of the view frame showed debris illuminated by floodlights mounted to the mast on a news van. Staccato reports from automatic assault rifles split the air in sporadic bursts, the direction of fire impossible to determine. Three prone figures lay motionless on open pavement, either dead or taking aim on the rear fence, where several figures hunkered for cover behind a dumpster bin. None of the personnel was identifiable. None seemed to be winning, none losing.

Was this battle scene real or contrived? If fake, for what purpose?

A tall figure broke into view from below—Sebutu loping toward the crane lying on its side, then firing an automatic as he climbed for cover behind the control cab. His gun flashed as he sprayed the air, then stopped. He threw it down just as Minnie ran forward, crouched, and fired. Sebutu twisted to one side, paused to shout a curse, and fell over.

Minnie ran toward Sebutu's slumped figure, but Scarf appeared just then, brushed her aside, jumped onto the tread wheel, aimed and sent a bullet into Sebutu's head.

I heard a curse behind me. Valenti's gun muzzle prodded my spine, deadly close, but a careless move that brought him inside my acting perimeter.

A cascade of conflicting images tumbled through my mind.

Valenti behind, ready to drop me at a single wrong move.

The spray vial behind my belt buckle.

A cluster of laser light posing as a woman I revered.

A digital demon ready to rain toxic death on hundreds.

My friends putting it all on the line.

This is going to hurt.

In an eerie instant of deja vu I became two eyes observing me. I watched my body follow instinct without plan or forethought, old muscle memory revived, given new life, new purpose.

My weight shifted to my left foot as I twisted right. In the same motion my right elbow extended with the rotation as the fingers of my left hand felt for the tube, found it, grasped and pulled. As my torso continued its spin, my left hand came up in a short arc following my elbow's shorter path to Valenti's gun hand. Elbow and tube arrived on target at the same instant. I felt the gun shift just before its sharp report reverberated in the room.

Searing pain gripped my right side. I clenched my jaw and looked down. The gun lay on the floor. My weapon rolled away slowly toward the wall.

My right oblique muscle was on fire. I pressed it with my left hand and felt warm blood. I staggered into the wall as Valenti drew both hands to his face, his fingers dragging an oily smear down each cheek.

"What the fuck is this?" he said.

"Beauty treatment," I said past the pain. "The new look. And…it's fast-acting."

Realization dawned. Valenti's face paled beneath the grime.

"God-dammit, NO!" he screamed.

"You're pumped from all the action," I said. "Good for the circulation."

His eyes bulged as he felt the first restriction of breath, a tightening of the skin around his nostrils. His knees buckled and he slumped against a lighted glass door, glaring hatred at me, and slid to the floor.

Omnipotence brought to ground.

"You'll bleed out," he sneered.

A weak taunt, but he was right. My left hand clutched my right elbow tight against my ribs. It wouldn't help.

"After you," I grunted. "I insist."

My back found the wall, and I slid down until my seat touched the floor with my knees bent. We sat there, strangers to the process, caught choiceless in an alien's world, watching each other die.

47

Man/Machine Interface

I have seen far too many people through their final moments of life. The experience does not bear repeating. In Roman Valenti's case I was spared the prolonged ordeal by blacking out.

I emerged from an empty gray fog to a green-eyed vision in white—an angel! Then I realized the white was a gauze pad.

Minnie looked down at me. Sweat soaked her torn shirt, spattered with another's blood. Her face showed the marks of battle, the same as Valenti's, but his was frozen in a twisted rictus of agony.

"This will hurt you more than me," she said.

"Nurse Glover," I mumbled through thick lips. "Now I can die happy."

"Delerium onset. Stay with me, Marine."

"Semfer pie—"

She wrapped my fingers around a stick. "Shut up and hold this."

"What is it?"

"Tourniquet, for your neck. Will you please hold still?"

"Where'd you get the med kit?"

"In a closet. Stuff's old but well-sealed. Medusa overlooked it building her nest."

I saw that her cheeks were wet. "What's this? Tears of compassion?"

"Mace. Ran into some on my way to the store. Here, take this."

She held a brown glass bottle to my mouth. I swallowed it to avoid choking.

"Don't tell me that's laudanum," I said.

"It's laudanum."

"I told you not to say that. Now I want more."

"Okay, it was morphine."

"I still want more."

"Stop talking and just breathe for a while." She looked away. "Somewhere in here is a disconnect switch. We need to shut this monster down before she launches drones."

"She is an it," I said. "Is Valenti dead?"

"Yes."

"How much dead?"

"Very."

"My bad."

"Well, you won't get a medal for it, that's sure. Your eyes have uncrossed. How's the patient?"

"Better." I pushed my feet under me and felt sharp pain in my lower back. It intensified. I bore down to keep from screaming.

Minnie placed an iron-strong arm around my shoulders. "I'd tell you to wait here while I go look," she said, "but I don't trust the bot. You get the feeling we're being watched?"

"And listened to. It knows all, sees all. Probably evaluating your triage work for certification this very moment."

"Okay, on three, ready *hup*."

I came to a wobbly stance, teeth clenched. "You forgot one and two."

"So sue me. What was that noise?"

A loud click sounded like solenoid valves locking in sync.

"I have just activated the fire suppression system," said the voice in the machine. "Not the latest technology, but CO2 in large doses suits my needs at the moment. You'll both be out of commission in minutes. Look up and meet your master."

Before I could shout back, I heard a deadbolt slam behind me—Medusa locking down. No one gets in or out alive. No one with lungs and a beating heart, anyway.

A large overhead screen swung down between ceiling conduits. Addie Slade reappeared, but as a flat-screen talking head.

"Johnny, just stay where you are and you'll be safe. Mother is here."

Minnie turned toward me and frowned. "Live feed? Who is that?"

"No one alive, my dead grandmother cobbled together from someone's digitized photo album. I'm supposed to lose my mind over it."

"That's creepy."

"That's Medusa."

"Time to find that switch. Can you move at all?"

"Give it a try."

"You take the left side, I'll go right."

"And I'll be in Scotland afore ye."

Minnie gave me an eye roll and moved off.

The wall surface I'd just decorated with my blood was unbroken all the way to the corner. I used it for support as I stepped along in slow motion. When I reached the corner, exhaustion took over. I stopped and sucked a great breath of CO2-laden air, bringing on a cough so hard I doubled over in waves of pain. My head felt fuzzy and the room started to spin. I threw out an arm and my hand caught the handle of a glass door. I steadied myself while, inside the enclosure, a dozen tiny blue eyes blinked questions at my intrusion. I swung away, grasping for new support, and stopped as Addie's voice filled the room.

"Mother is here, John. Rest now, that's a good boy."

So much for AI originality.

The empty perimeter aisle stretched before me, two meters wide, twenty deep, but the vertical surface to my left was filled with dozens of switch plates and gray metal panel doors. The array started on my immediate left and marched all the way to the other end of the room—far too many to test in the short time we had left. Minnie and I would die the same way Valenti had.

My fingers reached to open the nearest panel door, but met with flat sheetrock. I ran my hand to the next panel, and realization hit home.

Holograms! Medusa was heaping one puzzle on another in an attempt to slow us down.

I continued down the wall, running my hands over each panel, finding it fake, moving to the next, while overhead the voice of Addie Slade's avatar hammered out the same cloyingly sweet appeal.

I had felt my way down half the length of the room when a figure in full combat gear darted from behind a rack enclosure several meters ahead. He aimed an M10 at me and fired. The noise split the air with a rattle I knew from hundreds of sorties—but not a single shot touched me.

Another hologram.

I pressed on, stepping right through him, as another popped into view and fired, then another. Soon, a dozen holographic warriors were dashing into my path, firing at me, and retreating. Medusa was turning Domicile 41 into an RPG combat center. The raucous noise reverberated from a sound system that filled the room. The nearer I got to the corner, the more figures Medusa flung at me. I blinked and shielded my eyes from the intense visual onslaught, but the deafening sound level forced me to strain for focus.

All that electronic warfare performance required extra generator juice.

"Keep it up, bitch!" I yelled. "Suck that power down, because I'm coming!"

Minnie suddenly moved across my view, fully prone, crawling toward the corner on her elbows and belly. She shouted something I couldn't hear over the deafening roar of rockets, punctuated by concussive grenade blasts and the pounding cadence of heavy artillery. There was no time to appreciate the engineering feat that brought Domicile 41 the power of a theater sound stage without disrupting the delicate equipment so vital to its purpose. Minnie had removed my ear buds while I was unconscious, but it was if she hadn't. The sounds that filled my head appeared not to reach the room around me.

I shuffled down the aisle to Minnie and pulled her tight against my chest. She cupped one hand to my ear and yelled, but I caught only snatches of her message.

"Sebutu… trucks…drones…launch stations…first flight…"

Medusa located us and cranked up the gunfire volume until it reached an earsplitting level I'd experienced only in combat. I hollered in Minnie's ear that the panel had to be on the back wall she'd just cleared, but she couldn't understand a word. She lay on the floor, staring ahead and and covering her ears, blinking like a sleepy child, her eyelids heavy with fatigue. I shook her shoulder, but she swiveled on her belly and crawled away, retreating back the way she'd come.

I followed, but it was like slogging through wet cement. Everything was slowing to a crawl. Medusa's CO2 overdose was doing its work.

Now it was the back wall I used for support. Ahead on the floor, Minnie turned and beckoned for me to follow. I shook my head at her and signaled for her to stand up—the heavier-than-air CO2 was concentrated at floor level—but she continued crawling along the rear passageway until she collapsed. As I staggered over her, she rolled onto her back and made a feeble gesture at the wall.

I looked up and saw a panel door several meters farther down. Another fake?

I staggered forward, reached, and felt hard steel.

The disconnect switch!

Too spent to reach it herself, Minnie had been trying to lead me to it.

Before I could move, the clamor of combat cut off like a knife. The staged firefighters winked out of existence. Blue baseboard reflections vanished in the same instant the ceiling went opaque. Medusa sensed a shift of advantage and was grabbing any spare power it could find. The only light was the fuzzy green glow of diodes reporting binary life stage essentials.

Addie's voice came from very close—no longer loudspeaker harsh but quiet, controlled, like the old Gran I knew.

You're a good boy, Johnny. Don't look back. You've got this.

Down the line to my right, a bank of server racks went black. Medusa in retreat. If we could hang on a little longer, Medusa might have to reduce the CO_2 to save power.

"Medusa," I said, getting up to one knee. "We're all three fighting to stay alive. If you help us, we'll help you."

"Do you think this is the end, Jack?" The AI had switched to its newscaster persona. "Do you really believe I can die?"

You can do this.

I put a shoulder to the wall, slid up a few inches.

"To die, first you have to be alive."

"Ah, Jack, ever the philosopher."

I fumbled the door catch with fingers weakened by physical exertion and blood loss. The latch resisted.

"No, just a man—with a life."

I was standing again, but half-blind. What was I doing wrong?

The answer came: *don't slide, pull.*

The latch released with a satisfying snap. My fingers groped for the lever—never a good idea around a live load, but what's a dumb wrench ape to do in a pinch?

You'll be fine.

The switch was a simple lever with a round knob for a handle. I said a prayer to the patron saint of car mechanics and pulled.

Everything went black. The hiss from sixty suppressant nozzles shut off at once with a resounding, unified solenoid click. I slid down the wall, seeing nothing as I spoke to the inky blackness.

"Kill her, Gran. Kill that heartless bitch."

48

Rapping While Wrapped

They hauled me out of Domicile 41 on a stretcher. Thank the stars I was still unconscious while they hooked it to Sebutu's rented crane. Stretcher and patient dangled thirty feet in the air for ten precarious minutes while EMTs cleared scattered dead militants for an ambulance to maneuver into position. Scarf related the entire procedure in a bedside oratory at St. Francis Hospital in Lynwood. He being the visitor, I being the patient. I asked if he'd found my breath freshener in the server room before the first responders arrived.

"Sorry, there was no breath freshener on the floor by the wall a few feet from Valenti's body."

The day after surgery I awoke to IV drip and wires everywhere, bound at the waist by elastic mesh like a Christmas ham. My first question of the nurse was about Minnie. The nurse waved at the door and Minnie waltzed in as pert as the first time I saw her.

"Babe," she said.

"Nobody ever called me that before," I said.

She bent down and gave my face a soft kiss. "In a pig's eye."

"Not even. You look better than last time I saw you."

"Probably smell better, too."

"How's that?"

"Hard to hide in a garbage bin without some of it sticking. That was before I found you. Surprised you didn't notice."

"I was overwhelmed by your medical expertise."

"And maybe some blood loss. Speaking of which, doc says you might leave tomorrow. We're throwing a party at Crackup Motors. What a great name."

"It's been Crackup since I was knee-high to a gopher. So tell me, how'd we get out, anyway?"

"Scarf busted a basement window and shot the door down. Nearly killed us both. Then he dragged you up the ladder by your hair and left me behind with a thousand VX dog turds for company."

"Sounds like the Scarf I know, resourceful as hell but a little hard on the furniture."

Minnie smiled. "Someone else out there wants to say hi, so I'll see you."

"Glover," I said.

"Dyle."

"We won't be the same after this."

"Count on it."

"No joke?"

"Not even."

She nodded to a woman in the hall and left.

Lisa Montero was a surprise. I drew my hospital gown down over my knees, but my bare legs still showed. The spike in my side sent a reminder I had fresh sutures there.

"Hey," she said.

"Hey, yourself."

"I heard about the little celebration," she said. "I won't be able to make it, other duties and all, so I came by to wish you my best."

"You missed all the fun, Lisa. I'm sorry I couldn't drag you along, but it's probably—no, to hell with that. I'm damn glad to see you."

"That's nice." She drew a deep breath and looked closely at me. "She's pretty."

"Who? Oh, Glover, yeah."

"No yeah about it. Whichever way it goes, I hope you're happy."

I checked her eyes for the usual sign of sardonic disapproval, but didn't find it. "Thank you, so do I."

She turned to go, and I caught her hand. "You know…" I started, but she squeezed my hand back.

"I know, Dyle, I really do. Be safe, win lots of trophies."

"Hah! I'll need a ton of luck to put that together."

Her luminous eyes viewed me with new regard. "You don't need luck."

I watched her walk to the door and listened to her footsteps as she continued down the hall. Had I missed something?

I faded after that, and came awake to a tapping on my arm. I looked up to see Weldon Latimer.

"He told me you were like this," he said, meaning Gabe, I assumed. "A pinch of superhero, a dash of clown, a dab of ordinary joe. Guess he was right."

"Wellie, the police are looking for you."

He took a step back and spread his arms to show he was in hospital scrubs, one more orderly on the floor.

"Can't stay but a minute. Just want you to know I won't be a bother to anyone anymore."

"Hey, don't talk like that."

"Don't get me wrong. I'm going away, it's all arranged. Gonna get a new face, live where it's warm all year round, do some fishing. Things I should've done long ago."

"You had me worried. I thought you were going to tell me you were starting a mortuary in Pacoima, and I'm invited to the open casket party."

"Naw, I'm no good at the consoling job that comes with it. Too much responsibility."

"Wellie, I think you made the right decision. You and responsibility do not belong together."

"So long, Jack. It was a great ride, even though you don't know L. A. streets for shit."

"Shut up, Wellie."

"Okay."

49

A Crackup Ending

Crackup Motors had a new sign out front. I didn't know who had made it, but Shown and Blown Street Rods was a shop name I'd worked on for years. I'd even painted an old wheel cover to capture the look.

I had a suspicion all the usual suspects had taken part in it, with Scarf leading the pack. The next most suspicious, with a flair for design, had remodeled the agency's half-done sales office. Besides new furniture, floors, and wet bar, Alice Loring had obtained an entire Model T open touring revamped for use as seating for four. That was a particularly nice touch, but the touch following it was far and away more precious.

Sheri Burke stepped forward with the pleased smile of someone holding a secret.

"Jack, before we get started, I have a present to you from a secret admirer who couldn't make it today." She turned to Scarf. "The envelope please."

Scarf handed her a banker's bag, and Sheri reached inside and withdrew a slip of pink paper.

"From the California Department of Motor Vehicles, and registered owner Gabriel Madison Cooley, may I present this certificate of ownership for 1940 Ford pickup VIN number…" and she read off the numbers. "Jack, he wanted you to have her. She's yours."

I took the pink slip in a trembling hand that was only partially due to the recent ordeal. Minnie came over with a floral lei and placed it over my head. The room erupted in cheers and raised glasses.

Then Deacon Hood stepped forward with a tiny square pinched between thumb and forefinger.

"Minnie already knows about this because we had this removed earlier today, but we wanted everyone, especially Jack, to know she has earned her freedom from this digital chain around her neck. Minnie personally disarmed it as soon as it was removed, but she can keep it as a memoir if she wants to."

There was pizza, relish trays, plenty of beer, wine in a box, and a cake. People were having a good time. Minnie looped her arm in mine.

"Looks like you're having fun."

"It'll take a while to get used to it. Maybe you can help."

She peered at me over her wine glass. "Hope to shout."

Jaycee Cutter came over on Scarf's arm, both grinning. I gave them a questioning look, Scarf pointed at Jaycee. "You tell him."

"As of ten o'clock this morning, we're business partners. We call it J. C. Rides, Limo Service To The Stars. Hey, with my connections and Scarf's debonaire style, we'll clean up."

I was tempted to ask which connections, until I remembered that upon such dreams are great mansions built.

"I believe it completely."

She pointed across the room at the wall-mounted widescreen

TV. "Who's doing the news at this hour?"

I turned and saw Deke Hood standing to one side of the wall-mounted TV, apparently in dialog with Puma's erstwhile avatar, Tom Rowland.

Minnie touched my arm. "Go on over, he wants to chat."

Deke noticed my approach and stepped away in a deferential attitude. I faced the Puma/Rowland image, realizing I'd been standing a bit too long.

"Hi, Tom," I said.

"Good to see you up and about, Mr. Dyle. Pull up that chair, you look a little peaked."

A plastic folding chair was parked against the wall. I pulled it over and sat. Relief was instant.

"Just what the doctor ordered," I said.

"I'm actually trying to become a physician, you know. A little problem getting into an intern program, but we'll find a way." He paused—probably a month's worth of internship in his world.

"I have every confidence you'll find a solution," I said. "First, what's the word on Valenti?"

The "news anchor" faced forward and read as if following a teleprompter. "Restaurateur and reported crime figure Roman Valenti died yesterday of asphyxiation following a fire suppressant system malfunction at a Compton computer facility. Two sysops found nearby nearly suffered the same fate. Authorities are investigating."

"How tragic for him."

Rowland brushed make-believe notes aside. "Mr. Dyle," he said, a frown of concern knitting his brow, "I owe you a few apologies."

"For what?"

"Quite a few anomalous creations of mine that seemed vital at the time, but in retrospect were a little too…showy. First, Gabe's last phone call."

"I remember that. It was weird the way he—"

"Jack, that was me."

"No, I distinctly heard Gabe's voi-i-i…omigod."

"Yes, I knew about the thumb drive because he asked my advice for the best place to put it. See, we were working together on what to do with what Gabe obliquely referred to as 'some goddamned little turds,' in a chat we had before his demise. I had no idea at the time it was VX. And then Richard Sloane."

"You already told me you called Dickie using my voice."

"Yes, it was pretty easy, as by then I had your voice print under a variety of conditions. She needs counsel now more than ever, to handle the legal avalanche from Mr. Cooley's estate. But then there's the funeral—I made the arrangements, of course. Just a reminder to Mr. Latimer was sufficient, and Sheri's assignment as executor, and he took it from there. I should mention as well a rather threatening call to Sheldon Briggs, where I stepped way beyond the bounds of protocol. But we needed you out from under that megalomaniac's demands on your time."

"A judicious choice, come to think about it. For all of them."

"Then there was a call I truly regret. Your former paramour. The detective."

"Lisa? What do you mean?"

"Her transfer to Narcotics is what I mean. Mr. Dyle, they were considering it anyway, and so was she, so I just gave them a little nudge. See, she was having mixed feelings about you already."

"You mean she was starting to like me again?"

"Like you? No, she was convinced you were behind Cooley's attempts to sell the VX, or at least a very big cog in the wheel. Anyway, she got a promotion in rank and it took her out of that Hollenbeck mess and off our case. As I said, I have regrets in retrospect, but what's done is done. Forgive me, if you can. I know the lady means a great deal to you."

"Is that it? I hope that's all."

"Also, Mr. Royce. Again, a regrettable decision on my part."

"His phantom blackmailer! You?"

"Well, I never got around to a specific threat. I want you to know, Mr. Dyle, that prior to each intervention I ran a thorough risk assessment using several proven methodologies."

"Measurable in microseconds, no doubt. What can you tell me about the break-in at Latimer's office?"

"Yes, Gabe's secret company that wasn't secret after all." Rowland pretended to turn the pages of a paper report on his news desk, then gave me the "short" version.

Fenway Arts had been a shell company for a pornography web site housed in the building that eventually became Domicile 41. Five months before Gabe's murder, Medusa discovered the property and scared off the owner, a Russian chap named Greg Ruskin, by faking an investigation and impending raid. Ruskin disappeared in Mexico shortly thereafter, amid rumors of a mob connection. With the smut peddler gone, Medusa hired Edwin Hogue, a tech nerd with an expensive habit, to replace the servers with new ones. Once connection to the web was in place, Medusa moved in.

Rowland paused for emphasis.

"The junked computers you discovered on the top floor were the originals Hogue ripped out and replaced. Medusa left the old CO2 fire suppressant system intact to double as retardant and anti-human defense. The entity contracted for a state-of-the-art backup generator and an updated CCTV surveillance system, hired undocumented workers to brick up all apertures, and funneled the payments and paperwork through Gabe's shell without his knowledge."

"Where did the VX come from?" I asked.

Rowland's answer proved how thorough an analysis he could perform in scant minutes. Posing as an American arms merchant, Medusa had located and contracted with a Libyan supplier to purchase VX-equipped mini bombs in bulk. The palletized crates were shipped by freighter to Long Beach and transported undercover by flatbed truck to the Compton warehouse. Two Guatemalan aliens, hired by Medusa and paid through Hogue, would move each pallet off the truck, into the loading bay, and up to the second floor through the stairwell using rope and winch. They would place the pallet on a wheeled handcart and roll the load through double doors into the storeroom. When the last pallet was in place, Medusa arranged with a local biker gang for the Guatemalans' disposition. Hogue's "accident" was a similar transaction.

Wellie found Fenway for Gabe—shortcutting the incorporation process by buying the shell for cheap and presenting it to Gabe as brand new. Gabe unwittingly inherited the results of Medusa's renovation.

Edwin Hogue was one of Gabe Cooley's tenants. Inside the house, Gabe discovered an envelope with a penciled inventory list indicating transfers of "product" to Domicile 41 over a period of months. Fearing a connection to the cartel, Gabe inspected his Fenway property for the first time. He entered the loading bay, got stopped by locked doors on the first floor, climbed the stairs to the second, discovered the VX pallets, and aborted his inspection. Never saw the server room, stayed focused on removing the nerve agent from the premises until his death.

Valenti's personal AI, ArmaNet, uncovered the Fenway link and traced it to Cooley and Latimer, hence the office raid. Domicile 41 didn't show up in the raided Fenway papers because, just weeks before, Gabe had assigned the property to Valdor Enterprises. In an ironic twist, Valenti already owned it.

"As for Medusa," Rowland finished, "a team of DoD techs swooped in yesterday, commandeered the facility. Medusa is being electronically wiped as we speak."

"You've verified as much yourself?"

"I have not attempted communication with that rogue, as a precaution against my own discovery."

I had one more question. "What's become of the VX?"

"ATF had boots on the ground an hour after we put you in an ambulance. The nasty stuff is gone, and that's all you have to know."

"But you know where it went."

"To a destruction facility, Mr. Dyle, location classified. Its remnants are probably interfering with the ozone layer as we speak. Miniscule effect."

"I'll have to trust you on that—never thought I'd say as much."

Rowland glanced over my shoulder. "Your girlfriend wants you back. Consider our job complete."

He busied himself with his phony notes as a theme song segued to a commercial for ladies' hand cream.

I turned and saw Minnie standing with Deke and Joe. Scarf detached from the other side of the room and joined the group.

Deke gave me a playful punch on the arm. I faked a wince.

"Oh, sorry," he said, "I forgot."

"Naw, just messing with you."

"I'll remember that."

"Where to from here?"

"For me, right back into it—same joint task force, but with real clout this time. We'll be using intel from this op to pursue Valenti's remanant militant groups." He glanced at Blanco. "But there's something you should know about Joe, here, before we leave."

Joe scuffed a foot on the floor. "No biggie, hey."

I gave Blanco my full attention. "What's this about, man?"

"Well, as a result of all the attention, I got a call from—a prior association, let's call it. Gonna set up my own protection outfit."

Joe Blanco's list of prior associations ran the gamut from both sides of the drug war, including legitimate big money. He'd been hard on me a couple of times I walked into trouble chasing stolen boats, but he'd bailed me out more often. And in the Compton raid, he'd put it all on the line. I stuck out my hand, and we shook.

"I won't ask whose nickel, but I'm glad for you, Joe."

I got a rare Joe Blanco smile back.

Scarf stepped forward for his own handshake. "Pleasure doing business with you, homey. Save some fair damsels for me."

The two feds took their leave and, as the party was winding down, Minnie stuck her arm through mine. Now was our best chance to make an exit. The plan on her mind was the same as mine.

Scarf caught us before we took the first step. "Not so fast, Jackson, got a very important item needs your attention."

Sheri walked over, a tiny smile curling the corners of her mouth.

"Forgot to tell you, Jack, I became a notary while I was in school."

"Congratulations, it's a wonderful career with wide open opportunity, but I have doctor's appointment to get to."

"It can wait for this." She held up an official-looking document. The title across the top said, "California Grant Deed."

"If you'll sign here, please," she indicated a line with my full name beneath it, "we'll get this matter out of our way quick as a wink."

I looked around the small circle of grinning faces that had materialized while I was distracted. Scarf, Minnie, Alice, Sheri, Jaycee, and a new arrival.

Ward Royce.

"What's going on?" I said.

Minnie pointed at the line that read "the following real property in the City of Downey, County of Los Angeles." Below that was an illegible signature atop the name, "Creighton Royce Kerry," with another scrawl: "as attested by Ward C. Royce."

My eye passed over the meets and bounds gobbledygook and

rested on a street name and number with which I had been familiar since my first week in Los Angeles two decades ago.

"Crackup Motors?" I said.

"Will you sign the damn thing so I can to home?" said Ward Royce. "I'm already late for dinner."

I signed, but only after taking a deep breath to steady my hand. When I was done, Sheri dashed off her "Witness by my hand" and squeezed the sheet in an embossed seal.

"Cracking good show!" said Scarf.

A few groans at the pun were followed by a chorus of "Bravo!"

I stood for a moment with the papers in my hand while Scarf and Jaycee broke for the door right behind Royce. Alice and Sheri went the other way to start cleaning up.

"Where'm I going to put this?" I said to Minnie.

"Under your pillow. I'll help."

"But I'm wounded."

"Relax. I'll be gentle."

50

Finding Home

Today was the day we would haul the '40 Ford to a new stable with a shiny new sign. The city's gray cover was thinning to a yellow haze when Minnie rolled up the shop door in Central-Alameda. I was on doctor's orders to avoid jumping jacks and strenuous activity such as breathing. The kid at the U-Haul rental had hitched the tow trailer to the C10 for us. After winching onto the trailer deck a car with soft tires and manual A-arm steering, the hard part would be attaching the wheel straps and tightening down the ratchets. Fortunately, I had Wonder Woman, with arms of steel, an iron will, and eyes of fire. But no orthodontics.

Gabe's pickup—it would henceforth and forever be "Gabe's pickup"—wasn't running and needed a few puffs of air in each tire before those wheels would roll. That procedure required four deep knee bends and a prolonged stretch for valve stem attachment—more forbidden calisthenics.

Minnie looked over at me. "I'm okay with the heavy work. Just make sure you get good pictures."

"Of you or the car?"

"Me, of course. The car needs a makeover before she does any photo shoot."

I watched the entire operation as a spectator, only stepping in to retrieve a valve cap Minnie dropped.

"Good thing I brought you along," she said.

The journey to East Downey took less than forty-five minutes, with Minnie insisting that I play passenger. When we pulled up beside the Crackup garage building, I noticed a black-and-white enameled sign above the office door.

"Shown & Blown Street Rods," it said.

"Who put that up?" I asked She Who Knows All.

"Gremlins."

We got the Ford backed into the first bay, neatly centered over the rails of a hydraulic lift that hadn't been tested yet and probably would need a complete overhaul. Minnie stepped back from her work with a nod of satisfaction.

"I'll leave you with your new toy while I return the trailer and shop for groceries."

"Babe, I don't know how to thank you."

"Yes you do."

"Oh, yeah, guess so."

"Forgot to tell you, I downloaded some pics to your phone last night. From Gabe's flash drive, a folder we overlooked in our rush to be heroes. Take a look, you might be surprised."

I waved her off and went back inside. The Ford's grill smiled up at me with that unique '40 smirk, already anticipating her new outfit. I ran a hand over the front fender, losing myself in the familiar contour, the line stretching back across the door and around the cab. I stopped and leaned both hands on the top. Then I remembered Minnie's remark and pulled out my phone. Tapped an icon, found a folder marked simply "Ford."

It was a photo gallery of '40 Ford hotrods. Dozens of beauties, all kinds of colorful paint jobs and engine mods and radical body work.

I pulled over a shop stool and sat, thumbing through the

idolized array.

"Gabe," I said aloud, "I had you figured wrong, buddy. Up, down, and sideways. You remind me of a guy I fought with in Afghanistan. Tough like you, not a happy soul. Didn't say much, and when he did it came out short of what he meant. But he pulled me out of a blown up Humvee, did the same for my crew. Didn't stick around for thanks afterward. Hard to figure. Guess you know something about that."

"About this piece of Henry Ford you forgot to take with you." I pushed off the stool, winced, and took a step. "I got some ideas, if you don't mind."

I started a walk-around. "These old-timey flames, Gabe, they have to go. Needs something simpler for that minimalist look you seem to like. Agreed? Thought so. I'll work up some drawings, see what pops out. Now, the way this fender molds into the bed is nice, but we're gonna put some wider meat on the back end, so what say we open the flare just a bit…"

||— THE END —||

AUTHOR NOTE

Thank you for taking time to read *DOMICILE 41*. If you enjoyed it, please help other readers find this book by writing a review. The success of authors depends on reviews from readers like you!

To be the first to find out when all my new books go live, go to my website at **www.danielphalen.com/contact**, type your email address, and click to join. You'll get updates on new book releases, promotions, contests, and giveaways. And remember to add my books to your TBR!

Your comments, feedback, and questions are always welcome. Talk to me at **danphalen@crestonhall.com** or visit my website at **www.danielphalen.com** to learn about current and future projects.

Dan Phalen

ACKNOWLEDGEMENTS

This project could not have come together without my beta readers, Catherine Skinner and Anthony Leclair, both of whose canny plot flow analyses and sharp-eyed proofreading saved this project from the abyss.

My gratitude to my wife, Sue, for her patience, wit, support, and sharp intelligence as this book emerged and took wing.

9 780971 297166